SOMETHING WICKED

A Sinclair Mystery

Jane Hurst

Copyright © 2022 Jane Hurst
All rights reserved.
ISBN-13: **9798446311781**

Chapter 1

Autumn had been hard at work, donning its costume and making a stage entrance overnight in the Oxfordshire village of Kington. The field opposite Wheelwright Cottage was dressed in a soft gauzy cloak of fragile mist, the stage scattered with the first signs of decay, the chilled air scented mellow with fruit.

This was to be Miri Sinclair's first autumn in her cottage since relocating from London in the spring of the same year. She had taken early retirement from a successful career as a clinical psychiatrist in the city, on health grounds, intending to give herself up to the steady pace and beauty of this stunning village location. Then life happened, or rather death, and Miri had found herself at the centre of an investigation into a paedophile ring, and the consequent murder of a young girl. Miri's professional skills had been invaluable, and she had made her mark in the village rather more dramatically than she had intended.

DCI Mike Absolom had developed a deep and enduring respect for Miri during the investigation, and publicly acknowledged her role in solving the case on several occasions, without a shred of irony. So as the village began the long journey towards recovery, Miri found herself playing a key role, several key roles in fact, in the process. As part of the rehabilitation programme in the village primary school, Miri had been asked to develop the new post of school counsellor. The brief was to respond to the social and emotional needs of the children in the wake of the murder of one of their peers, from bereavement to irrational fear and everything in between. Miri was delighted with the offer, taking great pleasure in the prospect of shaping the new post from scratch, serving both the needs of the children and their families in a very real and practical way.

During the summer when Miri was approached about the role, her eldest son Joe had interrupted during one of their long telephone conversations when Miri had been expressing her excitement at the prospect of her new place in the village.

"Mum, haven't you forgotten something? You're supposed to be recuperating after a major operation. Wasn't the idea to stop work and relax? What if the tumour takes off again because of over exertion? For God's sake! Isn't the trauma of recent events enough excitement for now? Near death experiences, chasing round the countryside like a maniac, not to mention nearly losing Will!"

"It's fine Joe, honestly. I need to do something with my time, and it's only two or three days a week."

"Sure. I know you. Once you start, you'll just keep taking on more and more work until you're back where you started. I'll have to come and keep an eye on you, there'll be no chance of any adventure then. Most of that stuff wouldn't have happened if I'd been there instead of Will."

Miri smiled at the sharp contrast between her two sons as she breathed in the new season and watched the mist undulate and clear, a watery sun bleeding over the horizon. Will, who had been staying with her during the recent tragic events, had been concerned for her, certainly, but at the same time had relished the chase and the excitement of it all, so much so that he had nearly lost his own life. Joe was much more cautious and serious of mind, and Miri had been touched by his genuine anxiety. She had taken on board his words and reassured him that she would only do what she felt was well within her comfort zone. However, Miri's success as a member of staff at the school had, as Joe predicted, resulted in her agreeing to additional duties such as covering for absent teachers, helping Michele in the office, lending a hand with the end of term play. And so it went on.

"I enjoy it, Joe!" she would argue whenever her son challenged her over the phone. "It's therapy for me as well as the kids. I need to keep busy and it isn't stressful; someone else higher up the food chain is always there to take the rap and make decisions if it's out of my league."

"Really? Has that ever actually happened, Mum? Out of your league? Come on, Mum."

"Well, it hasn't happened yet I admit, but I do have to consult with the management team and keep detailed records. Let's face it Joe, if I didn't do this work it would be left to an outsider, possibly from an agency who doesn't know the families or have any real understanding of what the kids have been through."

"I guess." Joe conceded. "Finding the body, narrowly escaping death and playing a key role in luring the killer from her lair should leave you with a good understanding, I suppose."

The irony hadn't escaped Miri. Joe always pacified her good humouredly, whilst forcing her to acknowledge her tendency to become over involved with things, a kind of blind spot within her, a snowball effect which unconsciously gathered momentum. Joe knew that it was his mother's skills and intelligence that caused this to happen, and he was proud of that, but felt duty bound to keep a check on it.

With that in mind, Joe decided to take advantage of some time off, ostensibly to relax in his mother's beautifully refurbished cottage and stunning rural backdrop, in reality, to get a genuine feel for her well-being. His brother Will, though still disturbingly excited about the 'chase' as he called it, and somewhat over-casual about his own near-death experience, had told Joe enough to raise alarm bells and to galvanise his plans for the autumn.

Joe's job as a professional sound engineer for bands and artists, offered him constant worldwide travel and all the experience and variety that goes with it, a lifestyle he had been prepared to take advantage of until such time when age or fatigue caused him to re-assess. He had been involved with a number of girls over the years, life on the road not being particularly conducive to stability, Miri reasoned, and she was yet to learn the present state of play with regards to the romantic side of Joe's life.

Given that he spent most of his time in towns and cities, it came as some surprise to Miri when Joe asked her if it would be okay if he stayed with her for a few weeks.

"That's the whole point Mum," Joe had protested. "It's exactly what I need. A proper change and a good dose of fresh air."

"Well, you're very welcome, Joe. It will be lovely to have you around, just don't want you to be bored that's all."

"No way, I've got some recordings to mix, plus a live gig to engineer in Oxford before Christmas, so I'll be fine. Most of our work coming up is next summer's festival stuff so I'm pretty keen to take it easy for the next couple of months."

Miri suspected that Joe was thinking of her as well as himself. She was looking forward to sharing quality time with him and began thinking of ways to keep him entertained when he wasn't working. How would the folk club at the village hall do as a substitute for Glastonbury, she wondered, or quiz night at the Kington Arms?

Much of Miri's summer had been spent either gardening under the auspices of her eccentric and dear next door neighbour Edie, or researching and planning for her new job, and although the seasonal events that marked out rural life continued; harvest, country shows, fayres and so on, there was still a muted pall over the village which would take a long time to lift, a grief and shock shared by all.

Miri had volunteered to help out at various events, usually on the organisational side, and had found this a very effective way of getting to know the families in the village. 'Just preparation for the new job,' she'd told Joe, and it was on the strength of her growing reputation as a good all round and hands-on planner, that she was invited to a village committee meeting in the Kington Arms on this, the first real evening of autumn, two days before Joe was due to arrive.

Chapter 2

Isolated and abandoned leaves, the first falls of the season, eddied and stilled at intervals along the short path leading from Miri's cottage door. Though the day had been dark, the final remnants of natural light persisted, and sickly patches of lime and purple hovered low along the horizon; the eruption of a bruise.

Since moving to the village, Miri's senses had expanded to fully appreciate the beauty and wonder of the natural world. This seasonal adjustment would have passed relatively unnoticed in London during her previous life. Rarely would there be any point in looking at the sky, whitewashed as it was with light and chemicals. Rarely would she notice a tree as it shed its summer mantle, and seldom would she breathe deeply and taste the sweetness of new growth, or the natural processes of the annual decay which heralds it.

Fortified by a mug of creamy hot chocolate, Miri made her way down the path and through the fading garden gate leading to the adjoining property.

The door of Blacksmith Cottage creaked open in anticipation as Edie materialised to greet her friend.

"Darling, you look wonderful."

Edie worked as a theatrical costume designer and enjoyed a renowned reputation, certainly within Oxfordshire, and especially amongst theatre goers in the city. However, Edie's creative talent often seeped into her private life and she was regularly spotted sporting eccentric outfits, wigs and theatrical makeup, much to the amusement of the villagers.

At first, Miri had found this tendency somewhat disconcerting and had been shocked when Edie had first revealed herself bare-headed and without make-up. Since then, Edie had proven herself to be a most loyal and stalwart friend during the tragic events that had taken place earlier in the year, and Miri loved her dearly. Recently, she had endowed Miri with a spectacular hooded woollen wrap, lilac and shot through with subtle silver threads, 'Don't ask where it came from Darling, but did I ever mention a certain Ms. Dench?' Miri had uncharacteristically chosen to wear it tonight for the meeting in order to show her appreciation, despite being well out of her comfort zone. She took solace from the fact that when she took it off later at the pub, her usual uniform of casual jeans and Breton t-shirt would discourage any unwelcome attention.

"It really suits you, Darling," Edie continued. "I fully intend to transform you! You shall be my personal project."

Six months ago, this comment would have seriously thrown Miri off balance but now she took it in her stride and even made an attempt at some sort of twirl. "Really, Darling, you should make more of yourself. All that potential." But Edie knew when to stop, and they walked arm in arm down the path, at ease in each other's company and excited about the prospect of the forthcoming seasonal events.

Gavin and Craig, joint landlords of the Kington Arms, civil partners and all-round wonderful hosts, greeted them warmly and showed them through to the snug at the back of the pub, a space often reserved for business meetings and village committee events. Miri surreptitiously folded the wrap, placed it on the back of a chair near a wall and gazed with pleasure at the scene.

The room was furnished with a variety of mismatched easy chairs and two-seater sofas, each painted in a different pastel shade and upholstered in a range of vibrant linen prints. There were many fascinating original features in this room which had been thoughtfully restored and accentuated, such as the black leaded fireplace set back into a small inglenook, low thick undulating beams, and an ancient flagstone floor made warm by a scattering of ethnic rugs, each fringed with wool which had been dyed to match the chairs. Miri's friend Diane had designed the room and the effect was both stimulating and cosy. She owned the interior design shop in the village and had created Miri's dream cottage during the first few weeks of her new life. They had liked each other immediately and their friendship had grown, not least because Diane's niece Melanie was the child Miri and Will had discovered, murdered and buried in a shallow grave on the nearby Frankland Estate. Miri had supported Diane in the days and weeks that had followed, acting as a buffer against the scrutiny of some of the villagers, and being there for her when she needed to talk.

The Chair of the village committee, Nadya Begum, had invited about ten people to the meeting, a perfect gathering for the size of the room. Gavin and Craig had provided a wonderful finger food buffet, and as Miri and Edie were the first to arrive, ('It gives one such an advantage, Darling.') they had time to settle in and observe as the remaining chosen few were ushered in.

Nadya's organisation skills were well known. During the murder investigation when the village hall had been used as an incident room, DCI Mike Absolom and his team had conducted their interviews and press conferences from there, and Nadya had borne the brunt of the organisational burden with calm efficiency and good humour; she was capable, level-headed and energetic.

"Hi everyone." She swept into the snug followed by Gavin, who raised his eyebrows meaningfully at Miri, presumably to communicate his awe at Nadya's eternal energy. "Just grab these will you, Miri? I need to make some space! Now where–?"

"Let me help you," said Miri, getting up and rescuing a pile of files. "There's a spare table over in the corner we can use for paperwork and things." Miri was glad to have something to do, partly to escape the inevitable titbits of gossip that Edie would whisper to her as each person came into the room, ('You would simply never guess, Darling.') and partly to be useful in a practical way.

"Brilliant. I might ask you to hand a few things out later if that's okay, Miri."

Miri watched as Nadya, with her long athletic limbs, systematically organised the paperwork into neat piles, mentally counted the chairs as she moved a few slightly, and smiled at the impressive buffet.

"Aren't they marvellous? Always such an imaginative spread. I do hope that everyone genuinely wants to roll their sleeves up and get on with it rather than just coming along for the grub and then ducking out afterwards!"

Miri laughed, secretly suspecting that Nadya's fears may have some foundation, especially as she knew that Constable Jane Peters had been invited in her role as family liaison officer. Jane was a junior member of DCI Mike Absolom's team and an endearing young officer; transparent, homely, forthright, efficient, caring, and fond of her food. Miri now remembered with a wry smile how Jane had eagerly devoured a plate of toasties in her cottage during the recent investigation.

Guests drifted in, greeting those they knew, whilst Gavin, ever the genial host, spun around the room ensuring everyone was warm and comfortable. "Stunning wrap love, absolutely stunning. Sets off that luscious red hair." he whispered to Miri behind a theatrical hand. So much for blending into the background, she thought. Reminding herself that she had relinquished anonymity when she left the city, and that dodging the village radar was something she had yet to embrace, she settled back and tried to relax.

"Told you, Darling." Edie said, triumphantly.

Miri recognised most of the committee members, either as a result of her leisure activities, such as choir, or because of the investigation into the murder of Melanie Crew. Jane arrived noisily, flopped into a chair near the buffet, eyes popping, smile wide and genuine, and mimed a greeting to Miri before taking out her notebook.

Helen Tripley, the vicar's wife, and her cousin Beatrice, arrived together, inseparable since their husbands had been sent down for heading up the paedophile ring which had resulted in Melanie's death, and it was with great satisfaction that Miri observed the transformation in each of them. Beatrice no longer scurried or stooped, buried inside old-fashioned drab woollies and long skirts. Here she was, alert and animated in jeans and a red top, a hint of lipstick and a flattering new haircut. Helen, the butt of her husband's relentless bullying and put-downs, looked renewed with self-esteem and confidence, ready to put her undoubtedly considerable skills to good use. To the credit of the locals, no-one that Miri knew of had laid any blame at their door, though both of them must have known what their husbands were doing. Even Mrs. Duggan, owner of the village shop and loudhailer of village gossip, had heeded the warning and kept her thoughts to herself. Most people understood that the women had been in constant fear of their lives and sympathised accordingly. "Like two phoenixes, rising from the ashes. Marvellous," said Edie, reading Miri's thoughts.

Michele Cavendish, school secretary, arrived, iPad at the ready, having been duly given administrative responsibility for notetaking, sending memos and so on. She was followed by a selection of minor committee members who were responsible for a variety of aspects of village life; sport, music and entertainment, neighbourhood watch, and the ubiquitous health and safety.

Nadya called the meeting to order, thanked everyone for coming, and reminded them of the agenda, which was to discuss the forthcoming Halloween and bonfire night celebrations. There was the usual murmuring as folk finished their conversations, resettled in their seats, switched off their phones and kicked bags under seats. Nadya's initial delivery of the aims was entertaining and enthusiastic, so by the time she opened up the meeting for suggestions, everyone was buzzing with excitement.

"We've had a horrendous year so far," she added. Silence fell. "Tremendous work has been done to help the village heal," she continued with a meaningful look in Miri's direction, "and we have a long way to go, but keeping up this tradition will give us all something to focus on. Let's make it the best Kington Halloween yet. Get creative everyone!" Nadya sat down to hearty applause and the guests began to discuss ideas in pairs or threes, moving around occasionally to check details with their fellow committee members.

"So, this is an annual thing then, is it?" Miri asked Edie and Jane, who made up their group.

"Oh yes, Darling. Goes back centuries apparently. You know about the witch hunts around the time of the civil wars that took place in certain parts of the country?" Miri nodded. "Well, legend has it that during that time several burnings took place in this very village. I don't know the details, but what began as an annual celebration of the burnings back in the day, continued through the centuries, gradually losing its significance and becoming what it is today, a procession through the village with a burning tree and everyone chanting, 'Burn the witch! Burn the witch!'"

"What?" Miri was appalled.

"Just a bit of fun and an excuse for a party, not unlike bonfire night, Darling," Edie said with a nervous laugh as she saw the horrified look on Miri's face. "No-one is seriously suggesting that we should celebrate a plot to blow up the houses of parliament. It's just tradition, and good business too. Look at the profit generated from Halloween outfits and fireworks. Our celebrations are much like everywhere else these days."

"Yes, I know. It's just the idea of celebrating the death of innocent young women in the light of, well, you know."

"Yes. See what you mean," Jane said leaning forward so that she could speak in confidence. "But I do think the village should go ahead with the event. If we don't, firstly it will leave a gaping hole and draw more attention to the misery of the last few months, and secondly the village really needs something to look forward to and concentrate on. All the families I've worked with over the summer have said the same thing. I'll have a word with Nadya after the meeting in my role as liaison officer." She paused, flicked her big eyes around the room and drew herself upright to indicate a position of power, much to their amusement, "I shall suggest that we keep the entertainment light-hearted." Jane slumped back in her chair to denote a job well done.

Over the soft smoked salmon and cream cheese sandwiches, richly flavoured olive bruschetta, salads and cakes, conversations broadened, legs were stretched, people mingled and caught up on news. The aim of the second part of the meeting was for each pair or group to create and submit a shortlist of ideas to Nadya and Michele for processing. Miri, Edie and Jane made a list of three things for consideration; a short drama to be presented by the village school, skittles or Aunt Sally tournament with jacket potatoes and hog roast, and musical entertainment by the resident folk group. Miri was happy that none of these suggestions would have any impact on the grief of Mel's family and she privately thought that the musical event might provide Joe with a role.

"Please keep your group papers anonymous and resist the temptation to discuss your ideas with other groups at this point," Nadya began as she drew the meeting to a close and collected the papers in. "Some of you will be disappointed if we don't go with your idea, I know, but this is the most democratic way we could think of, and we promise to consider all suggestions carefully before deciding. Thank you all so much for coming. We'll reconvene here, as arranged, to discuss the next steps. Hope to see you all then. Good night, all!"

Miri and Edie prepared to leave as they bade their farewells to the dwindling crowd and thanked their hosts for the wonderful food.

"Don't tell Craig." Gavin whispered. "I hate it when he gloats. I like him where he is, in the kitchen out of sight out of–"

"I heard that!" called a disembodied voice, creator of all things culinary at the Kington Arms.

Gavin took it upon himself to arrange Miri's wrap on her shoulders, though not before parading around the bar in it himself, escorted them through the huge oak door and waved them on their way.

A chill had set in during the evening and the sky glowered behind the steeple causing the edges to fray, ragged and pinkish.

"I wonder what other ideas will be written on those bits of paper, Edie. What usually happens?"

"Well, this is the first time it's been open for discussion. Don't forget, until recently, Lord Frankland and his cronies would have decided everything. Now that he's banged up for his part in the paedophile business, it's an open book. Good bloody riddance, I say. That's another reason the villagers want this to be a success you see; we're free of him at last. The National Trust has taken over Frankland's estate and renamed it after the village, so it's a new start. Some of the villagers have already applied to buy the lease on their properties and they feel empowered. I doubt if anyone will want to upset the applecart now. I hope it all goes well, I really do." Miri took this as a declaration of firm allegiance to the project and a warning that if Miri decided to object to it on the grounds of bad taste, then she was unlikely to find an ally in her neighbour.

"I'm sure you're right. I've enjoyed this evening, Edie. Let's hope everyone can be as dignified and generous of spirit as you are if their suggestions are turned down!"

"Ha! Includes you, Darling."

As the two friends negotiated their own pathways in the darkness, an owl hooted, crisp leaves rustled and moaned, and the waxing moon peeped out, bloated and creamy.

Chapter 3

Joe arrived as planned late in the afternoon two days after the meeting, ruck-sack bulging, wide toothy smile, short fair hair sticking out every which way.

Miri, who had been periodically looking out for him, walked briskly down the path to greet him, waved at Edie who was pretending to rearrange a curtain, relieved him of a carrier bag and shared her joy at the prospect of spending some quality time together. Miri thought her son looked tired and a little pale; dark patches had etched themselves beneath his large blue eyes and his lips were dry. Life on the road had taken its toll.

"This is lovely, Mum!" he said as he dumped his rucksack, stretched his spine and gazed at his mother's new home. "Will was right. I thought he was just being over emotional about it because of what happened here, but it really is as cosy as he said. No wonder he can't wait to get back here."

"What?"

"Oh, didn't he tell you? Typical. He's hoping to come down for a few days while I'm here so we can have a catch up. He said he can work from here." Joe grinned. He knew what that would probably mean to his mother; long nights in the pub, noisy jam sessions and a chaotic kitchen.

"Err, no he didn't tell me, but it will be great, don't worry. You'll have to share a room though. Now, tell me all about what you've been doing while I finish getting supper ready."

Miri was secretly thrilled at the prospect of having her two boys to stay. They would be company for one another and their easy and close relationship was something she was extremely proud of and loved to be around. Any opportunity to consolidate that was time well spent in her book.

Joe told her about his recent European tour with a grunge band from Surrey who were supporting a more famous act, The Pilots, from the Midlands. "Most of the time it was okay, but there's not much time to see places. By the time we've set up, done the sound check, worked the gig and packed up, it's time to move on. I was happy with the sound balance in most of the venues though. Couple of awkward buildings where it was impossible to get it right, but you get that from time to time, goes with the territory."

"Not as glamorous as everyone thinks, ay? Don't tell me you had to sleep in the van again."

"Nah. Luxury this time, Mum. A mixture of cheap hotels, hostels and some pretty rough dives." Joe rubbed his eyes and sighed wearily. "It'll be a treat to stay in the same place two nights in a row to be honest."

"Stay as long as you like. Here, tuck into that," she said, placing a casserole and jacket potatoes on the table. "We'll talk about it later." Miri got the impression that Joe was tired of being on the road and was on the verge of contemplating a new future. All in good time. Here he would have all the time and space in the world. The casserole hit the spot and Joe appeared to revive in front of Miri's eyes, much to her relief. A bowl of fruit crumble later, and he was almost back to normal.

"Christ, that's better," he said, leaned back in his chair and groaned with satisfaction. "Man cannot live on pizza alone, that's for sure. If I see another bloody cardboard box with plastic food in it, I'll–" Joe was interrupted by a light tapping on the back door.

"Ah. I wondered how long it would take her. That'll be Edie from next door," Miri whispered. "She's, well you'll see."

Edie was playing her 'quiet neighbour who never interferes but just happened to be passing' role, dressed in what she referred to as her 'blending in' costume; combats with sweater, homely headwrap to conceal her wispy receding hair, and minimal makeup. Praise the Lord, thought Miri. In his present state, Miri wasn't at all convinced that Joe wouldn't pass out if she'd turned up in one of her more exotic creations.

"Darling," she whispered from the doorway, peering over Miri's shoulder, "I hope you don't mind, but I thought I'd–"

"Come in, Edie! You know very well I don't mind." Miri steered Edie, who had adopted a rather uncharacteristic slouch, over to the table where Joe was rising to greet her.

"Hi Edie. Heard a lot about you from our Will. Great to meet you at last." He gestured towards a chair opposite and drew it back slightly for her.

"Oh, I say," she giggled. "How charming you are. You must be so proud, Darling." She turned to Miri who was grinning and pouring coffee. "I'm enchanted, I really am.

How lucky you are to have two such wonderful sons, Miri."

"We have our moments," said Joe with a wink to his Mum. "Will's coming down soon so you might get a different picture of us then."

Edie accepted a mug of coffee from Miri before responding vehemently. "Now, I will not have a word said against either of you. Your brother was nothing short of heroic while he was staying here, wasn't he Miri? At least this time he'll be able to relax and have a good time. Plenty of nice young ladies in the village would drop their hankies for you two to pick up, I'm sure." Joe roared with laughter at the old-fashioned image Edie had conjured up.

"Well, I'm sorry to disappoint you but I already have a girlfriend," he said, still amused by her match-making efforts. Edie leaned forward and was just about to begin a full-blown interrogation, when Miri stepped in to prevent further embarrassment.

"If you'd like to unpack or take a shower, Joe, just carry on. You'll find everything you need upstairs." Joe, grateful for the escape route, excused himself politely and disappeared upstairs with his bag. Edie said she was looking forward to seeing more of him, expressing anew her admiration for the boys. "You raised them on your own as well, Darling." Edie stopped short, embarrassed by her clumsiness. They rarely spoke of Miri's husband who had died of cancer when the boys were young, and Edie was relieved that she hadn't made the comment while Joe was there. "So sorry, Darling," she said, reaching over and touching her hand.

"Oh, don't worry," Miri replied, collecting dishes and plates ready to load the dishwasher. "We're all quite open about it. Don't be afraid to speak freely; it's better that way." Miri smiled. She was happy to talk about her late husband. It was Zack, her partner in later life that she preferred not to be reminded of.

The tension dropped and Miri, by way of changing the subject, asked Edie if she'd had any more thoughts about the forthcoming celebrations.

"Well, I don't expect it'll be as democratic as Nadya was making out. I mean, someone will have to make the final decision, just as Frankland used to, unless there's a vote, which I doubt. We've only got six weeks to get it all done, after all. And in my experience, Darling," said the wise old bird, leaning forward for dramatic effect. "There's always someone with a private agenda when it comes to these sorts of events." Miri turned and looked up from the dishwasher puzzled. "Oh, you know what I mean, someone wanting to upstage someone else because one of their kids got a higher grade than theirs God knows how many years ago. You know the kind of thing." Miri laughed at Edie's portrayal of village life. "Oh, I doubt it, Edie. Surely, with everything we've all been through?"

"You mark my words, Darling," said Edie, gathering herself to leave. "Somebody somewhere will be thinking about how to use this opportunity to stick the knife in." With that, she grabbed a cake knife and twirled dramatically around the kitchen, glaring with menace, teeth clenched, just as Joe appeared at the bottom of the stairs, bare chested and asking for a clean towel.

"Edie is just leaving."

Chapter 4

The following morning, Miri and Joe planned their day. Miri's only commitment was her weekly session with Adam, which was booked in for three o'clock at the village hall.

Adam was Miri's friend. They had met earlier in the year on the day she and Will had discovered Melany Crew's body. At the time, Adam had been employed as a casual labourer on the Frankland Estate, ostensibly to look after the birds and keep the hedgerows under control. However, Adam's history of abuse, together with his learning and speech difficulties, meant that Frankland soon had him marked out as an easy target, using him to keep guard over the new teaching facility at the back of the Victorian institution, which at the time was being used as a cover for heinous crimes against the most vulnerable children in the village. Adam had been set up for Melony's murder, and it was largely due to Miri's intervention that the real murderer and associated paedophile ring, headed up by Frankland, had been caught. DCI Mike Absolom had recognised Miri's skills and, as part of the rehabilitation programme for the village, had asked her to take on the role of Adam's mentor to continue work on his speech, build his self-esteem and prepare him for meaningful employment.

Miri knew how much Adam loved the birds and trees on the estate, how much he knew and respected them, so she had used this as a starting point and asked him to teach her about the species he knew. He had taken the bait, excited at the prospect of being 'teacher', bringing along pictures and talking about them. Miri had been genuinely impressed by his knowledge, and Adam's communication skills steadily improved. She also managed to arrange for him to resume his work on the estate as a junior groundsman under the wing of a splendid chap called Tom who, Miri was told, was patient, kind and understanding. It would probably be some time before Adam could trust a stranger again, but with her guidance, they were making slow and steady progress towards his recovery. Miri was yet to meet Tom, but she thought it best to give them both space to develop a relationship without her interference. Adam was a young adult after all, and Miri had decided quite early on that she would wait for him to invite her to his place of work.

"How about," said Miri, "a tour round the village and church, extended walk if the rain holds off, followed by lunch at the Kington?"

"Sounds just the job," said Joe. "I'll be hungry again by then, making up for lost lunches. How's the weather looking? I haven't got any proper walking boots." Miri lifted the pretty pastel blue blind at the kitchen window and peered out. She never tired of the view into her back garden, especially now that she and Edie had worked some shape into it. A sky shrouded with bright clouds gave promise to a low diluted sun, streaked with layers of frayed silver.

"Looks okay," Miri said, turning back and rummaging in the small cloakroom between the kitchen and living room. "Showers are forecast for later, but we can prepare for that. I'm sure Will left some boots here which might fit. Oh, and don't be surprised if you see Edie materialising before your very eyes and not looking anything like she did last night. She likes to shock people."

"Learned the hard way, did you?"

"Yes, something like that."

As they set off, Miri was reminded of her first walk with Will back in the spring and how different the landscape had looked. Fresh buds, which heralded their inevitable rainbows of colour, had flourished and were now retreating to make way for a more sombre palette. Golds, reds and oranges fringed the leaves, and pathways were stained into a myriad of mosaics where the few that had already fallen had bled their colour. The breeze was fresh, musty smells from the nearby fields lingering, pungent and heady.

Joe breathed deeply. Weary as he was of life on the road, his senses were particularly susceptible to the allure of the natural world. Diesel, fried chicken, smoke and sweat had taken their toll temporarily. Now in the crisp outdoors it felt as though he was expunging poison and absorbing perfume.

"No sign of Edie," Miri whispered. "I love her dearly, but... Let's start with the church." Miri didn't want to exclude Edie and had willingly invited her for supper later, but she unapologetically wanted this time with her son. They had talked till late the previous night about the events that had taken place during Will's stay, so Miri didn't want to make it the focus of the new day, and if Joe wanted to talk about his own life and future then what better than a long walk? For now, she allowed herself to be struck by the beauty of her surroundings anew.

"Cool!" said Joe as they approached the great door of the church, it's squat tower strong and defiant. "I wonder what will happen to it now. Will said the pervy Rev will go down for years. Should be crucified if you ask me. Whoever takes it on after all that is gonna need a shed load of balls, that's all I can say. Who'll trust another vicar here?"

"It won't be the first challenge in the history of this building, I'm sure," she said, twisting the huge hand-forged ring to activate the latch. "Damn! It's not budging," she said. "I expect the parish council thought it best to keep it locked until the future of the church has been decided," she said, clearly frustrated but resigned to the situation. "I should have realised. Mrs. Duggan, village shopkeeper and fount of all gossip, has been heard to say, by anyone who'd listen, that the council are concerned that parents of victims might deface the inside of the building in their grief and anger, or that neighbouring villagers might have a macabre desire, fuelled by the media no doubt, to find where the murder weapon, the candle snuffer, originally hung. I'm not surprised it's locked. Never mind, Jo. let's have a look around the church yard anyway."

They picked their way down the worn steps towards the path which would lead them to the churchyard, hands in pockets, scarves tightened against the strengthening wind. Miri stopped to put on some gloves just as the sound of someone singing reached them, vague and tremulous on the wind, but clear enough to cause them to share a frown, at once puzzled and amused.

"That's the single off Adele's new album! Not a ghost then."

"No indeed," said the voice. "Very much alive, I think you'll find."

Miri and Joe looked around attempting to locate the source, as a young woman approached from behind a tall grave marker, half-walking, half-running, and giggling with delight.

"Hi! I'm Zoe Deans, the new reverend. Pleased to meet you both. If I'd known I had an audience I would've shut my mouth. Singing isn't my strong point unfortunately, but I just can't get that song out of my head." She shrugged, shook her head as if she were a lost cause and offered to show them round, assuming that's what they'd come for.

Miri introduced herself and explained that she knew the church quite well but would welcome the opportunity to show Joe the inside. "Ah, I know who you are, Miri! Your reputation precedes you," said Zoe, fitting the huge key and hefting it until a loud click released the lock.

"Oh dear," said Miri. "Not the village shop, I hope!"

"Oh no. I know better than to source my information there. Well, usually," she added with a wink. "No, I only arrived yesterday but I was thoroughly briefed about the recent history of the village and the church at my interview, so naturally your name came up as the brains behind the investigation. And you," she said, swinging round to face Joe before Miri had the chance to confirm or deny the accolade, "you must be the guy who rugby tackled Constance Fielding and saved the day. I sincerely hope you don't try any of that nonsense with me. I have a brown belt in kickboxing and I wouldn't fancy your chances." To prove the point, she offered them a short display of her skills, managing to clear a nearby gravestone with one leg, revealing a flash of the skinny black jeans she was wearing under her calf length robe.

"Er, no," said Joe, bewildered but impressed. "That was my brother, Will. I would have done the same of course if I'd been there, naturally."

Miri smiled to herself at the inevitable male bravado, and raised an eyebrow to Zoe, who shared her amusement. They trooped inside, single file in the dim light, their clothes criss-crossed by bars of refracted colour from the stained-glass windows.

Miri liked Zoe already and took the opportunity to observe her more closely as she flitted this way and that, quickly and efficiently grabbing dust sheets from some of the pews and turning up a few of the lights. The air was cold and stale, and Miri was taken back to her first visit here and her initial meeting with the Reverend Tripley, a meeting which had catapulted Miri into the heart of a murder mystery.

The new reverend was young, probably about thirty, Miri thought, slim and light on her feet, reminding her of a sprite; Puck from a Midsummer Night's Dream perhaps. Her black hair was cut in a simple bob tucked away behind her ears, her skin pale and clear. The facial features were small and well defined, like the rest of her;

thick black lashes, perfectly arched brows, pert nose and small even teeth. Her face was neither striking nor plain. The accent was difficult to place, though Miri thought she could detect the merest trace of Yorkshire, which might account for her forthright manner. She was dressed in the regalia associated with her calling, at least on the surface, the black of the robe and jeans and the white of the collar adding emphasis to an overall monochrome look.

She must have sensed that she was being scrutinised, though Joe had wandered off in search of the missing candle snuffer shape on the wall and could be heard periodically testing out the acoustics. "Please excuse my weird outfit," she said, rubbing dust off her sleeves. "It's all I could get to tide me over I'm afraid. Do you know Diane?" Miri nodded. "I've asked her to make me a fitted collarless jacket with matching cigarette trousers so I can dispense with this archaic balloon, and rock up to the pulpit looking cool and chic."

"You went to the right person, Reverend. If Diane can't fix you up, no-one can. You'll look amazing." Miri couldn't have conjured up a more contrasting image to that of the disgraced Reverend Tripley. She didn't know what to look forward to most, seeing the new rev 'rock up' in her new designer outfit, or hearing Mrs. Duggan's appraisal in the shop the following morning. "No better than she should be. You mark my words!" The pews will be jam packed for that service, Miri thought with a smile.

"You've quite a job on your hands, Reverend."

"Zoe, please. We're going to be friends, right? It's not going to be easy, that's for sure. I need to get the people on my side. Clean sweep. New ideas. Fresh approach.

And I'm gonna start," she declared, spinning around dramatically, arms outstretched, "by cleaning this place from top to bottom and filling it with flowers. The grain on these pews is amazing and I want to scrub away all the grime, literally and metaphorically, and make it beautiful again." Joe and Miri smiled, absorbing her energy, and Miri looked down at the patina formed by centuries of congregations on the wood and stonework.

"I hope you don't mind me saying this Zoe, but you might like to think about putting the brakes on a bit, just to start with." Zoe cocked her head to one side, an idiosyncrasy that Miri would grow to recognise. "You'll have some great ideas Zoe, and I would hate for them to go to waste, but if you go in full throttle, you may unsettle the very folk you want to draw in." Joe was hoping that his mother wasn't going to launch into one of her lectures, and shot her a look of mild disapproval, one he knew she would interpret positively. "I totally get what you are aiming for, and I think you're right, one hundred percent, I really do." Good. She's toning it down, thought Joe. "It's just that the village is still coming to terms with recent events and a 'softly softly' approach might be more effective in the long run, that's all. It only takes one troublemaker in a community like this and you've had it. I'm still unpopular with some people for helping the police dislodge a paedophile ring and catch a child murderer! They see it as somehow my fault, that it was my meddling that led to the murder in the first place, that things would have been better left as they were and so on."

"Mm, I see," said Zoe, crestfallen, deflated and a little embarrassed at what she now regarded as her hitherto naivety. Joe pursed his lips in thought.

"I think cleaning the church is a good plan to start with anyway. No-one can object to that, surely?" he said, holding up fingertips thick with dust and pulling a comical face. "Needs doing."

"Absolutely!" said Miri. "One step at a time. Maybe you could ask the village committee to help you set up a group of volunteers? That way you'd create a few allies and friends to strengthen your cause, putting you in a better position to do the things you want to do in the community later on."

"Sounds like a plan," said Zoe, cheering up.

"You missed the meeting earlier this week when we discussed ideas for Halloween and bonfire night, but how about coming along to the follow up meeting this Friday with me and my neighbour?" Joe just about managed to stifle a snort. "I can introduce you to the committee and we'll take it from there. I'm already pretty sure of at least two ladies who will be more than happy to help you shift the cobwebs out of here." Miri was thinking specifically of Helen and Beatrice, former wives of the worst offenders in the investigation and both keen to make a positive contribution; therapy for themselves as much as anything else.

"I'd like that, Miri. Thanks. I do get carried away sometimes, I know."

"Don't worry," said Miri, touching her arm as she gathered her bag and gloves. "You're just what the village needs. You're going to need help, that's all."

"Or a shed load of balls?" Now it was Joe's turn to be embarrassed. Zoe's laughter still prevailed as her diminutive figure emerged from the great oak door, into the gathering gloom of the late morning, and scurried off in the direction of the vicarage where she was planning to spend the rest of the day unpacking. "See you on Friday."

Outside the wind had strengthened in their absence, a persistent and horizontal drizzle setting in, misting their faces and hair and glossing the lichen on the gravestones to a deep velvety green.

Chapter 5

"Joe! You must be brother of the celebrated Will, 'hero of the moment!'" Gavin said as he ushered them to Miri's favourite table and handed them a menu each. Joe answered politely, privately planning to wring Will's heroic neck if he heard another word about it. "Specials are on the board as usual," he added. "Craig's done a superb chicken in orange and tarragon, bless him, which I can highly recommend. Lovely to see you both."

"Wow! This is some pub." said Joe, gazing at the cosy inglenook, exposed beams and ancient stone. Fit for a hero."

Miri laughed and nudged him playfully. "I'm afraid you may have to put up with that Joe, especially when he gets here."

"Jesus. We won't hear the last of it."

"Well, he was quite brave, Joe. Don't forget, he was already injured himself, his hands were still bandaged, and he had been in hospital after being dumped in a dungeon and left to die. Come on. You should be proud of him."

"Alright. Alright," he conceded. "Thank God he's okay," he said and quietly shivered, physically shaking off the unthinkable.

Despite further interruptions, Miri being obliged to introduce her son to a handful of acquaintances during the busy lunchtime period, they still managed to talk at some length over their meal, and Joe grew relaxed enough to open up about his immediate future.

"I know I told Edie that I have a girlfriend, but I only said that to stop her match-making," he grinned. "I'm still friends with Deb, but we agreed just before my last tour that we probably wouldn't live together when I came back. It's no big deal. I think the novelty of sharing a life with a muso was wearing a bit thin." Miri looked askance at Joe to gauge whether he was just putting on a brave face and hiding the hurt; she knew him well enough to suspect he was making light of it but decided not to pry too much.

"Okay, Joe. You may be right about that. It's not easy for the person on the other end of the kind of lifestyle that you are leading at the moment, I guess." When Joe offered no further comment, Miri tactfully steered the conversation towards more prosaic matters. "You can talk to me about that whenever you want to. You know that, don't you? So, what about London? Do you still want to go back?"

"Not sure. That's where most of the big recording studios are, but there are others. Computer software means you can work from just about anywhere, at least for part of the time. I don't know. I'll do some research. I know a lot of people, so I'll just take it from there. I've had enough of being on the road, that much I do know."

"Good. There's no rush, Joe. Take as much time as you need. When Will gets here, you'll be able to talk it over. He knows loads of people in the business as well. Working freelance might be a route worth considering for you, Joe. He may even be able to put some work your way."

"Is there no end to his talents?" said Joe, smiling sweetly.

"Let's order coffee," said Miri, giving his arm a squeeze.

The rain had eased to a weak, misty drizzle and both Joe and Miri were keen to take a detour after the meal, if only to walk off some of the rich and delicious food.

"Is the food always that good?" said Joe as they wandered around the centre of the village, Miri pointing out various shops and buildings of interest.

"Yes," she said simply. "Always a warm welcome too. But it's more than a pub. It's the hub of the village. Gavin and Craig cater for whatever the village needs; meetings, celebrations, anything."

"Live music?"

"Well, yes if you count the occasional folk night with old Tom Jessup and his accordion. Nothing grand. Maybe you could change that, Joe?"

"Hmm. I'll think about it. Depends how long I'm here."

Miri was pleased that Joe was thinking positively about the future and, mindful of her late afternoon appointment with Adam, suggested a different and slightly longer route home which would take them round the back of the church before skirting the perimeter of some farmland leading back to the cottages.

The churchyard was tended regularly by Michael Swain, a ruddy faced man in his sixties who had worked on the estate during Frankland's time. He had left as soon as the news erupted of his boss's involvement in child abuse but his excellent reputation had resulted in him being quickly re-employed by the National Trust. The upkeep of the churchyard was one of the duties he would have been most loathed to give up. It was his patch, as familiar to him as his own backyard.

This particular afternoon, Michael was weeding, sweeping and tending the graves with as much care and pride as he had shown since he was a boy. He and Miri had passed the time of day many times during her walks and she had learned a lot about the history of the village from him. When he saw Miri and Joe approaching, he paused, leaned on his shovel and waved his customary silent greeting. His face under his ancient oily cap was moist from the drizzle, his cheeks more ruddy than usual, and his battered old wellies caked in mud.

"Good a'ternoon, my dear. This must be Joe. Heard a lot about you, young man," he said and held out his hand, calloused with years of toil, for a firm and honest handshake. "Take a look around, lad. That bit over there is newly turned over so keep off that, but the rest is fine to walk on."

"Thank you." Joe nodded and left Michael and his mother to chat. He'd always felt a calmness when trailing the paths of graveyards, ever since he was a child, always wandering off into the maze of grass and stone, alone yet comforted by a different kind of company. Reading the names and dates on the stones, Joe was fascinated by the clusters of graves bearing the same name, and was touched by the proportion of markers for siblings who had succumbed to disease in the same year, parents who had died in their twenties and young women who had died in childbirth no doubt, buried alongside their tiny bundles.

One solitary grave attracted his attention, standing out from the rest because it was so overgrown, streaked green with slimy lichen and almost horizontal, like a broken tooth. The stone was tucked away near the perimeter fence on the northwest side, exposed to the cross winds from the fields, chipped, porous and so faded that Joe could only just make out the name. He wondered why this grave should be so neglected when all the others were tended so regularly; recent ones by living relatives, ancient ones by Michael. Joe wasn't sure how much time had passed, but he was jolted back to his senses by an icy wind, sudden and squally, which chilled him to the bone.

At the northeast corner, a section had been fenced off and contained the graves of six siblings and their mother, all dated from the year 1665 and presented in a circle. The sight caused tears to well in Joe's eyes and he had to blink furiously as he heard Michael and his mother approach. He was not ready for an explanation about the graves yet, still thinking about the pain of losing a brother, and privately promising to allow Will all the hero status he wanted.

As he moved on, slowly so that his Mum could catch up, he waved to Michael and decided that he would revisit the graveyard the next day to learn more. He had read somewhere about families who had succumbed to the black death being buried at a distance from other graves, but his knowledge barely scratched the surface and he felt sure that Michael would be a rich vein of local information, the kind that you rarely find in a book or on the internet. He knew such ancient graves were rare, especially those set out in family formations. Michael was also bound to know about the isolated and untended grave. Joe could just about make out the date, 1676-1698, but the name was far too faded to make out.

"Great day so far Mum, thanks," said Joe as they settled in the sitting room with a pot of tea. "I think I'll do some work this aft, email a few contacts and try and get the ball rolling. To be honest though, I don't know if I'll be able to concentrate. Must be all that fresh air. I feel quite light-headed."

"Well, use my study area if you get round to it. The view is so lovely. I need to leave for the session with Adam soon, so make yourself at home. Joe? Are you listening?"

"Oh yeah, sorry Mum. Jesus. I can hardly keep my eyes open." Nor could he remember the walk home.

Chapter 6

Back in the summer, DCI Mike Absolom had given Miri carte blanche regarding her role as Adam's mentor. 'Do whatever you think will be most useful Miri,' he'd said, shortly after Adam had been released and the true culprits arrested. 'Just make sure you log everything and meet me for lunch once a month at least, to discuss progress.' Miri had ignored the blatant reference to an ulterior motive, leaving Mike with a redundant smile on his face that he'd had no choice but to let casually fade.

"It's progress enough that you are finally trusting my judgement, Mike. This is no longer a police matter after all, this is my area of expertise."

"It's still my neck on the block if things go belly up!" he'd argued, leaning forward, placing his palms flat on Miri's kitchen table and looking intently up at her. "I initiated the specialist roles that have been created for you with Adam and the school, I'm still accountable for the outcomes and I still have to submit written reports. Procedure must prevail, even when it just seems like pointless bureaucracy. I still have to do it like everyone else, to cover myself. You would do well to remember that just in case something goes wrong." Mike's tone had been light, but Miri had taken his words seriously.

Miri knew all about procedure from her career as a psychiatrist and she hated the pettiness of it all; the meaningless box ticking and the slavish adherence to a system which didn't allow for initiative, creativity or spontaneity. Toward the end, even before her illness, she'd felt confined and stifled by it. In this case though, she knew that Mike had her best interests at heart, so she'd agreed to keep detailed notes, as much as a strategy to address her short- term memory loss as anything else.

So far, she and Adam had completed eight sessions since the arrest of Melanie Crew's murderer, and Miri was looking forward to their meeting. He usually waited for her outside the village hall by the main entrance. Miri had a key in case the hall was locked, and they would usually begin by brewing a pot of tea together before settling down to work. Miri felt that Adam valued the sessions, that he trusted her as far as he would trust anyone, and that he would confide in her if something was worrying him.

On this increasingly cold afternoon, Miri expected Adam to be sheltering in the small open porch at the front of the building where there was a boot bench and a few rudimentary coat hooks, used mainly by local farmers. She was surprised, therefore, to see him pacing around, throwing his arms randomly around in his distinctive yellow jacket, and stamping his feet. Miri knew Adam and his needs well enough to recognise this as a display of excitement rather than agitation, so she wasn't particularly alarmed. Greeting him in her usual way she reached in her coat pocket for the key.

"N-no! N-no!" Adam urged, tugging her sleeve, gently pushing her hand towards her pocket and indicating that he wanted her to put the key away. "C-ome with m-me!" he said, waving his arms and grinning.

"Okay! Okay! "Is it a surprise?"

Adam nodded, latching onto the game and giggling with excitement. He ran away backwards, beckoning Miri to follow, impatient at the time it was taking for her to replace the key and put her gloves back on. "Woah! Hold on. I can't keep up with you," she shouted. He stopped and ran around in circles, unable to contain his excitement as Miri caught up and fell into step. "What's all this about, then? Aren't you going to give me a clue?"

Adam was enjoying taking the lead. There was no way he was going to say any more, so Miri did her best to stay close as Adam led her towards the fence which bordered the school and marked the perimeter of the estate.

This was the path that Miri had taken alone just a few months before, her curiosity aroused by a 'Keep Out' sign, her subsequent discovery of a derelict Victorian institute adding fuel to a growing suspicion that the village was harbouring a secret. The institute, protected by a preservation order, was now in the process of being restored by the National Trust, in the hope that it would serve the village in a positive way yet to be decided. Some people Miri had spoken to, Edie for example, felt that the building should not be used as an additional facility for the school, that any associations with children should be severed and never revisited. Others thought that using the revamped building to fulfil positive outcomes for the children of the village was entirely appropriate; a place where visiting theatre groups could perform, for example.

Miri was silently debating this issue in a deliberate effort to divert her thoughts away from the awful memories, when Adam drew her attention to a row of tied cottages situated along the eastern boundary. Miri had noticed them once before as she had driven around the outskirts of the estate on her way to the manor house, but she hadn't had the time then, nor the inclination, to observe them closely. She believed, quite rightly, that the cottages had been rented by Guy Frankland's labourers in time-honoured tradition, a precedent set by generations of his family before him. Now that Frankland was in prison and his land given over to the National Trust, Miri assumed that the cottages would be repurposed, possibly as some sort of historical attraction for visitors. Adam was pointing to the cottages, running backwards again, encouraging Miri to speed up.

"L-ook! L-ook! Adam's h-ouse! Adam's h-ouse!"

Miri stood still and watched as Adam ran towards the second door along from the left in the row of eight, all freshly painted in a different bright colour, and unlocked it. He signed for her to follow him, shrinking back from the door, shy and reluctant to make eye contact.

It had been his dearest wish for Miri to see his new home and now that she was here, he didn't know what to do. Miri, used to Adam's abrupt changes of mood, was practiced at restoring his equilibrium and swiftly took the lead. She knew it was his new home because he had told her, but she decided to play innocent and treat it as a game.

"This is your friend Tom's house isn't it, Adam? Is this where Tom and his family live?" Adam giggled and hid his face in his hands. "Are you there, Tom?" Miri called. "May I come in? I'm with Adam. We've come to see you. Hello!" Adam ran ahead of her into the tiny sitting room.

"No Tom! No Tom! Adam's house! Adam's house!"

"Your very own house? That's wonderful, Adam. It's beautiful." Adam wiped his tears away with the palm of his hand and showed her the ancient stove and old-fashioned square sink which was built into solid stone just beyond the low half wall which separated the kitchen from the rest of the downstairs space. A set of wooden steps, a unique groove worn into each one, led from just inside the door to an open loft space just big enough for a single bed, a tiny sink, and a cupboard which was built into a sloping wall. The toilet was outside, accessible by a stable door which led to a tiny backyard. The miniature rough walls had been whitewashed, but apart from that, Miri supposed it looked pretty much the same as it had when they were built, sometime during the eighteenth century, she guessed. The sloping flagstone floor and bulging walls made Miri feel slightly disoriented, as if she were at sea, and there was a distinctive earthy smell, moist and rotting, as if the walls were slowly oozing their secrets.

To Adam, it was a palace of boundless luxury and Miri, though curious as to how it had come about, was delighted for him. The few possessions he had were neatly arranged on hooks, much as they had been in the bird hide where he had slept in Frankland's time; plate, mug and spoon, clean and dry on the board next to the sink. The physical distance from the memories was enough to endow each and every item with a new lease of life, and Adam presented them as if Miri was seeing them for the first time. There were also two chairs, faded and sagging, and an upturned crate which served as a table.

"Adam! Adam love! Are you alright?" Someone was calling from outside.

"N-ettie. N-ettie," said Adam quietly. "Tom w-ife."

"Ah," said Miri. This was a good opportunity to check on Adam's welfare and find out a bit more about how he was getting on at work. Miri stepped out of the cottage and introduced herself to the young woman. Miri recognised her face but couldn't place her so she decided to start from scratch and let the details emerge naturally. She was more likely to remember them that way, rather than trying to make connections that may or may not exist.

"Ah, Miri. Yes, of course. I've been expecting you."

"You have?"

"Yes. Tom told me about your involvement with Adam, so I assumed you'd be coming to see him at work at some point." Nettie was smiling and her manner was friendly and efficient. "You've got the look," she said, laughing and resting her hands on her hips. Miri shook her head. "The look that says, 'I know you, but I can't think where from. Am I right?"

"Well, yes as a matter of fact," said Miri, feeling a little embarrassed and hoping that her own lack of clarity would not have the effect of making Nettie feel insignificant.

"I'll put you out of your misery. It happens all the time, don't worry. Nettie Hopkins," she said, shaking Miri's hand. "District nurse, based at the surgery in the village, but often seen peddling around the houses doing home visits, baby clinics at the village hall and the like. I'm usually in uniform, that's what confuses people, I reckon."

"Of course," said Miri, raising her eyebrows at her own inability to put two and two together. "I must have seen you at a distance many times." Adam was standing closely behind, a little overwhelmed at being the centre of this little drama.

Miri estimated Nettie to be somewhere in her mid-thirties, a large, fleshy woman with a pale face, large pale blue eyes and natural white frizzy hair that puffed out like a dandelion clock. Her lashes, eyebrows and lips were also colourless, the overall effect that of a face in need of definition. Out of uniform, Nettie presented herself in plain joggers, sweatshirt and trainers.

"Well now. What do you reckon, then?" she said in her broad Berkshire accent. "New 'ouse! New job. Doing great aren't you, love?" she added loudly, turning to Adam who was half hiding behind the open door, hands covering his cheeks. Miri touched Nettie's elbow lightly and began to walk slowly back along the narrow path with her, partly to allow Adam some privacy and spare him further embarrassment, partly to engage Nettie in a conversation that would further her own understanding of Adam's current situation.

"Hope you didn't mind me turning up," said Nettie. "We live in the old game-keeper's lodge just beyond the manor now," she said with pride. "Tom's been promoted to head groundsman as you probably know, but we used to live in the end cottage here." Miri followed Nettie's gaze. "It's bigger inside than the rest, with a bathroom built onto the side so it wasn't so bad. The rest of the cottages were just empty, a proper waste my Tom says, so he had 'em painted up, seen to some basic repairs, and offered 'em up for a few of the labourers. Well, I thought of Adam straight away, didn' I? Dossin' down in that filthy old hide all the way over the other side of the estate with all them bad memories, poor lad. At first, I thought he wouldn't want to make the move, but he took to it like a duck to water. He loves it! And it means I can drop in every now and then and make sure he's alright, like."

"Sounds perfect," said Miri, striking a more measured tone. "I'm so pleased for him. As Adam's mentor," she added, keen to make it clear that she would not be backing off just because the Hopkins' were nearby, "I shall monitor how he settles and continue to work with him on his emotional and communication needs. Thank you for thinking of him, Nettie. Adam seems very happy, and it's been a pleasure to meet you at last. Please pass on my thanks to Tom as well, would you? I will need to speak to him at some point, but I must be getting home now. My plan for today's session seems to have taken an unexpected turn."

"Adam!" Nettie yelled, "Miri is going now! Come and say goodbye."

"That's quite alright, leave it to me. I have a few things to say to him before I go," Miri insisted, waving to Nettie as she retraced her steps towards the cottage door. Adam had retreated inside, not surprisingly, so Miri was able to say her farewells undisturbed. She praised his home again, told him she was pleased with him and checked that he knew about their next meeting. "I'm so glad you brought me here, Adam. Thank you." Miri still judged it to be too early to raise the subject of Adam's silver pendant. He had dropped it into Miri's pocket to help her solve Melanie's murder, a personal item of much sentimental value. At some point Miri would return it, but not until she felt that Adam was resilient enough to withstand the resurrection of the horrific memories with which it was associated.

Miri smiled to herself walking home, reliving Adam's delight. This was a real step forward for him and she was almost as thrilled as he was. Mike might be inclined to suggest that Miri's input was no longer needed now, and she was planning her defence, for reasons she couldn't quite articulate, even to herself. There was something about the way Adam had shrunk back when they had been interrupted, that was concerning her. He had been overwhelmed, and this was an aspect of his needs that Nettie had clearly not understood, though she had meant well.

Miri could see from the path that Joe was not working in the annex. He probably wouldn't see her approaching, so she fumbled for her key. Stopping short, just before the porch, Miri took a sharp intake of breath, her hands flying to her face, dropping the key. On the slab of her front step lay a dead raven, a watery red stain spreading out from beneath its wing.

Chapter 7

"I just don't understand why anyone would do such a thing though, Darling. Surely the bird must have been attacked and fell from a tree or something?"

Though the edge had been taken off their appetite, once Joe had buried the bird in the back garden, they had quietly set about preparing for Edie's visit, sharing theories and trying to make some sense of it before she arrived. Joe was all for keeping it to themselves for the time being, but Miri knew that it wouldn't be a secret for long, and there was every chance that Edie had seen something herself. Over quiche and salad therefore, the grim discovery was the main topic of conversation.

"No way," said Joe. "There was a single wound, as if the poor thing had been stabbed, the rest of it was intact and it was placed neatly in the middle of the stone step. If it had been attacked, its body would've been in a terrible mess. Birds, especially big ones, don't get stabbed mid-flight. The poor thing must have been dead already and the stab wound is obviously some sort of message. There wasn't a feather out of place, was there Mum?" Miri shook her head, holding up her hands to express her bewilderment. "I must have nodded off, I'm afraid. If I'd been working by the window, I might have seen something." Joe hung his head to hide his embarrassment.

"Well, I certainly didn't see anything," said Edie. Miri and Joe exchanged a glance. Edie wasn't in the habit of missing anything, and Miri suspected that whoever had delivered the gruesome gift, was well aware of that. "So, let's just forget all about it, Darling. It's probably some odious adolescent creature playing a prank for Halloween, or a dare. Anything for a bit of excitement. Village life is wonderful in many ways, but for teenagers it can be a bore. That's my theory anyway. Let's have a top up Darling, and talk about all the events we are looking forward to in the coming weeks. Cheers!"

Miri pretended to soften her mood; Edie's theory was as good as any, after all. But beneath the light-hearted banter and optimism, the incident had shaken her deeply. A dead raven, a well-known symbol of death, had been placed at her door, and to Miri it was as powerful as receiving an anonymous letter. She knew that she had made enemies, the village would never be the same again, and to some that was reason enough to hate her. Strong-minded, capable women had been perceived as a threat and driven out of their communities, or worse, for centuries, and Miri wasn't about to give in to that kind of intimidation. However, she had been very ill, perilously close to death in fact, so the fear was not only real to her, it was all too familiar.

The following morning, Joe could see that his mother had not slept well.

"Come on, Mum," he said, guiding her to a chair at the kitchen table. "You're not going to let this thing drag you down, are you?"

"No. I'm fine, Joe. Just a bit tired. It spoiled a good day, that's all."

"Hmm. Well, good news. Our very own hero will be here tomorrow, so you'll have serious protection. Just had a message. That should cheer you up."

"Oh, it does, Joe. It does. What could possibly go wrong?" They laughed and Miri sat down while Joe made breakfast.

"Thought I'd explore a bit more today, if that's okay with you Mum? It's a better day weatherwise," he said, peering through the picture window at the calm blue sky, "and I could do with the exercise. Shall I pick up some shopping on my rounds? We'll need some extra grub with Will coming."

"Yes, that's fine. I need to pop into school this morning for a session with a small group of year one kids, and there's some admin I need to catch up on, but I'll be back by lunchtime." Miri smiled and tried to keep her spirits up, telling herself that she must not allow this, whoever and whatever it was, to spoil the precious time ahead with her boys. Striding boldly down the garden path with her head held high, a mere glance at the pale red stain on the step, Miri concentrated on the session she was about to deliver; she had her resources ready, the room was booked, and the kids would be waiting to tell her their news.

Joe cleared away the breakfast things, stacked the dishwasher and prepared to leave, taking the spare back door key from the hook. Both Joe and Will loved to cook together, and Joe was looking forward to picking up some fresh local ingredients from the village. He'd messaged his brother about the dead raven and Will had sent a vomiting emoji in response which had made Joe laugh, but he hadn't forgotten the shock he'd felt when he'd first seen the size of that bird, nor the first signs of a rancid smell as he'd scooped it onto the shovel. Joe knew that ravens were big, he'd seen pictures of course, but nothing had prepared him for the size of those claws and beak, the thick shaggy neck, and above all, the blackness. The shiny blackness.

Joe breathed deeply as he walked around to the front of the cottage, metaphorically and literally ridding his system of the image. The plan was to acquaint himself more thoroughly with the layout of the village, taking in a visit to the churchyard along the way.

Joe was hoping that Michael would be working there again so that he might discover more about the history of some of the ancient families, particularly that of the solitary grave, alone and neglected as it was, that had so captivated him. Something in his subconscious had linked the raven with the gravestones, maybe something he had read in a book as a child.

The village looked new to Joe beneath the brightness, a black and white drawing magically exposed into muted colour overnight. Thatches reflected their undulating shades of gold, and stone walls suddenly paled creamy and thick by the light, played host to their russet and ginger climbers. Hedgerows dripped, trees shuffled off their dead, and a new wetness varnished the lane.

Michael, bent double over his hoe, cap bobbing in time with his slow and steady action, paused as Joe approached and smiled a greeting.

"Thought I might be seeing you again, lad," he said. "I keep a spare shovel for visitors. Puts 'em off and keeps 'em from trampling all over my paths."

"Oh, sorry," said Joe. "I wouldn't want to cause any damage."

"Nah, I'm only teasing, lad," said Michael with a wheezy chuckle, making it necessary to spit on the ground behind him. "I don't mind. There's a lot to do this time of year, what with the leaves blowin' all over the place and the prunin' an' all, but it's always nice to pass the time o'day. I often stops to 'ave a chat with yer mother if she takes this path 'ome."

Joe took this to mean that his time as a visitor was limited, so he offered to lend a hand, sweeping and scooping some of the dead leaves onto the compost heap which was sheltered from the winds on the far side by the east wall. Michael made no comment about this and they fell into a silent working rhythm until Joe felt comfortable enough to ask what he had come to find out.

"I expect you know all the names here on the stones by heart, Michael."

"Should do, been tendin' 'em since I were a lad. Reckon I know every chip an' crack in every stone, ev'ry date, ev'ry name, who's related to who, what they died of, who visits, who don't." Michael rested on his hoe, one rough hand on top of the other. "I know more 'bout these dead 'uns 'ere than I know about the live 'uns out there, and that's the way I like it."

Joe smiled. There was no sensible answer to this. "Many ancient family names I see, and many young children who must have died of disease."

"See that circle of graves yonder, set apart from the rest, lad?" Michael was warming to his subject, proud of his expertise and happy to impart his knowledge to a youngster. "Whole family died of the black death. They say the head of the family, probably a drover, walked to London to sell his sheep at market, came back with the disease and the whole family died. The church would only agree to bury them if they was well away from the rest, fearing they'd spread it after death, and the village would be cursed. They say," he added with emphasis, "that they was buried in a circle 'cos of the 'ring 'o roses' like in the rhyme, which was supposed to keep the bad smells away."

Michael continued to turn over the damp ground, feeding in the nutrients provided by the rotting vegetation, and breathing in the familiar odours; decay and death. A pocket full of posies.

"Fascinating," said Joe. Then more casually as he continued to scoop up the dead leaves, "Know anything about the grave over there, away from all the others, the one that's neglected and looks like it's falling over? I noticed it yesterday."

Michael turned his back. "Don't know nothin' about it, don't go near it and never shall," he grunted. Then he turned and looked at Joe, close up, intense and menacing, a filthy finger in his face. "And if you know what's good for yer, you won't neither! Do you 'ear me, lad? That's the grave of Lavinia Whitlock. Burned at the stake for a witch. It's cursed." Joe stepped away respectfully as Michael turned his back again, spat noisily, and resumed his rhythmical sweeping. "This is my place," he said over his shoulder. Don't want no trouble."

Chapter 8

Miri's friend Michele was stationed in her usual position behind the screen in the school foyer, ready to spring into action by welcoming visitors to school, answering the phone, relaying messages, rescuing soggy lunches and wiping tears.

Miri first met her when she had enquired about a job there, ostensibly to help out, but in reality, to delve a little into the welfare of the children. On that occasion, Miri had found her to be rude and officious, but it later transpired that Shel, as she was known, had been under a great deal of pressure at the time, torn between maintaining her position and therefore her mortgage, or whistleblowing about what she suspected was going on. Later in the investigation, Shel had been a great help to Miri, they had become firm friends as a result and always greeted each other as such. The two women spent a couple of minutes catching up on their news and Shel was delighted when she learned that both of Miri's boys would be staying in the village for a while. Miri didn't tell her about the raven though. It was neither the time nor the place; an isolated incident hopefully.

She signed in, grabbed a quick coffee from the staff room and made her way quickly to the usual small annex room, uncharacteristically flustered, distracted by the raven business, and aware that her usual setup time was now briefer than usual.

Miri's sessions were all designed to improve the children's communication skills and she liked to have the chairs arranged in a circle. The six children who regularly came to the sessions were identified by their teachers as those who would most benefit from this kind of booster session, where they could practice talking, without the pressure of writing anything down. The aim was to encourage self-confidence, turn-taking and listening skills, and Miri had been surprised by the variety of needs within the group. It meant she had to plan each session carefully to ensure that each child had the chance to improve on their weaknesses.

The focus of this session was going to be turn-taking and being heard, and Miri had brought some enlarged photographs for them to talk about in case any of them did not have any interesting news of their own. As the children arrived, flushed from their outside play, Miri welcomed each by name and guided them to their chair. She had worked out a strategic seating plan based on who was best kept away from whom, and the children knew what to expect.

Miri started the session with a few word games based on the photographs to get the children warmed up, then invited them to share a sentence or two about something that had happened, or a place they had visited.

"It doesn't need to be anything exciting," Miri coaxed, "just as long as you say something. If all you did at the weekend was visit your nan, or walk the dog, that's fine, okay? I'll give you a minute to think about it but don't speak yet," she said, and pressed her finger to her lips. Miri set an egg timer going for them to focus on while she gathered her pictures together.

The little ones swayed on their chairs, screwed their faces up, swung their legs, sucked their fingers and wiped their noses on their sleeves as the endless minute slipped away, but it was all part of the learning.

"Okay, now. Let's start with you, Billy." Billy rarely gave any thought to what he said, a breathless torrent of unfinished sentences about anything and everything, so Miri was trying to encourage him to think and select before he began to speak. "Remember there are lots of other children who want to speak as well, so just a sentence or two please. Can anyone remember what this is for?" Miri held up a large shell, or conch, which was to be passed to the child whose turn it was to speak. If you didn't have the conch, you weren't allowed to speak and each child had to use both hands to hold it because of its size which, Miri hoped, would prevent them from picking their noses, at least while they were speaking.

Next up was Sadie, who could speak in proper sentences and often had interesting things to say but whispered so quietly that she could not be heard.

"Let's use our massive voice today Sadie, and put the tiny voice in our pockets, shall we?" This worked for the first two words, the rest of the speech being totally inaudible, but again it was an improvement, so they all gave her a clap. David hadn't interrupted yet which was another improvement, and Miri was planning to leave him last and give him extra encouragement for waiting his turn. The conch moved around to Tilly now who needed to straighten her tights and skirt and pull her jumper down before she could begin. "Okay sweetheart," said Miri with a smile. "Off you go."

"My mummy'th a witchth. Thshe maketh thsmellth," said Tilly, wriggling in her chair, tiny hands flying up to her face, either with embarrassment or alarm at knowing that she'd told a secret.

"Do you mean 'spells', sweetheart?" Miri asked, the only thing preventing her from laughing being the desire for clarification before the moment was lost. Tilly nodded slowly, legs swinging, nose running.

"That's interesting, Tilly," said Miri, gathering her wits. "Well done." Again, the other children did not respond; it was clearly just a matter of fact. She may as well have said, 'my mummy workth in a shop,' so Miri drew no further attention to it.

"You've all done very well today and I'm going to give you all a special sticker."

On any other day, Tilly's remark would have remained an innocent source of amusement, if registered at all; Miri assuming that Tilly and her mother had been playing a game or preparing something for Halloween. But this was today, the day after a well-known symbol of witchcraft had been deliberately levelled at her and her family. Deep in thought as she approached her cottage, she lifted the gate latch, waved half-heartedly to Edie, glanced at the step and went in.

Joe was already home, unpacking some shopping and waiting for the kettle to boil.

"Hi, Mum. How did it go?" he said casually without looking up.

"Oh fine, thanks Joe," she said, hanging up her bag and coat. "How about you? Did your exploration of the village live up to expectations? I see you've been shopping. Thanks, Joe."

"No problem." Joe knew there was no point in keeping quiet about his morning with Michael; his Mum would know there was something wrong and it would come out sooner or later. "I er, had an interesting meeting with Michael in the churchyard earlier," he began.

"Oh yes. What happened?" Miri had noticed Joe's reserve and was relieved that he was about to talk without the need for her to question him. He told her about it, slightly playing down the intensity of Michael's passionate warning, but even so, Miri could see that he had been shaken by the experience. Will would have been more inclined to laugh it off, she thought, treat it as deep-rooted ignorance and superstition, and then imitate Michael's voice with uncanny accuracy. As if reading her thoughts, he added.

"I probably wouldn't have taken much notice, except..." Miri looked at him, eyebrows raised, not wishing to rush him. "Well, I know it sounds daft, but every time I go near that grave, I feel a sort of weariness come over me. I felt it yesterday when I first saw it. I kind of lost track of time, as if I'd zoned out for a bit. Weird," he said, shaking his head as if to clear his mind. "And then sleeping yesterday afternoon. I never do that. Even after a gig. The same thing happened today. While I was working with Michael, I felt almost compelled to keep looking over to that corner where she, you know, the grave is, and every time I did, I felt a sort of calmness and couldn't hear when Michael was calling me. I saw his lips move but heard no sound." Joe sat down, pale and preoccupied. Miri's concern for her son eclipsed any nagging concerns of her own, and she sat down opposite, poured the tea in silence and chose her words carefully.

"Whatever it is Joe, I'm sure there's a rational explanation. You've been on tour for months. You're re-adjusting, that's all. Your brain is fatigued, that's why you're sleepy, and your body is probably wondering why there's so much nutrition inside it. You've no need to go there, anyway Joe, if it upsets you."

"Yes, but what if it's got something to do with this bloody raven business? What then? We can't ignore that."

"What makes you think they're linked? Probably just a coincidence."

"Or not," he said grimly, twisting his cup round and round in his hands.

Miri felt a bit guilty for not sharing Tilly's revelation, justifying it on the grounds that it would merely add fuel to the fire and might not mean anything anyway. Even so, privately she intended to arrange a coffee meeting with Shel, to see if she knew anything about Tilly's family that might shed some light on the matter.

"You two are in fine spirits I see," Edie shouted through the window, hands shading her eyes on either side of her face. Both Miri and Joe jumped at the sudden intrusion into their private thoughts but managed to rally round and behave as near to normal as they could. "You look like you've seen a ghost, Darling," she said.

"Sorry, Edie. Miles away. Tea?"

"Super. Brought some Welsh cakes. Still warm."

"Lovely, thanks Edie. Might have them after lunch if that's okay. We've both only just got in."

"Oh yes, that's fine. I won't keep you. When is Will due to arrive? Bet you can't wait, Joe. Be company for you."

"Yeah, haven't seen him for a while. Tomorrow as far as we know."

"Lovely. Are we still on for choir tonight, Darling?" she said. "That's what I came round for really, and to see how you are, of course."

"I think I'm going to give it a miss tonight, Edie," Miri said firmly. "I'm rather tired and I need to prepare a bit for Will's arrival. I don't want to miss the meeting in the pub tomorrow night, so I suppose I'm prioritising."

Edie had come to recognise this decisive tone in Miri and didn't attempt to persuade her. "Of course. I'll fill you in if we start anything new, Darling," she said helpfully, "and if I don't see you before, I'll swing by about seven tomorrow evening. How does that sound?"

"Could you make it half six? I said I'd call in at the vicarage to take Rev Zoe along."

"Yes, by all means. Be a good opportunity to have a nose round. We can take the shortcut to the pub round the back of Jack Whitlock's place," she added as she made her way to the door. Joe almost dropped the cups he was carrying to the dishwasher but rescued them just in time.

"Who's he?" Miri asked, not remembering having heard the name before.

"He's the old boy who lives alone in the cottage on the edge of the graveyard just behind the church. You can't miss it. He's a bit of a local legend, but as with most people who keep themselves to themselves, whatever folks don't know, they make up," she said bitterly.

Joe still had his back to them, rummaging around in the dishwasher, but he was listening intently.

"Like what?" he asked nonchalantly.

"Well, he's the only living member of one of the oldest families in Kington; that's enough for some people to single him out as weird, Darling. He's a bit grumpy and taciturn, so naturally that makes him a potential threat. The only person who has anything to do with him is his old school chum, Bob Whittle. You know Bob, Miri, runs the repair shop in the village." Miri nodded. "Let me see, what else?" said Edie, ramping up the tension and swinging one of her bright wraps around her shoulders as if delivering the final speech in act five of a play. "He refused to have his cottage modernised because it meant he would have to move out while the work was being done, and of course anyone who still gets water from a well must have a screw loose, surely? Oh, and because he is almost entirely self-sufficient, living off the land, rearing pigs, chickens, keeping a cow for milk and growing herbs for his aches and pains, he must be some sort of wizard, right? See you later, Darling!" Stage exit left.

After Edie had left, Miri and Joe silently set about preparing lunch.

"This Jack Whitlock, he must be a descendant of hers Mum. I bet he knows all about her." he said.

Miri was finding it increasingly hard to ignore the recent onslaught of evidence that Kington was still, four hundred years on, somehow inextricably linked to the supernatural, whether real or imagined. But if she were to investigate the extent of this phenomenon, assuming her suspicions were correct, she would need to tread very carefully. Someone had already singled her and her family out. A warning perhaps? She had already nearly lost one of her sons.

"Forget it, Joe. Do as Michael says. Forget it."

Chapter 9

"Just going for a walk, Mum." Will and Joe were delighting in each other's company, and now Miri found herself putting recent events into perspective. If people wanted to prance through the village following a branch and shouting ridiculous rhymes, fine; if Tilly's mother wanted to brew up a storm, fine; if someone out there was getting a kick out of leaving odious birds on people's steps, fine. Nothing was going to spoil this day. She even managed to stay quiet when she heard Will ask Joe to wait while he got his foraging knife out. She suspected that their walk would take them in the direction of the graveyard, but she refused to let even that prospect bother her. She might have a quiet word with Will later about Joe's preoccupation with the grave of Lavinia Whitlock, but for now she had work of her own to do, and a couple of hours alone was just what she needed.

Will wanted to show Joe the cellar where he had been 'left to rot,' as he put it, the copse where he had found Mel Crew's body, and the bird hide where almost the entire local police force had been waiting for the killer to strike, only to be faced with a decoy, whilst the real killer was in their mother's house with the murder weapon. It was important to him to have the opportunity to offload to someone he was close to, someone who hadn't been there. Will found it a cathartic experience to relive some of the scenes from his own unique point of view, entertaining his brother with snippets of conversations he could remember, using his brilliant talent as a voice artist. Joe was suitably impressed and awestruck, seasoned with the kind of relief one feels when we know all is well, and those we love are safe. They both expressed a keen sadness for the dead girl.

When they arrived at the institute, still bleak and repellent but humanised by workers erecting scaffolding and cladding, they heard someone shouting.

"Wi-ll! Wi-ll!"

"It's Adam! Come on Joe. Have you met him yet?"

"No, but Mum talks about him so much, I feel I know him anyway."

"Just give him time to finish his sentences."

"I'm not a complete idiot, Will. Give me some credit."

"Hey!" said Will as Adam ran towards him, arms flailing like windmills. "Come 'ere." Will hugged Adam and they laughed and clung to each other, bonded by a traumatic experience shared. "This is Joe, my brother."

"J-oe! J-oe!" Joe hugged him as Will had, though not so enthusiastically, and the three of them fell into step, Will taking care not to mention anything that might cause pain. Joe suggested that Adam could show them some good patches to forage for mushrooms and wild berries, and they spent an enjoyable hour with him, including a tour of his cottage.

"L-ots of spe-cial pl-ants!" said Adam, showing them his patch. "Nett-ie gr-ows th-em. Nett-ie makes dr-inks w-th the pl-ants!" He made a sour face and they all laughed, Adam delighting in their reaction. Will was pleased to see

Adam so happy and resisted the temptation to worry him about the diversity of plants there. Some of the species were quite rare; one or two he had never seen before.

They had gathered enough mushrooms for the baked pasta dish they were planning to cook later, but Joe wanted to show Will Lavinia Whitlock's grave before they went home. Will could tell that Joe was interested in her and had, by his own admission, been deeply affected by the sight of her grave. He listened attentively to his story, but when he heard about Michael's allegation that the grave was cursed, he snorted with derision and agreed to help with some research on the matter while they had some time together.

"Sounds like a crock o' shit, Joe. What harm can it do?"

"See that cottage over there?" said Joe. Will craned his neck over the boundary wall.

"That old wreck of a place? Nobody lives there, surely?"

"Yep. None other than one Jack Whitlock."

"Jesus! That'd be as good a place to start as any. Rather you than me though, mate."

During the short walk back, Joe told Will about the dead raven incident. "I know Mum doesn't want to talk about it, but just in case she does. She was really upset."

"Some nutter trying to put the frighteners on ahead of Halloween, I expect. I bet half the cottages in the village have been targeted. Probably bored. I bet nothing's happened here since—"

"Since you, 'hero of the moment', saved everyone from a fate worse than death?" This resulted in a play fight which continued all along the lane, fading naturally as they neared Wheelwright Cottage.

***

Edie, punctual as ever, had clearly given due consideration to her first meeting with the new reverend. She had chosen an uncharacteristically conservative outfit; mustard woollen dress with matching jacket, subtle blonde hair piece and dainty shoes.

"Don't want to create the wrong impression, Darling," she said.

"That's exactly what you're doing, Edie." And Miri, rather mischievously, eagerly anticipated the moment when Edie met Rev Zoe and realised her error. If Edie was expecting a conservatively styled vicar, she was in for a shock. Miri thought it served her right. Who, in the light of recent events, would care a hoot about impressing a vicar? Edie.

The night had become still, warm air made heavy by fruits of the oncoming season, rich and mellow. Miri had never been inside the vicarage and it had remained empty since the arrest of George Tripley. His wife Helen had been offered the choice of staying on until a new vicar could be appointed, but she had chosen to move out and stay with her cousin Beatrice, wife of another key player, Vic Burton. Much of the evidence, mostly in the form of photographs on computers, had been retrieved when the church was searched. Helen hadn't been able to face another night in the vicarage, so she and Beatrice had cleaned and polished it from top to bottom and left, Helen taking no more than her personal belongings away with her. Edie had attended a garden party there once, many years before, but the house itself had been out of bounds on that occasion so neither of them knew what to expect, should they be invited inside.

From the sweeping and gently elevating approach, the house was impressive. Dating back to the turn of the eighteenth century, the creamy stone, limestone tiles, mullioned windows and spacious storm porch, endowed the house with immense charm, and both women were secretly hoping to be shown around.

When Zoe opened the beautiful oak panelled door and welcomed them, Miri was required to nudge Edie discreetly, alerting her to the fact that her mouth was gaping open. Maybe it was Zoe's diminutive and unimposing stature? Maybe her youth and delicacy of features? Maybe. Miri strongly suspected that the leather jacket and patent biker boots were to blame, and when Edie finally did close her mouth, she shot Miri a withering look. "Why didn't you tell me?" she hissed as they followed Zoe into the drawing room. "I look like a reject from the local women's institute. I'll never forgive you!" Miri grinned, hoping it would teach Edie a lesson, and pleased that for once, she had the advantage over her neighbour in the presentation stakes. Miri had chosen the 'coolest' outfit she possessed, leggings and a long denim tunic, and couldn't resist teasing Edie a little by briefly adopting a catwalk style wiggle. She knew that Edie would not forgive her for this and imagined with dread the fright she had in store from one of Edie's bizarre transformations.

"Great to have visitors," said Zoe. "This place is ridiculously big for little old me," she continued, twirling around, arms outstretched to emphasise the point. "I feel a bit guilty really. I'm happy to share or move somewhere smaller, but when I suggested it to the parish, they wouldn't hear of it, so I guess I'll just have to get used to it. When I've settled in, I shall set about planning how I can make best use of the space to benefit the village."

"Parties? How wonderful!" said Edie, clapping her hands.

"Maybe. I was thinking more of fundraising events and the like," said Zoe, suppressing a smile. "I'm hoping that most people will want to see the back of the old ways," she added, cocking her head to one side in that characteristic way of hers.

"Don't bank on it, dear," said Edie.

The room felt very grand with its high vaulted ceilings, panelled walls and ancient floorboards. The furniture and rugs were a little old fashioned for Miri's taste, and certainly incongruous with the new tenant, but the atmosphere was homely and comfortable. Zoe was thrilled to show her guests round, commenting on various idiosyncrasies she had discovered so far, such as clanging pipes, creaking stairs and a dodgy cistern.

"Gosh! Don't you feel a bit nervous here on your own with all those spooky noises going on?" said Edie, and Miri nudged her for the second time. Edie made a puzzled expression and raised her hands, palms up. "Just asking, Darling."

"No way," said Zoe immediately adopting what she obviously considered to be her most threatening defensive kickboxing stance, leather jacket squeaking, boot buckles rattling.

"Oh, I see," said Edie, backing away slightly. Miri was enjoying this.

The huge kitchen had clearly been modernised in stages over the centuries, the strata of evidence visible in the exposed brickwork, the beams and rough plastering, juxtaposed with modern appliances and 1960's plumbing.

"I'd like to redecorate as soon as I've finished unpacking," said Zoe. "Thou shalt not live by magnolia alone, saith the Lord!"

"Couldn't agree more. I'm rather good with colour myself if you ever feel you need any help," said Edie, negotiating several packing crates in the small conservatory, clearly a recent addition to the property.

"I think we'd better be going Zoe," said Miri tactfully, looking at her watch. "I need to introduce you to the meeting and time's getting on."

"Yes, of course," she replied as they headed back towards the front door. "But you must come again, for coffee one morning maybe, and I can show you the rest of the house. Hopefully, I might be a bit better organised by then. It's clean thanks to Helen, but the police search team certainly didn't stand on ceremony when they turned the place over. There's damage to the paintwork and chips knocked out of the bannisters. Don't think they found anything though."

***

The pub lounge was busy for early evening, wonderful smells of sizzling steaks, roast vegetables and fruit compotes mingled with the charred earthiness from the open fire.

"This is fantastic!" said Zoe.

"Good evening. Good evening." said Gavin, rubbing his hands together and steering them through to the snug meeting room, totally unfazed by Zoe's appearance. "You must be the new rev. Love the outfit. I love black and white, don't you? The collar really sets off that jacket, it really does." Zoe made a theatrical bow and followed Miri and Edie in.

A handful of the committee had met Zoe before, during the selection process, so there were some friendly faces, offers of seats and so on, which served to put her at ease and offset the raised eyebrows and furtive whispers from some of the more traditional members. If asked why they had reacted so, they would have been unable to answer; a vague reference to a leather jacket maybe, a blustery sarcastic and wordless sneer, a shallow and above all, unchristian response. Miri was expecting this, she was not a church goer herself for many reasons, but she was determined to support Zoe and was ready with her own armoury of caustic remarks, should she be called upon to use them. However, she bit her lip until Nadya gave her the nod and she stood up to address the meeting. She waited a few seconds for the conversations to peter out and for everyone to look at her. Edie, who was sitting as close to Miri as she could get, tapped her hand lightly to show her support and prepared to glare at anyone who dared to interrupt.

"Good evening," Miri began with a smile and what she hoped was an upbeat tone, her 'teacher voice'. "I have been asked to introduce our brand-new reverend this evening." Everyone looked at Zoe and back at Miri, much like the timed shift of gaze one sees at a tennis match. Helen, uncomfortable as the situation must have been for her, sat with dignity and poise, smiled warmly at Zoe and triggered a round of spontaneous applause. This not only broke the tension but gave Miri's speech the positive kick-start it needed and set the tone for the evening.

"The village has been through a difficult time," she continued, once everyone had settled again. "We are here to plan ahead for the forthcoming season and beyond. The Reverend Zoe Deans has been appointed to lead our church and represent that fresh start right at the heart of the village. I'm sure we're all looking forward to the new and exciting ways the church can serve our community and I have no doubt that Zoe," Miri paused for the smattering of giggles to die down, "is just the breath of youthful fresh air we need. Please make her welcome!" Miri turned to Zoe, initiated another round of applause and checked that she was happy to say a few words.

"Thank you so much," she began. "I'm sorry if I have disappointed some of you with my outfit tonight." A low murmur ensued which Zoe allowed to run. "My leopard skin bodysuit is in the wash, but I promise you—" Jane Peters, who had surreptitiously reached for a piece of Craig's homemade lemon shortbread from the buffet table, guffawed loudly and succeeded in spraying two of the adjacent tables. Good-humoured laughter rippled through the room as Zoe's next move was eagerly anticipated, poker faces clearly in the minority. "I am dedicated to helping make this village the happy place we all want and deserve it to be. For our children, our parents and our friends, Christians and non- Christians alike, let us work and play together. I can't wait. Please come along on Sunday morning for the service, when I will be outlining some of my ideas and enlisting some help. In the meantime, if anyone would like to give me a hand cleaning the church, I would be very grateful!" Robust applause ensued as Zoe sat down.

"Well done, Darling," said Edie, eyeballing someone at the back who wasn't clapping.

The rest of the meeting ran according to the agenda, business matters being swiftly dealt with before the break, long awaited decisions about the forthcoming celebrations to be announced at the end.

"We have deliberated long and hard," said Nadya. "We had loads of terrific suggestions and we've settled on the following. Please don't be too disappointed if your idea hasn't been taken up; we have kept a record of everything and hope to include them all in future events. For now, the Halloween celebrations will consist of the following: First, the traditional burning tree and procession through the village by the children." Miri kept her head down, not wishing to show her disapproval too strongly but making her feelings clear by not joining in any celebratory noises or gestures. "Secondly, the bonfire, jacket spud, hotdog and fireworks night on November the fifth which we usually host." Everyone cheered, relieved that this popular family event was not about to be axed. "An idea we have chosen which is different this year is this: a short performance of the 'three witches' scene from Macbeth, involving the year six pupils. Now, for those who don't know, a famous actor, retired now, called Dexter Steele was born in the village. He lives in Oxford these days and has agreed to come along to help the children with their play and maybe deliver a couple of suitable speeches himself. Jez has been in touch with him and is following up on the arrangements. We thought it would be positive publicity for the village and great for the kids." There were murmurs of agreement here though not everyone knew who Dexter Steele was.

"He used to be in a few of the soaps in the seventies and eighties," whispered Edie. "Plus a few productions at the Oxford Playhouse. He was rather a dish in his day. I knew him in my London days."

"We particularly wanted the focus of this event to include children and be as much fun for them as possible," Nadya added, as if justification were necessary, Miri privately questioning just how much fun an aged theatrical 'has-been' would be for the youngsters. However, positive publicity was always welcome, and overall Miri felt there was a good variety of events lined up. Nadya reminded everyone that the Aunt Sally tournament would go ahead as usual during the celebrations and that the hosts of the Kington Arms would, as ever, be catering for all events with seasonal fayre for all. No-one argued with that. Nadya and her team had made initial notes about who might take responsibility for the various events based on previous years, but she asked for additional volunteers to contact her over the coming days by email or text.

Most people were happy with the decisions but there were a few sour faces as the meeting broke up and one or two negative comments. "Who the hell is Dexter bloody Steele anyway?" Good question.

"Will you be joining us for a drink, Zoe?" asked Miri. "I'm meeting the boys in the lounge. Edie, are you staying?" No-one could think of a good reason to go home, so a cosy alcove and a bottle of red was duly commandeered, and the evening was rounded off by interesting conversation and good company. Just when Miri thought she couldn't be happier, DS Kate Woodley joined them, deliberately squeezing in between Will and Zoe.

"Oh! Sorry!" said Zoe, pleasantly. "I'll budge up."

"Yeah, thanks." Trendy new vicars with perfect facial features were all very well, in their place; a narrow window seat, cosying up to Will, wasn't one of them.

Chapter 10

Joe couldn't remember the last time he'd been up and about so early. He told himself that he hadn't wanted to disturb his brother's hangover nor his mother's rest, but the real reason was that Joe wanted to be alone for a couple of hours. This was part of Joe's nature and not particularly unusual, but there was an ulterior motive on this occasion, an inevitable meeting with Jack Whitlock. Miri was also up early. She drew her tiny curtain and lingered, as she always did, to absorb the view and note the changes engendered by the changing season. She saw, with some surprise, her son emerging from the side of the cottage, hands in pockets, beanie pulled down low over his ears, and wondered what could be important enough to drag him from his bed at this hour.

The autumn sun had barely risen, and a harvest moon was still visible, suspended huge and pale against the brightening sky. Murmurings were already afoot in the fields as the long day began on the farms, and as the mist swirled and eddied around Joe's feet, almost to his knees, he wondered how the drivers negotiated their tractors in such conditions. He paused to savour the solitude and stillness, the mellow scents, the otherworldliness of this time of day, and pulled his hat further down over his ears against the chill. Nascent yellow light penetrated the grey swirls and created a unique pattern, drawing Joe closer to the natural world again; if the day had ended there and then, it would not have been wasted.

He was fully prepared for a long wait, having no idea of Jack's routine, but there was plenty yet to discover in the village and he would simply return later if there was no sign of life at this early hour. No rush.

Joe took the route through the graveyard, a shortcut which led to the back of the cottage. Mist rose high enough here, so that Joe could barely make out even the very tips of the stones as he tentatively negotiated the path which wound around the church, stumbling from time to time on a protruding flagstone or small rock, startling tiny nocturnal residents as they made their way to their nests or burrows. By the time Joe reached the solitary grave of Lavinia Whitlock the mists had begun to clear, and the cottage stood well defined against the deepening sky, trademark embellishments along the ridge of the thatch as unique as the building itself. Only the grave remained partially shrouded, the final swirls reluctant to leave its resident unprotected, a persistent chill allowing a thin frost to remain there. It was from this vantage point that Joe was able to absorb the scene in more detail without either interruption from Will, nor reprisal from Michael.

The lack of modernisation was clear, even from the outside, the many ancient and unidentifiable tools leaning up against the cottage wall were testament to that. Will would love those, thought Joe, remembering fondly his brother's interest in living off the land. It was like stepping back in time, a window into how people would have lived three centuries ago, at least from the outside. Whatever else Jack Whitlock may prove to be, Joe gathered that he must be a meticulous and highly organised man.

The tools were clean and neatly stacked against the shed. A vegetable patch set in the sunniest corner of the garden was arranged in neatly trimmed rows with hand crafted markers. Bean poles were uniform and tightly bound, and the short path was swept and weed free. A squirrel played among the branches of a gnarled and twisted apple tree in the far corner. The sun rose, and a fox alert to Joe's presence, peered from behind the low hedge that separated the small garden from the graveyard before darting out, his thick bushy tail sweeping the earth.

Joe had barely moved. The clunk of a latch brought him out of his reverie, and he took a step back not wishing to startle Jack at this early hour.

"Go on girl, out you go." A gruff voice followed by a throaty cough heralded the appearance of an old collie dog, arthritic and slow, before the clunk of the latch again. Joe watched as the old companion negotiated the familiar surroundings and settled in a warm spot by the root of an ivy which was slowly crawling across the west wall of the cottage. A twig snapped. The dog raised its head and cocked an ear.

"Hello there," said Joe gently, stepping over the hedge and walking slowly forwards, bent low, arm outstretched. The dog fidgeted a little, uncertain of the threat and no longer able to act. It whimpered gently and the clunk of the latch came again.

"Hey! What are you up to?" said Jack, growling and reaching for a pitchfork. The dog slowly got to its feet, ever willing to protect the master, however impotently. "Clear off before I pin you to this wall 'ere!" Joe raised his hands and found his most winning smile.

"Mr. Whitlock, please. I'm sorry to disturb you. I was walking around the churchyard and saw your dog so I, er—"

"An' you thought you'd come trespassin' on my land!" Jack was shouting now, anger lining his face, mistrust etched in every crevasse, his broad rural accent stronger than before. "Get out!" followed by another jab of the pitchfork. Joe backed away; hands still raised.

"Of course."

"Always one of your lot poking their noses round 'ere. I've said all I want to say! Do you 'ear? I don't know any more about 'em. Poachers come and go. Let that be the end of it. I won't be so bloody gracious next time." Gracious was not the word Joe would have used to describe Jack's behaviour, but he quickly worked out that this was a case of mistaken identity.

"I'm not a journalist," Joe ventured quickly, reluctant to leave on these terms. "I'm Joe Sinclair, Miri's son. I'm staying with Mum for a few days. I'm sorry about being on your property. I just saw your dog. I didn't mean to disturb you." Jack paused before lowering the pitchfork. His sudden spike in temper had subsided and he even looked somewhat abashed.

"Well, I 'ave to look after meself. She ain't much good now." The poor dog raised its head as if to object but settled back down again. "Well, sorry lad," Jack continued more thoughtfully. "I know a bit about your mother and what she done to make sure them bastards got banged up. I seen 'er about. Nice lady. That 'headstrong lad must be your brother then?"

Joe laughed, still nervous but keen to take advantage of Jack's change of heart. "Yes, that'll be Will. He's been through a lot but we're spending some time together now." Jack nodded. He was a man of indeterminate age. He could have been anywhere between fifty and seventy-five, tall and wiry, though slightly stooped, with a full head of thick hair the colour of a pearl tied back in a low ponytail with a piece of rough twine. Joe thought he must have been handsome in his youth, good cheekbones, brown skin and a well-shaped nose. His old clothes had long ago moulded to the shape of his body, and his boots were caked with the same earth that he devoted his days to tending and protecting.

Jack rubbed his white whiskers with the palm of his hand. "So, what do you really want?" he said, levelling a stare at Joe, clear grey eyes still a force to be reckoned with. "I knows you ain't 'ere at this blessed time o' day to pet old Bess 'ere." Once again, Bess raised her head momentarily, decided it wasn't worth the effort and placed it back down. Joe knew better than to insult Jack by trying to blag his way out of the situation and decided to be straight with him.

"To be honest, Mr. Whitlock, I don't really know." The sun was fully risen now, mist burned off, long distorted shadows forming along the path. Unconsciously, he turned towards Lavinia's grave. "I'm interested in the history of the village," he continued, suddenly inspired, "and I assumed, because of your name, that you would know more than most. Edie says you are the last surviving member of one of the oldest families."

"Ha! Edie! Bloody woman drives me mad," said Jack. "Lives in a fantasy world of costumes and," Jack paused, searching for the right words, gesticulating wildly, "characters in some bloody play."

"She's been very kind to us," said Joe, feeling it necessary to defend Edie.

"Oh ay, she's alright in that way but," and he tapped his temple to illustrate his meaning. "You'd best come in then."

"Thank you," said Joe politely. "Beats being impaled with a pitchfork," he added.

Jack grunted. "Don't push yer luck, son."

The cottage door was tiny so that Joe needed to duck, and the ceiling was low. He thought this may account for Jack's permanent stoop. There was a stale smell inside, a combination of damp, burnt wood and neglect; clearly Jack's meticulous organisation was confined to the garden. The flagstone floor undulated from years of wear, and Joe felt a little disoriented as he followed Jack through the kitchen area to the small sitting room at the back.

The kitchen consisted of a wood stove, a large sink with one tap which was green with rust, and a shelf for two battered cooking pots. Various implements such as a ladle, an enamel jug and mug, knives and cleavers, hung from an array of hooks drilled into the one huge beam which ran across the ceiling. The sitting room, reached by stepping down and ducking through a narrow passage, contained two faded easy chairs, sunken and oozing their stuffing, a gas lamp, an open fireplace and an old brown wireless that looked like it dated back to World War Two. There was hardly any natural light, and the only fresh air had curled in by accident through the gaps in the rotting window frames.

Joe was relieved that Jack made no offer of a drink but sat, when invited, on one of the chairs, sinking almost to the ground, knees uncomfortably high. "I finds it beneficial to stretch the legs out lad," said Jack observing Joe's discomfort and demonstrating the move. Joe smiled, thinking that whatever wildlife was thriving inside this nest of a chair was just as likely to invade his trousers wherever his legs were. A black cushion, which turned out to be a cat, unfurled and stretched at Joe's feet, green eyes half closed, all seeing.

"Well, what d'ya wanna know, son?" said Jack, striking a match on the wall and picking up a crusty pipe. Joe wanted to get as near to the point as politeness would allow. The smell from whatever it was Jack was smoking was making him nauseous and his legs were itching.

"Oh, you know the sort of thing, the age of the church, the families who are at rest in the churchyard?" Joe unsuccessfully tried to stifle a cough and began to feel hot. "Do you mind if we take a walk outside, Mr. Whitlock? There's something I'm particularly interested in that you might be able to help me with."

Joe held his breath as Jack led him through the back of the cottage, followed by the ever- faithful Bess, past a rudimentary washroom, outside toilet and tool shed. The fresh air revived him, and his head began to clear. Jack grinned, revealing a surprisingly good set of teeth. "Well done, lad. You lasted out in there longer than most. I don't 'ave many visitors. I goes to my old mate Bob's for a chat sometimes though. Old school pal o'mine." Jack pointed towards Bob's repair shop across the churchyard. " 'e don't come 'ere though." There was no polite answer to that, so Joe returned a smile and reflected on the life of this man and what might have happened to him to make him so solitary.

"Right, spit it out now lad, I've work to do," said Jack, stopping suddenly and rounding on Joe, the menace returning to his eyes. Joe knew his time was limited so he pointed to the neglected grave of Lavinia Whitlock which was standing a few feet from Jack's garden.

"Well, as the last surviving member of one of the oldest families in the village, I wonder whether you could tell me anything about Lavinia Whitlock? Why her grave is so far away from the rest, for example."

Jack rubbed his whiskers with his palm, an idiosyncrasy of his that Joe took as a positive sign, and to Joe's surprise, put an arm around his shoulder, the noxious smell of his tobacco rising from yellow fingertips, nails bordered with grime. "Take my advice son, and don't be concernin' yerself with 'er. She were a young woman who died at the hands of an ignorant mob for bein' cleverer 'an them. That's all. All a very long time ago." Jack's grey eyes looked far off into the distance, or possibly the distant past, Joe couldn't tell.

"You mean, she was burned for being a witch? Michael said…"

Jack laughed, a deep throated rumble which caused the need to cough and spit. "Michael! Don't be takin' no notice of 'im. He's as damn foolish as them who tied 'er to the stake all them years ago." Jack stood close to Joe, face to face, his gnarly hands weighing down on his shoulders. "She was clever, a doctor by rights," he murmured. "Gave folks the cure, grew her own medicines and the like. So, they burned 'er. It's that simple, lad."

"But how do you know all this, Mr. Whitlock?"

"I was doin some delvin' into the land registry, a private matter I ain't about to be tellin' yer," said Jack, leaning on a nearby post while he considered just how much information he wanted to reveal. "Except to say that a good deal o' land belonged to the Whitlocks' in her day," he continued, nodding in the direction of the grave. "There were a dispute over borders with another family, the Tanners, and she cursed 'em by all accounts. Two weeks later two o' the children in that family died o' the fever. That were enough. They took 'er, led by the Tanner menfolk. People were dyin' every damn day of fever, especially little 'uns, but they took 'er, and she cursed the family over again as they tied 'er to the stake, promisin' they'd all die a terrible death before their time, for as long as their name survived. 'Course that were difficult to prove 'cos everyone died a terrible death in them days, accidents on the farms, disease, fires an' the like." Jack picked up the pitchfork again, Joe feigned a defensive position and they both laughed. "Ain't your time yet, lad."

"Thank you, Mr. Whitlock. I'll let you get on. It's been a pleasure to talk to you." They shook hands, Jack's callouses scraping harshly against Joe's soft skin.

"Think on lad," said Jack. "Forget about it. The grave is separate from the rest through ignorance; ignorance outlives us all."

Joe nodded and began his walk home, the long way.

Chapter 11

"Ow! Stop clanging that bloody pan!" said Will, head in hands, semi-naked at the breakfast table, black curls tumbling down.

"Serves you right, mate. If you can't take it, don't drink it." said Joe. Will groaned.

"Thought you were still in bed, anyway."

"I've been up for ages. Went for a walk."

"It's Kate's fault," said Will, one beat behind in the conversation. "Went back to hers."

"Woo!" said Joe. "Getting pretty cosy with the Detective Sergeant, are we? You'd better watch it. She might handcuff you. With any luck." He threw a tea-towel at his brother's head, just missing the milk jug.

"We're not quite there yet," said Will, swirling a soluble painkiller in water and grabbing the towel irritably.

"Leave it, Joe," said Miri. "At least until the hangover's gone," she added with a smile. "Actually, I meant to have a word with Kate myself last night about the raven business, but I'll wait for a more appropriate time. I'm seeing Mike later anyway for an update about Adam and the school. I might mention it to him instead. I want to talk to him about this wretched witch burning mock-up as well."

"Leave it, Mum," said Will wearily, massaging his forehead. "It's not your place to go trying to change everything. You might find something even more unpleasant on the doorstep. Just do your bit with the kids n' stuff and let them get on with what they usually do. It's none of our business."

"I agree," said Joe, causing Will to raise his eyebrows. "Now, who's for pancakes?" Will groaned.

"Just me, you and Edie then," said Miri as Edie tapped on the back door, her voluminous headwrap bobbing at the window.

"Nice timing, Edie," said Joe.

"Oh dear! You look a little worse for wear, Darling," she said to Will. "Good night, was it?" Will groaned, baulking at the sweet smell wafting from Joe's frying pan and Edie's signature scent. "I wouldn't bother trying to keep up with our new reverend in the boozing stakes again if I were you," she added, more gently. "Boy, can she drink. Walked home ahead of me as if she hadn't touched a drop."

"Yes, I noticed that too," said Miri, a puzzled frown on her face.

"Such a tiny little thing." Edie went on. "I hope you've learned something, Darling." she said, turning to Will with a sympathetic smile.

As the pancakes were served, Will excused himself, hoping a cool shower would help, and while the rest tucked in, the conversation revolved mainly around forthcoming events. Miri reinforced her dismay about the 'Burn the Witch' spectacle. "I told Nadya what I thought too."

"Like I said, Darling," Edie interrupted. "It's a tradition. You're not the only one who wants it banned but it still goes on every year, regardless."

"Oh?"

"Let me see, there's Nettie, Tom's wife. She's often said she thinks it's in bad taste. Then there's Sarah Clarke, her friend, she's not happy about it either." Miri let Edie go on, but her own attention was diverted by a link she was trying to make in her head. Clarke... Tilly Clarke. Maybe it was her mother?

"Does Sarah have children in the village school? I think I may know one of them."

"Yes, two I think," replied Edie. "Nettie and Sarah are very close, they run the Pilates classes at the village hall, and there are a few others who support your view, Miri. But like I say, it goes on, despite the protests. I guess it's just one of those things that has always happened so everyone expects it, a bit like cheese rolling in Gloucestershire."

"Hardly the same thing, Edie," said Miri lamely. She was losing the will to argue and was far more interested in this group of women who were known to have protested to the spectacle before. Edie sensed the lull and made a conscious effort to raise everyone's spirits. Joe had zoned out anyway; up since dawn, ravenous and focussing on his third pancake.

"I'm looking forward to seeing my old partner in crime, whatever happens," she said with a mysterious air, adjusting the angle of her headwrap for emphasis. Miri and Joe looked blankly at each other, eyebrows raised, waiting for the inevitable details. Edie made a move to leave, which both Miri and Joe knew was fake. "Go on, Edie," said Joe, pushing her gently back in her seat. "Tell all."

"Not all, Darling. But I'll tell you that 'Dexter Steele' is not his real name."

"Oh, him," said Miri. "I'd forgotten you said you knew him."

"Oh yes," she said coyly. "He was born here and won a scholarship to study drama at the London Academy straight from school. I grew up in Surrey and went to London to study art and design in Kensington at around the same time. My flatmate introduced him at a party one weekend, and he became part of our social group."

"What was he like?" said Miri politely, her interest limited to the possibility that she may find herself working with him during the coming weeks.

"Well, it was the seventies, Darling. He was a colourful and key figure when it came to organising our social lives; tickets for concerts, theatre and so on. He was a few years older than me and when he got the call to his first TV role, we sort of lost touch." Edie's voice faded to a whisper and Miri suspected that Edie was holding something back. "But I never forgot how he described the village he grew up in," she continued, more animatedly, "and when I wanted to move out of London, I looked it up and bought Blacksmith Cottage. He's the reason I'm here, I suppose."

"Does he know you're here?" asked Joe.

"I don't think so. I certainly never told him."

"Wow! That'll be a surprise," said Joe. "How famous was he?"

"Oh, he did pretty well for himself during the late seventies and eighties; soaps, a few minor parts in films and some theatre work," said Edie wistfully. "He lives in Oxford now, but I've never seen him at the theatre, so maybe he just prefers a quiet life these days."

"So, what is his real name, then?" asked Joe, reaching for some fruit and yoghurt.

"Bill Tanner. Not very show biz, I'm afraid."

"Tanner?" said Joe.

"Yes, Darling. Why? What's the matter?"

"Oh nothing," he said casually.

"This Pilates," said Miri. "Do you know the times of the classes by any chance?"

"Not off the top of my head," she said with a wobble of her turban, "But there's a notice in the village hall foyer, and I'm pretty sure they have a Facebook page. It's very popular."

"I don't doubt it," said Miri.

After Edie had left, Miri and Joe sat together enjoying a pot of coffee.

"Is there anything you want to tell me, Joe? You seem a bit distracted," Miri said. She knew her boys well, could sense their moods accurately, and they knew she was there if they needed her. When they were teenagers, she had tended to watch, assess and monitor from a distance, only intervening where she felt it would help to do so. The boys had sometimes felt that they were at a disadvantage having a parent who was a psychiatrist, and she hadn't wanted them to feel that she was analysing them at every turn. But they were adults now, and they would tell her if she was overstepping the mark.

"Nothing wrong exactly, but, well there's no point in keeping it secret I suppose," said Joe, turning his mug round and round in his hands and looking down at the table. "I went to see Jack Whitlock this morning." Joe paused, waiting for a reaction, but Miri's eyes merely widened a little as she took a sip of coffee, giving him time to continue at his own pace. She knew he'd been out, of course. He gave her an accurate account of his visit; Jack's initial hostility, a description of the cottage and the link to Lavinia. "But here's the interesting thing, Mum."

"It's all interesting, Joe."

"Yes, but here's the thing," Joe continued, rising from his chair and pacing the kitchen floor. "The family who Jack's ancestors were in dispute with over their land all those hundreds of years ago, were called Tanner." He waited for the penny to drop but Miri had already forgotten. "Bill Tanner... Aka Dexter Steele."

"Ah, I see! He may be the last surviving member of his family, as Jack is the last of the Whitlocks. Quite a coincidence." Joe sat down again, relieved to have shared what he knew. He was a very open-hearted person by nature and harbouring secrets did not sit well with him. "Still," continued Miri. "There's no reason to think that a disagreement dating back to the Middle Ages would have any relevance today, Joe. I mean, it's centuries ago."

"I'm not so sure," Joe interrupted. "From what I remember from my history lessons at school, when the scattered strips of land owned by the peasants were rounded up and enclosed into fields, some families inevitably ended up losing out on the most fertile land, whereas some gained. That would affect the livelihoods of generations to come and disputes were common, feuds lasting hundreds of years and beyond."

"Joe, you've absolutely no evidence to suggest that there was any sort of feud going on between the Whitlocks and the Tanners, even then, let alone now," said Miri gently, placing her hand over his and smiling.

"What's all this about feuds?" Enter Will, a new man after a shower and shave. "Any pancakes left?"

"There's one in the pan to reheat," said Miri and quickly summarised what Joe had told her.

"Christ. Heads are gonna roll," said Will, sliding a pancake from the pan and squeezing golden syrup all over it. "What? Sugar levels are low," he said in response to Joe's look of horror.

"You should've seen Jack's face though when he was telling me about it," said Joe, determined to have the last word. "He blames the Tanners for Lavinia's gruesome death and the Whitlocks' poverty. He's got a point as well. If they'd got the land they deserved, they wouldn't have been poor and Lavinia would never have uttered the curse that resulted in her being accused of witchcraft."

"How do you know the land was rightfully theirs?" said Will. "People are always sayin' stuff should've been theirs by right. How do you know? Might just be some talk passed down the Whitlock generations to explain how poor they were."

"Whatever," said Joe.

"Seriously though Joe," said Miri who had been silently thinking this through. "It really is none of our business." Associations with witchcraft were beginning to stack up and Miri was determined to find out more about it. The arrival of Dexter Steele may cause more than a ripple if Joe's theory carried any weight.

"So why do I feel that it is?" he said quietly as he left the room.

"He's bloody bewitched by that gravestone Mum, that's what it is," said Will. "Whenever he's near it he goes all funny; I've seen it with my own eyes." Will put his feet up on a spare chair and watched as Miri stacked the dishwasher and put the kettle on for tea.

"I'm meeting Mike for lunch later at the Kington. I'll see what I can find out. I think whatever it is has upset him more than you might think, so don't tease him about it, Will."

"As if."

***

Miri, preoccupied as she was with her concern for Joe, prompted a comment from DCI Mike Absolom as he sat down in the alcove where he was waiting for her.

"Everything okay, Miri? You look a bit tired, if you don't mind me saying." Mike was a forthright copper, hard as nails when he needed to be, sympathetic and courteous the rest of the time and not too proud to admit defeat. He respected Miri, and her company over lunch was a pleasure he always looked forward to.

"Yes, thanks Mike. Bit of a headache, that's all."

"Let's get some grub down you then. What'll you have?" Mike rubbed his hand over his buzzcut as he scrutinised the menu, an endearing habit of his whenever he was concentrating.

"What can I do you for, Detective Chief Inspector?" said Gavin with a flounce and a twinkle in his eye.

"Just the steak," replied Mike with a weary, but friendly smile.

"Never mind, love. Hope springs eternal. And for you, Madam?"

"Same please, Gavin. How's Craig?"

"Oh, don't start me," he said with a toss of his handsome head, and waltzed off to place their order.

"Why are gay men always so good looking?" said Miri, sipping her soda and lime.

"Are they? I hadn't noticed," replied Mike in an unnecessarily deep voice. They laughed and Miri began to relax. "He's the real village heartthrob over there," he continued, pointing his glass in the direction of the bar. "Tom Hopkins."

"The same Tom Hopkins who is mentoring Adam at work? I know of him and I've met his wife, but I've never actually seen him." Miri's gaze finally fell upon this vision of manhood standing at the bar, enjoying a pint and a ploughman's lunch with a few workmates. In faded cords, open neck checked shirt and boots, he looked like he'd just stepped off the set for a Thomas Hardy film; Gabriel Oak in Far from the Madding Crowd. His dark curly hair, tanned skin, well-proportioned features and relaxed demeanour, as he shared a joke with his companions, said it all. Here was a man in his prime, comfortable in his skin.

"You can stop looking now Miri," said Mike with a grin. "Are you thinking what I'm thinking?"

"I doubt it," said Miri.

"Bet you're thinking, how did plain little Nettie Hopkins manage to bag the most handsome chap in the village? Am I right?" Mike took a long pull on his pint, peering over the top of his glass at Miri, eyebrows raised.

"Well, he is rather handsome. Who knows?" said Miri, exasperated. "She must be his type. It's not for us to judge, Mike." Miri would not be drawn further, but it did seem an odd coupling, looking at it from the purely physical point of view. Out loud she said, "There's a lot more to choosing a partner than looks, Mike. You know that."

"Whatever you say, Miri. You're the psychiatrist."

Their steaks arrived, smelling delicious and sizzling with a spicy sauce. "One of Craig's creations. Enjoy."

"Of course," said Mike, half way through his first mouthful, "she may have played the sympathy card with him."

Miri rolled her eyes. "You're not still going on about that are you? What do you mean?" she asked after a slight pause, her curiosity aroused.

"Well, Nettie had a terrible childhood, poor kid," said Mike, wiping his greasy fingertips on a black serviette. "An older sister in the family died when Nettie was very young, about six, I think. I don't know the circumstances. Nettie adored the older sister apparently, so she took it very hard."

"How terrible," said Miri, trying to imagine, without success, how one of her boys would have coped with the loss of the other.

"The tragedy caused the mother to spiral into a pit of depression and prescription drugs until she eventually sort of faded away to nothing and died. Their dad, who never had much of a backbone anyway by all accounts, took to drink, left the girls to fend for themselves and hasn't been seen from that day to this. Nettie would've been about sixteen when he left, I reckon. There was one older girl who went off to college and now lives miles away. Nettie raised the two younger siblings on her own, taking work where she could get it, help from neighbours and so on."

Miri was deeply moved by this account of a childhood blighted.

"If anyone deserves a knight in shining armour then," she said, thoughtfully.

"You don't begrudge her, then?" said Mike, laughing.

"Certainly not. May she have all the happiness she deserves."

Over a delicious portion of raspberry cheesecake each, they discussed Adam's progress. "I really don't think he needs me in any official capacity anymore, Mike. He is communicating well, he has a place of his own, and a job he loves. Nettie is keeping an eye on him and I can still visit him as a friend. I shall still be involved." Miri wasn't ready to cut the cord but kept her private concerns to herself.

"Fair enough, if that's what you want," said Mike. "Job done. Thank you for all you have done for him. How's the school thing going?"

"Oh, fine. I'm really enjoying it. I've had one or two counselling sessions with Trudie, Melanie's cousin, and her friends, and they talked quite openly about their grief, so I think that was helpful. They are keen to meet with me again, which is a good sign." Miri chose not to reveal any details about the dead raven after all, or her suspicions about Tilly's Mum. She would do a bit of digging on her own first. It may be nothing at all anyway. As for the tree burning ceremony, let it go, she thought, might prove illuminating, in more ways than one. Instead, she asked him if the investigation into the criminal activities of the Reverend Tripley and Vic Burton was wrapped up. Mike assured her that everything was under control.

"We're still looking into bringing additional charges against Vic though," said Mike. "His activities are much more widespread than Tripley's," he added, by way of explanation. "Fingers in a lot of pies. All sorts of rackets spreading far and wide."

"Really? What sort of things?" said Miri, conjuring up an image of the odious Vic Burton, the scene she had witnessed in his house as he bullied his wife mercilessly, not to mention the attempt on her own life, at his instigation.

"Embezzlement, fraud, theft on a grand scale, valuable art and jewellery for example," said Mike. "He'll be going down for a long time. We just need to uncover some additional evidence, the more the better, and we will. We found enough to get started when we searched the church, but I think there's more to come." Miri nodded and made a concerted effort to dispel all images of Vic Burton from her mind.

"There is something you could do for me Mike, if you don't mind." she said tentatively as Mike returned from the bar with their coffees.

"I knew there was something bugging you."

"It's about Jack Whitlock." This was obviously just about the last thing Mike was expecting to hear and his face betrayed his surprise. "Joe visited him. He has been curious about the grave of Lavinia Whitlock since he first saw it, and he seems to have got it into his head that Jack is still harbouring some sort of ancient grudge against the family who instigated her death."

"And took away all the Whitlock land? The Tanners? Don't say any more. We've heard it all before."

"You have?"

Mike put his cup down, turned to Miri and lightly rested his hand on her arm.

"There's nothing to worry about, Miri. Jack is a bitter old man, looking for someone, or something, to blame for the disappointments in his own life. He lives alone 'cos no woman could ever stand to be with the miserable bugger. He's poor because he blew every chance he ever had 'cos he wouldn't trust anyone, and he looks back instead of forwards to the point of obsession. Gradually, ancient history, or myth, or whatever it is, has taken over and rendered him incapable of rational thought." Mike gently stalled Miri from interrupting. "Hear me out," he said, hand raised. "There is no evidence whatsoever that the Whitlocks were unjustly robbed of their land or that the Tanners had anything to do with Lavinia's death. We know she was burned at the stake; there's a record of that, but that's all we know. Jack usually finds something to kick up a fuss about at this time of year. Jesus! It's hundreds of years ago."

"Try telling Joe."

"I will, Miri. If it gets to that point, I will bloody tell him. There's nothing there. Jack is a toxic piece of work. He lives next door to that forsaken grave and he feeds off its negativity. I'll tell 'im alright. You can count on me, Miri. I've had enough of Jack Whitlock spilling his poison around the village. If he sensed any kind of vulnerability or sensitivity in Joe, he won't be happy till he's sapped the bloody life out of 'im. And he wonders why people avoid 'him. The only person who gives him the time of day is Bob over at his repair shop. You know him?" Miri nodded. "They were at school together and Jack drops in to pass the time of day. If Bob is sick of hearing about the Tanners, he doesn't show it. Goes over his head, I imagine." Miri was trying not to betray any weakness, but where her boys were concerned, weakness didn't enter into it, and Mike understood this. "I'm sorry to be so blunt, Miri. Tell you what, how about if I offer to do the research with Joe, just to prove that it's all a load of nonsense? Would that help?"

"No thanks, Mike. I'll keep an eye on things and work with him if it comes to it."

"I can be subtle, you know."

"That makes me feel so much better," said Miri, an ironic smile on her face which Mike interpreted as real.

Chapter 12

Zoe's first sermon, and the church was bursting at the seams. After the frantic jostling for front pews had died down, there was standing room only, even beyond the huge door and into the porch. Most people were motivated by curiosity and the prospect of a good old gossip afterwards, undoubtedly at Zoe's expense; she was new, young and female, after all. Some were there just in case they missed something and would therefore be excluded from the gossip, and a handful were there because they were regular churchgoers. Edie, still smarting from her previous fashion faux pas, and declaring that Zoe needed her to be in church early 'for support,' had rooted out what she called her 'Emma Peel' outfit; black cat-suit, patent heels, bomber jacket, glossy sixties wig, and left her cottage an hour before the service to be sure of a seat from where she would be seen.

"Thank you all so much for coming, everyone. I must talk to the powers that be," said Zoe, raising her palms and her eyes upwards, "about getting more seats in here for this mighty throng. That is, of course, if you all intend turning up regularly," she said, smiling benevolently. Zoe waited for the general murmuring and shuffling of embarrassment to die down. She was standing on a box behind the lectern, yet even so, invisible from below chest level, her cassock stark against the dark wood. "I know those of you whom I have met so far, in the village and at the meeting in the pub the other night, will be desperately disappointed if I don't give you something interesting to talk about afterwards, but I'm going to make you all wait until after the service before I reveal my rather unconventional outfit. You must be patient, which you will be well aware is one of the seven virtues." She paused for the polite laughter to fade.

Zoe's voice was clear and confident. There was no nervous gulping or trailing off at the end of her sentences. The pace was even, her head was high, and there were no notes to refer to, which meant she was free to look at individuals. One by one the congregation, especially those who had come along to express their Christian charity by watching her fail, slowly absorbed the realisation that the failure was theirs and theirs alone.

"So, let's look in more detail at the other six virtues, shall we? This is a sermon after all, right?" Those who were standing began to shift their weight nervously from one leg to the other, those squashed together in the pews fidgeted, and isolated coughs rippled through the church like a Mexican wave.

"Chastity. Oh dear. Judging by the expression on some of your faces, maybe I'd better move on." There was another ripple of laughter at this, an attempt at relieving tension and diverting suspicion, Miri assumed. From her vantage point at the back, she could observe the reactions of some individuals clearly, and it didn't escape her notice that Tom Hopkins, who was leaning casually against the west wall, was laughing louder than anyone else. Nettie was sitting in a pew nearby, any attempt at taming her candy floss hair having failed, next to an adult version of Tilly Clarke. Miri wondered what kind of spells she would be cooking up after this and decided to approach the women after the service with a view to joining their Pilates class.

"Temperance? I know, that one's hard for me too." Zoe's strident voice brought Miri back to the present. She went on to compliment Gavin and Craig on their excellent choice of wines and real ales. They weren't there to hear it, of course, busy as bees preparing for the lunchtime rush. 'Make hay, love!' she heard Gavin say in her head.

"But it's something we should all be striving to control. We should be aiming to share what we have and not let greed overpower us." Jane Peters made a move to squeeze further into the end of her pew in an unconscious effort to appear thinner, and several beer bellies were pulled in. "Charity, another of the virtues, is linked to this, and I know that many of you are involved with all kinds of charitable works in the village, which is great. Unlike my predecessor, I intend to practice what I preach and be fully involved too." If Helen Tripley felt any kind of embarrassment, she didn't show it, though Miri did notice that Beatrice was holding her hand and her admiration for the two of them soared once more.

Zoe continued in this vein, citing the virtues as examples of the best we can be, with particular emphasis on kindness and humility, the crowd stunned into respectful silence. "So, if anyone here has an unkind thought as they leave church today," she added, "or thinks they are better than their neighbour, then please keep those thoughts to yourself. At least then, only you will know how 'unkind' and lacking in 'humility' you are. And never," she said, pausing and leaning forward for dramatic effect, "never assume that God is on your side." Zoe stood perfectly still for a few beats in the silence that ensued, the benevolent smile still radiant, eyes searching those who dared to return her stare. She had succeeded in completely deflating the pomposity of the voyeurs who, under the guise of Christian fellowship, had wished only to damage and destroy.

"I have displayed a list of forthcoming services on the noticeboard in the porch, everyone. I know how much some of you enjoy singing together, so I shall be enlisting the help of the choir and I do hope to see you all again," she said in a lighter, more business-like tone. "The parish council are working very closely with me to try and bring our community together after what has been an horrendous year so far. Please help us by getting involved with some of our projects and events, the first of which will be our autumn celebrations which many of you are working so hard to organise."

The spell was broken, and many people were nodding their support and sharing information. Even Mrs. Duggan, who had quickly worked out that she could create a higher profile for herself if she declared herself to be in favour of the reverend rather than against her, plumped up the two zeppelins that formed her mighty chest, in support.

"Oh! I almost forgot," said Zoe, and so it would seem, had most of the congregation. The diminutive reverend shed her robe in an ever-so-slightly provocative way as she made her way from the lectern, to reveal a beautifully cut trouser suit in black velvet, trimmed with red satin;

collarless short boxy jacket, cropped trousers and heeled patent ankle boots. She bowed to the congregation, setting off a spontaneous round of applause. and Miri gave a thumbs up to her friend Diane who had designed and made the outfit. Privately, she was relieved that Kate wasn't there to witness what she would perceive as deliberate and unnecessary exhibitionism. They had already got off on the wrong foot.

As the crowd dispersed, Edie made a beeline for Zoe. "Well done, Darling." Zoe looked blank. "It's me, Darling. Edie!"

"What? Oh, Edie! Of course, forgive me. You look completely different."

"You'll get used to it, Darling. Do you approve?" she added, twirling slowly on the spot.

"Well, yes. Lovely!"

"And you look wonderful too, Darling. You really won them over. Couldn't have been easy. Well done. Well done." Edie took Zoe's hands in hers. "Oh dear. You're shaking, Darling. And cold. Come and sit down."

"Just a touch of nerves. I'll be fine. Please," said Zoe, gently pushing Edie to the side. "I need to mingle a bit if you'll excuse me." With that, Zoe disappeared into the vestry, emerging a couple of minutes later, armed with a sheaf of leaflets, looking more relaxed, licking her lips, the colour returning to her cheeks.

Outside, the crowd was dispersing, mainly in family groups, friends gathering briefly to discuss Zoe's debut quietly. Miri could detect no tossing of heads, rolling eyes or defiant arm folding. No-one wanted to be seen to be the proud one, not in public anyway. The older members of the congregation were huddled in small groups, too far away for Miri to gauge their responses, but she'd hear all of that from Mrs. Duggan, no doubt. Zoe was busy handing out leaflets, copies of the notice she had pinned up, and judging from what Miri could glean from her position just beside the porch door, the brief exchanges were upbeat, and everyone took a copy politely, even if they had no intention of ever stepping foot into the church again.

Miri scanned the diminishing crowd for Nettie's hair. When she spotted it, she weaved in and out of the stragglers until she caught up with her. She was walking with Sarah Clarke, Tom being somewhere at a distance, laughing and joking with friends.

"Hi, Nettie. I'm glad I caught you."

"Now look, Sarah. Why won't my hair do that?" she said, indicating Miri's tamed chestnut waves with mock indignation. Miri blushed warmly and physically brushed the compliment away with a wave of her hand. Nettie introduced her friend, and a brief exchange ensued about Tilly's progress. "Honestly, I've tried every potion on the market, and some that aren't," continued Nettie, still focussed on hair, "and nothing works. Is it Henna or what?"

"Just genetics, I'm afraid," said Miri. "Mum was a redhead and my grandmother too. I think there's Irish blood in the family way back. Anyway," Miri could hear Edie's voice somewhere close by and she wanted to get to the point. "It's about your Pilates class, Nettie." Nettie and Sarah exchanged a fleeting look which did not escape

Miri's trained eye, partly because she was expecting something of the sort.

"Oh, yes? Are you thinking of joining us?" said Nettie smiling. "Great! We were saying only the other day, weren't we Sarah, that it would be good to have you onboard. We're always looking for new recruits."

"Yes indeed," said Sarah, head slightly at an angle, mesmeric pale grey eyes unblinking. "You'll be surprised by how much you'll get out of it, Miri. We're a friendly lot and we all support each other, don't we, Net?"

"Oh yes. You'll fit right in, Miri. Tuesday evenings, seven o'clock at the hall. Just wear comfy clothes, we have all the equipment. See you there." They waved their fingers, smiled, and backed away in step, and as Miri turned to face the church, she felt those grey, pearly eyes boring into her back.

***

"How did she get on?" said Joe, who was sweeping up some leaves from the front path as Miri and Edie approached from the lane.

"That's kind Joe, thanks," said Miri, scanning her tidy garden. "I'll tell you all about it inside. Come on." Edie tottered her way along the path to her own cottage, vowing never to wear her silly boots again, and Miri relayed the details of Zoe's triumph to her sons as they prepared vegetables for the casserole that was blipping away in the aga.

"Pilates?" said Will incredulously. "Since when have you been into that sort of thing?"

"She's up to something," said Joe quietly while Miri was in the sitting room looking for the leaflet Zoe had given her.

"What? Oh, I just thought it was about time I took a class, you know, to keep fit. My GP suggested it ages ago because it's non aerobic, but good for strength."

"Yeah, but haven't you got enough on, with the play and your job and stuff?" said Joe.

"Well, I'm not seeing Adam anymore, except as a friend, so that frees me up a bit," Miri argued. "Pilates is good for relaxation too. Nettie Hopkins runs it."

Will and Joe pulled silly faces at each other.

"What on earth are you doing?" asked Miri, aware that she was stumbling upon some private joke.

"That's what Adam did the other day when he told us about the drinks Nettie makes from the plants in his backyard," said Will laughing. "Best take your own bottle to Pilates!"

"Oh, I will, don't worry," said Miri.

"Have you got to buy a special kit, Mum?" asked Joe.

"No, just comfy clothes; they provide all the equipment."

"Ah, the mats, weights, bands and stuff. That's good," said Joe.

"Broomsticks, wands, and pointy hats, more like," said Miri.

"Ay?" said the boys, noses wrinkled, spoons mid-air.

"She's lost it," said Will.

Chapter 13

Joe and Will made a private arrangement not to mention anything about Pilates, potions or pointy hats. They would observe from a distance and if they thought their mother was getting into any danger, then they would intervene.

"You know what she's like," said Joe when the two of them were up in their room sharing ideas for a project that Will was working on. "If we say anything, she'll just clam up and do it anyway."

"Bunch o' nutters if you ask me. I wonder if this Pilates group had anything to do with that dead raven on our doorstep? "Double, double, toil and trouble," he added in an evil croaky voice as he stirred an imaginary pot.

"Who knows?" said Joe. "Will," Joe continued after a long pause. "I know you think I've gone a bit overboard, you know, about Lavinia Whitlock's grave." Will sensed Joe's embarrassment and knew that if he made fun of him now he'd never open up about it again, so he remained silent, attempted a serious expression and turned to listen.

"Thing is," Joe continued. "I really do think that Jack, you know, the old bloke who lives in the cottage by the churchyard, is somehow under the influence of her spirit, and not in a good way. Well, maybe 'spirit' is too strong a word, but you know, being so close to it, just seems weird somehow, Jack being as he is and nobody going near him."

Joe paused and looked down, prepared for the customary guffaw of derision from his brother. When that didn't come, he looked up.

"Go on," said Will. "Don't leave me hangin', mate. He's a descendant, isn't he?" Joe relaxed and laughed nervously.

"Apparently. The last surviving Whitlock. No children, by all accounts."

"None that we know of," said Will.

"Yeah well, let's assume there isn't. The reason I think he's somehow affected by Lavinia is, well, I don't quite know how to put it."

Will resisted the temptation to remind him that Lavinia had been dead for five hundred years and waited, with the nearest he could get to a sympathetic expression on his face, somewhere between a smile and a question mark.

"Thing is, I've felt it myself, Will," said Joe.

"Nothing evil about you, mate." Will already knew that Joe had been spooked in some way by the grave, he'd said as much to his mother, but when he finally absorbed Joe's words, concern clouded his face. "What the hell do you mean, anyway?"

"Not in that way, not in a negative way, but I certainly felt something, as soon as I saw the grave; a force, a magnetism. Oh, I don't know." Will put his hand on Joe's shoulder.

"It's alright, Joe. You talk as if you've got over it," he said hopefully.

"I think so," said Joe slowly. "When I was sitting in Jack's cottage, I felt really weird, sick and sweaty. I knew then that I had to shake the thing off, whatever it was, and when we went outside, I felt fine, back to my old self. If I'd stayed in there a minute longer, Will, I swear to God I'd have passed out." Joe raised his hands to his face and pulled them down his cheeks, as if wiping away a rash or a stain.

"Thank God for that," said Will, genuine fear in his eyes. "Are you sure you can handle this, Joe? I mean, we could get help, you know." Joe was touched by Will's use of the word 'we' and he smiled warmly.

"I feel better already for having shared it. I think I'll be okay now. I don't feel the need to go and look at the grave or anything like that." Joe went on to explain about the feud and the curse, just as he had told his mother. "I was going to look into the whole land business in the parish records, but I'm not going to bother now."

"Yeah, well I'd stay away if I were you, and if you start getting all weird again, more weird than usual I mean, we're in it together, okay?"

Joe laughed. "Getting back to Jack though, I think it's too late for him; he hardly ever leaves his spot beside the grave, his house smells of rot and decay, and his attitude stinks too. I thought it was odd when he asked me in, but now I think it might have been some kind of test, to see how I'd cope in there." Joe screwed up his face as his senses relived the experience. "He hates everyone, and he's got a real chip on his shoulder about Lavinia's curse, her death, and the whole land feud business. Don't tell Mum, but I wouldn't be surprised if it was him who left that bloody bird on our step. When I told him who I was, he said he liked our family, that was how I got invited in come to think of it, but that might have all been fake."

"But why? Don't read too much into it, Joe. Best leave well alone. If he wants to live like that, it's his business."

"Hey, you two!" Miri called from the bottom of the stairs. "I'm going into school for a couple of hours, okay?"

Will and Joe popped their heads around their bedroom door, one above the other, something they used to do when they were small that always made their mother laugh, as she did now.

"And," she said, grabbing her coat and bag, "the celebrated Dexter Steele is arriving tonight. Apparently, he's booked in for a week at the Kington. Interested?"

"Is Edie going to be there?" Will asked. Miri looked as if that was the most stupid question she had ever heard.

"We're in!" they said in unison.

Miri's two- hour stint at the village school was mainly taken up by admin tasks associated with the play that was to be performed by the year six pupils as part of the Halloween celebrations. The class teachers were responsible for the casting and any adaptations to the text, as they knew the children best. So, to save time for them, Miri and Shel had decided to spend the afternoon planning and printing a timetable of after school rehearsals, filling in health and safety forms, sourcing costumes, props and makeup, and discussing various options for scenery. The children had been involved with much of the decision making so far and had unanimously been in favour of performing their play on the back of a flatbed truck provided by one of the local farms. This truck was often deployed for fetes and village exhibitions, so it seemed like a sensible idea, especially as there was a ready-made canvas awning, should there be rain on the evening of the performance.

"It'll look great when it's decorated," said Shel. "The younger kids are making paper bats, witches' hats, lanterns and things, and there'll be no shortage of pumpkins."

"I'll talk to Diane again about the number of costumes," said Miri. "She's so imaginative and has tons of interesting fabrics and trims. Edie's has already started sketching out some designs I believe."

"Brilliant. Tick. Tick."

"Best wait till I've confirmed it," said Miri laughing.

"Oh, she'll do it. I've never known her to refuse. Look what she created for the new Reverend. In three days!"

"I know. Fine. Tick it off, then. What did you think of the sermon, by the way?" Miri asked as they reordered their list of priorities.

"I thought she did really well. Rattled a few feathers too, which is good. Couldn't have been easy for her. I must say, I was a bit surprised by her appointment to the role," she added thoughtfully. "I mean, such a contrast to George Tripley."

"Maybe that's the whole point. We don't want another one of him."

"Of course not. No, it's not that, it's just that I would have thought that all of the applicants would have been seriously vetted, you know, background checks, references going back to the crack of doom, the lot, precisely to avoid another George Tripley."

"Crack of Doom, eh?" said Miri with a grin. "Who's been reading Macbeth, then?"

"Well, I thought I'd better." said Shel, blushing slightly. "Don't want to look a fool!"

"Don't be silly, Shel. This school would close within a week without you. But getting back to Zoe. Are you saying she wasn't properly vetted before she was appointed?"

"Well, I'm on the parish council, as you know." They both laughed. Of course, she was. "And I just thought it was all a bit of a rushed job. I'm not saying there's anything wrong with her, but I did get the feeling that she was chosen precisely because of the contrast to Tripley, and that some of the procedures were glossed over as a result. There were some excellent candidates, other women too, but Zoe appeared to be so confident and, what's the word? Edgy. She stood out because of that. No bad thing, I'm sure. Maybe it's just what we all need but—" They were interrupted by the inevitable tap at the office door by a child in need of her medication, which was locked away in the office and administered by Shel twice daily.

"Oh, excuse me Miri," she said.

"No problem. Look, I need to get going now anyway, Shel," said Miri, grabbing her coat and bag. "Email me the revised lists later if you can. I'll talk to Di and be in touch soon."

During Miri's walk home, the bright sky that had characterised the morning, was giving way to a battalion of cloud, silvery and curdled, approaching far off behind the church. Miri quickened her pace, her mind quickly turning to the imminent arrival of the celebrated Dexter Steele and the possible effect on the village, not to mention Edie. She couldn't quite shake off Shel's words either. She had been a perceptive witness in the George Tripley case, and Miri trusted her judgement. A strengthening breeze began to lift the leaves that had settled during the day, reconfiguring their random patterns, playing with their shapes.

***

Edie had arranged to walk with them to the pub. "I'm rather nervous about seeing my old friend after all these years, Darling. What if he doesn't recognise me?" she'd said. Miri had pointed out that sometimes even she didn't recognise her and suggested, tactfully, that she should try to look as near to her real self as possible. "My real twenty-two year old self?" Edie had returned with a pout.

"No, Edie. Just yourself."

From the lane, the pub, festooned as it was with haphazard strings of coloured bulbs, looked like a floating galleon against the darkening sky. A waxing moon, milky in its haze, hung suspended from one corner of the squat church tower, washing the graveyard with its weak light. Only Lavinia, alone and apart, lay in shadow.

For a weeknight, the pub was quite busy. Word had got round, via the local independent news channel, Mrs. Duggan, that the famous Dexter Steele would be arriving that day and staying at The Kington. "He was born and raised here in this village, you know," she'd said. "Marvellous in Emmerdale!" Gavin had been busy introducing an autumnal theme into the lounge decor; burnt orange covers on the window seat cushions, bouquets of dried autumn fruits mixed with harvest stems hanging from the beams, and rustic wooden dishes full of cones and berries. These touches, plus low lighting and the scent of a pinewood log fire, created an ambiance of warmth and welcome that was unrivalled for miles around.

"Season of mists and mellow fruitfulness. My favourite time of the year. What do you think?" he said to Miri. "You'd tell me if I went over and above, wouldn't you, love?"

"Stunning, Gavin," said Miri, gazing around with pleasure. "The colours are simply gorgeous, a real feast for the senses. Just in time for your famous guest."

"I know. He's here, by the way. In his room, freshening up apparently," he said, pausing to peep behind each shoulder. "He's very dramatic," he whispered. Miri thought this comment must have been engendered by some sort of internal blind spot on Gavin's part. "Oh, well. Show must go on, love. Should be getting myself behind the bar before the rush or Craig will have a hissy. See you later."

Will had managed to secure an alcove for them, plus an extra stool for Kate, who was off duty and hoping to join them. Edie was uncharacteristically demur. She had taken onboard Miri's advice and was dressed, rather beautifully, in a long dress of riotously abstract print in mauves and oranges, black patent ballerina pumps, 'I've learned my lesson, Darling,' and a hairpiece with subtle copper highlights fixed with a broad band of matching fabric.

"You look lovely, Edie," said Miri. Edie fidgeted in her seat, clearly pleased by her friend's endorsement of her choice and waited patiently for her gin and tonic, while Miri, sensing the tension in her friend, continued to wonder about this mysterious relationship from her past that had so subdued her; she had not revealed all, she was sure of that.

"Glo!! I don't believe it! Darling!!"

'Glo?' mouthed Joe and Will. Miri noticed this and quietly informed them that Edie's real name was Gloria. "Diane told me when I first arrived in the village," she whispered. "Something to do with wanting to name herself after a famous Hollywood designer."

"Edith Head," whispered Will.

"Bill!" said Edie with a gasp, her hand flying instinctively to her throat. It was unclear whether Edie was using his real name to return the favour, or whether they were simply two old friends who would always call each other by the name they had used when they had known each other.

Dexter Steele was, as Miri had expected, a 'larger than life' character and if he'd had any notion of blending into the background, which she doubted, he had chosen the wrong ensemble. His mink fedora was, literally, 'strategically dipped below one eye,' just like the guy in Carly Simon's song, 'You're So Vain,' His scarf? 'Apricot', of course. The pale accessories were offset by the rest of his outfit, navy linen suit and powder blue cashmere sweater. There was no doubt that he had been a handsome man in his day and Miri could see why Edie had remembered him. He certainly had style. He reached his arms far and wide so that Edie had no choice but to get up and meet his greeting. For a few minutes they were oblivious to everyone else, locked in that precious world that only the two people involved can share, few words necessary, fingertips linked. Finally, Edie, flushed and slightly tearful, introduced Miri, Joe and Will, and invited him to join them.

"What an unexpected pleasure," said Dexter, settling his ample backside into a leather tub chair on the edge of the alcove. His voice was deep and resonant, the voice of an actor who was used to projecting his own voice, and hearing it. Several customers at the bar turned round to seek the owner of this unfamiliar, booming voice and whispered their theories. Word had circulated, again via the redoubtable Mrs. Duggan, about the impending arrival of the famous local boy, and a few extra customers had turned up out of curiosity, especially the older folk who might remember him from his TV days, but once they had seen, and heard, they turned back to their friends and continued with their evening. Miri and those who would be working with him had a vested interest, but apart from Edie, no-one knew much about him.

"Is that your car, Mr. Steele? The purple Daimler in the carpark?" asked Will.

"Indeed it is, dear boy!" he said, swirling a double brandy around a ridiculously large glass, observing at close range and with evident pleasure, its glossy amber film.

"Cool!" said Will.

"Ra-ther! I'd offer to take you for a spin, dear boy, but I haven't driven for years. I have a chauffeur," he added, raising his glass with a smile, emphasising the French pronunciation with relish. Will was just about to ask another question about the car when Kate entered, waving from a distance, and took her place at the bar.

"Oh, excuse me," said Will, tripping over a stool. "My friend has just arrived. I've saved a seat for her."

Joe and Miri shared a smile. "Love's young dream," said Edie, and immediately regretted it.

"Ah, yes! Those were the days, ay Gloria?" Edie attempted a coy look and took refuge in her gin and tonic, hoping that would be the last of it. At least for now. Kate was duly introduced, though not by her professional title, and the party settled down to fragmented conversation, the ordering of snacks and the general comings and goings that characterise a night out at the pub.

Miri talked with Dexter about the forthcoming play and he expressed his delight at having the opportunity to 'give something back,' as he put it. "Haven't been here for years," he said. "Too busy, you know. Now, in my dotage, I have more time to spend doing this kind of thing. I think I shall enjoy it very much, my dear." For 'in my dotage', Miri read 'out of work', and kept an open mind. Eventually, as the evening wore on, Edie and Dexter found themselves sitting next to each other, sharing memories and the inevitable giggles that ensue from such conversations.

At closing time, Dexter bade good night to them all and tottered towards the exit leading to the resident's staircase.

"Good job he's got a chauffeur if you ask me," said Joe. "He's as red as a beetroot!" Will and Kate were making other arrangements for what was left of the evening and Joe made some private comment to Will about handcuffs which earned him a shove back onto his seat. Miri, arm in arm with Edie, who was a little unsteady on her feet despite the sensible footwear, left first, Joe a few paces behind.

The moon was clear and crisp now, in silhouette against its black backdrop, unencumbered by the tower and free to cast its glow across the expanse of the church yard. The three of them were grateful for the light. Joe instinctively glanced back towards the graves. Lavinia was no longer alone and cold. A spotlight, broadening as it touched the ground, spilled wide enough to cast its silvery shadow, not only on her resting place, but also on the raven black cape of Jack Whitlock, perched birdlike at his garden wall.

Chapter 14

Miri, clad in an ancient black track suit, was reminded of Hamlet in the court of Denmark as she took her place in the queue. The foyer was a sea of pink jogging pants, pink tops, pink socks and pink trainers.

"Oh dear!" she said quietly to an acquaintance from choir practice. "I was hoping to blend in." The woman smiled and edged forward, indicating that she would need to fill in a form as it was her first session. Some of the tracksuits had the logo 'Pink Pilates' embroidered in white. Diane was there with her sister Clare, Melanie Crew's bereaved mother, and Shel was stationed behind the trestle table doing what she does best, organising the signing in book, new starter forms and various bits and pieces of admin. As Miri scanned the line, she recognised a few more faces from choir, a couple of teachers and, lo and behold, Mrs. Duggan, a sugar plum fairy on steroids, clad from top to toe in hot pink and poised to take on the world with her magnificent fluffy pink bosom.

"Where are Nettie and Sarah?" Miri asked, as she filled in her new starter form. "I thought they were leading the whole thing."

"Oh, they'll be in the hall, sorting the furniture out. Our instructor, Harriet, comes over from Abingdon for the class and she'll be in there preparing the music, mats and everything."

"Oh, I see," said Miri, stretching up to look through the glass panel at the top of the dividing door. Nettie's tangled nest of hair wafted around the room at lightning speed, stark white against her pink ensemble, reminding Miri of an old-fashioned sweet she couldn't bring to mind.

Nettie and Sarah waved in unison as the ladies filed in, a more frantic wave for Miri, because she was new, she supposed. Harriet was fixing a mini microphone to her pink 'Shut up and Squat' top, panpipe music played faintly in the background, mats unfurled with a slap on the hard floor, and everyone stood in position ready for the class to begin.

Harriet, a large solid woman in her forties, wore an almost permanent wide motivational smile, her blonde hair scraped back in the ubiquitous ponytail, her pure white trainers box fresh. Miri characteristically placed her mat as near to the back wall as she could get it, both to avoid attention, dressed as she was from top to toe in black, and also to give herself a vantage point from which she could best observe the behaviour of the other women. She was just wondering whether the pink theme was designed to deliberately discourage men from joining the class, when feedback from the small speaker indicated that the session was about to start.

"Okay, ladies! Let's get our breathing going nice and steady. Stand tall. Shoulders back and down. Good. In through the mouth, out through the nose." Miri tuned in to the panpipes and scanned the room. Pink bottoms of all shapes and sizes, ponytails of all colours, and Nettie's hair, partially held back by a sweatband, gradually gaining its customary momentum with every breath, sprung out defiantly at odd angles as the body heat rose.

The class proceeded much as Miri had expected; breathing exercises, stretches, core strengthening and balance. Harriet knew her stuff, and Miri was impressed by her ability to give an instruction, interpolated seamlessly with a slice of topical observation or local gossip. "Take a deep breath and bend at the waist for 'downward dog'. I hear you have a celeb in the village! And get those heels down! My Mum remembers him on the tele. And up we come. Slowly does it. Don't want anyone passing out. Hands up if you've met him." Interestingly, there was no need for any of the participants to speak; a nod, shake of the head or show of hands was the required response, and everyone seemed used to the game. Even Mrs. Duggan was wise enough to save her breath, cheeks puce as a result of both the unaccustomed exertion, and the steady flow of heat rising from her bosom.

When Harriet announced that the 'five-minute cool down' part of the class was about to start, Miri glanced at her watch for confirmation that nearly an hour had disappeared so quickly. With a frown, she realised that they were only halfway through the allotted time and scanned the room for signs of confusion from anyone else. On the contrary. Mats rolled up as if by magic, trestle tables flew into position, fluffy white cloths unfolded and handcrafted pink and white baskets appeared, full to the brim with pastel-coloured goodies such as candles, ribbons, cards, crystals and pots of herbs.

"An impromptu craft fayre!" said Miri. "How lovely. I hadn't realised." Was she fooling anyone? Probably not. She had known that there was something 'alternative' about the class all along, but she had been genuinely surprised at the brevity of the exercise session and the ensuing swift transformation from Pink Pilates to White Witches.

Someone had made cakes with pink and white icing, 'to restore your balance dear,' said Mrs. Duggan passing them round. "So good to have you here Miri," Sarah said softly from behind her shoulder. Miri could feel her hot breath on her neck. "Let me explain what this part of the class is all about." Miri, all innocence and curiosity, allowed herself to be led to one side, and braced herself for the shocking revelation that things were not all they seemed at Pink Pilates. "It's all about affirming our self-worth," Sarah continued, laying a hand lightly on Miri's shoulder. "A natural continuation from the Pilates session really, in that we're trying to find balance in our lives and learn how to deal with pressure or… or grief." Sarah spun round and looked Miri directly, her large watery eyes wide and unblinking. "You'd know all about that, I'm sure."

"What do you mean?" said Miri, failing to hide the fact that she had been caught off guard. As far as she was aware, no-one here knew of her husband's death.

"I mean," she said, eyes wide and unblinking, a reassuring but firm hand on Miri's collar bone, "that you've experienced a lot of pressure lately with the investigation and so on, and also as a psychiatrist, you must be used to all sorts of tricky situations. I bet you find it difficult to keep your professional nose out when you catch the scent." Sarah smiled without revealing her teeth and eventually removed her hand, but not before treating Miri to a little twist and squeeze at the base of the neck.

"Oh yes, of course," Miri replied clearly, keen to stand her ground. "I see what you mean. I must admit that I find it hard not to get involved when I see people being abused or manipulated. Can't see that changing anytime soon." Miri held Sarah's gaze for as long as it took her to back down. There was an awkward pause.

"We use crystals, candles and sometimes tarot cards, to help us find our place in the world and to believe in ourselves as worthwhile individuals," Sarah continued. "We support each other. We are a sisterhood Miri, and you are welcome." Sarah held Miri's hands in hers and stretched out her arms as she backed away, head averted, eyes and smile fixed. "If you think you need us."

There was no mention of witchcraft or spells of course, and there was certainly no suggestion that the 'sisterhood' was a secret. What possible harm could it do? It all sounded positive, empowering, and not unlike some of the work that Miri had been engaged in during the early part of her career; an alternative route to the same goal in fact. She tried to not allow her growing dislike of Sarah Clarke cloud her judgement.

Miri sat on a chair at the side of the hall and watched the ritual unfold. The women, including Harriet, sat in a circle on the floor holding hands, surrounding a basket of crystals and a small pile of fabric squares in various pastel shades. A few of them smiled at Miri, remembering their own initiation no doubt. She wondered what their motives were and whether any of the so-called 'sisters' were taking their artform beyond the pink and fluffy pastels and into the dark. Maybe all this deep breathing and mindfulness was purely for show, until they had the measure of new recruits like her.

"Choose your crystals please," said Sarah quietly. "Remember, rose quartz for love, citrine for happiness, amethyst for stress, clear quartz for clarity, turquoise for protection and malachite for transformation." One by one, the women made their choices, wrapped their crystal in a piece of cloth and returned to the circle. Sarah lit a gold candle in the centre and they all closed their eyes.

"Feel the vibration of your unique crystal. Focus on that alone," said Sarah, barely audible despite the silence. "You are now a vital part of the whole. As you feel the vibration, make a promise to yourself and let the power of the crystal help you to achieve your goal." Sarah allowed a minute or two to pass in silence. "Open your eyes and focus on the flame," she said, barely moving her lips. "Take your crystal from its cloth and place it in the palm of your hand. Good. Breath in for four beats and out for eight. Good. Now repeat. 'I matter because I am...' and finish the sentence yourself with one word of your choice. Good. Repeat five times and increase the volume each time. Begin. I matter because..."

Miri knew she would not have time to separate each of the women's words so she concentrated on those she either knew or had an interest in. Shel's word was 'efficient', unsurprisingly, Mrs. Duggan's word was 'necessary,' whether in the context of her role as village grocer or something else was unclear, and Nettie's word was 'skilled.' Nothing surprising about any of that, and Miri was even quite impressed by the positive effect these affirmations seemed to have on the women. Mrs. Duggan's bosom rose to even greater heights, Nettie's hair increased in volume and everyone there appeared to glow with confidence and goodwill. Clare certainly seemed to benefit from the class. She had chosen a turquoise crystal and her word had been 'strong.' Whether she believed it or not was debatable, but if it helped her on the way, surely that must be a good thing.

"Please keep your crystals, ladies. You may like to keep it with you in a pocket or bag, or you may prefer to place it on a shelf in your favourite room to remind you of your value to others. Next week we will be looking at the meanings of some of the tarot cards. Feel free to have a look at the display here before you go. Have a wonderfully fulfilling week, and we will see you next time."

The women calmly gathered their things, chatting amiably about the session, comparing crystals and catching up with plans for the coming week.

"I didn't know you were involved with all this, Shel. Quite a revelation!"

"Oh, it's no big deal. Just a bit of fun and female bonding; somewhere I can be useful. Do you think you'll come again, Miri?"

"Maybe. I came because I suspected that some of the women were dabbling in something of the sort, but I wasn't sure what and I'm still not, but I'm pretty sure it doesn't start and end with crystals and cards." Miri decided to confide in Shel about the raven. She trusted her and was sure she'd keep it to herself if she asked her to. She guided her to the far side of the hall and checked that no-one could overhear, continuing to pack her things as she talked so as not to draw attention to their conversation.

"Doesn't sound like anything I've experienced here," Shel said, thoughtfully. "I can't think of anyone I know from the group who would do something like that. Those two are pretty close," she added, nodding in the direction of Nettie and Sarah, "but it sounds to me more like the kind of trick Jack Whitlock would pull. It's not the first time either. Dead animals have been found on people's property before, but it's never been proved that it was anything other than a kid's prank or an animal leaving its prey behind."

"Why do you think it's Jack, then?"

"Well," said Shel, searching for the right tone. "He's been heard to boast about stuff like that, threatening talk, you know. Then shortly afterwards, something revolting turns up on the property of the person he's had a go at. He's a nasty piece of work. Most of the villagers think it's him when something like that happens. No-one goes near him."

"Why me, though? I don't remember him saying anything untoward to me, and he told my son that he had nothing against my family, that he likes us, even. I just don't understand it."

Shel shrugged. "Can't help I'm afraid. Probably a prank. Kids trying to set him up, maybe? Forget it, Miri. Hopefully, that's the end of it. See you soon in school, we'll chew it over then."

Miri thanked Sarah and Nettie and quickly made her way out of the hall before anyone had the chance to ask her whether she would be joining the 'sisterhood'. A quick visit to the loo would allow her to bide some time while the bulk of the class left, giving her the opportunity to cast a final glance around.

Through the window from the foyer, Miri could see Nettie and Sarah, deep in conversation, the back of their heads close together and looking down.

"Did I leave my glasses in here, Nettie?" Miri said loudly, feigning confusion and frustration. Sarah, startled, dropped something and both women fumbled, laughing nervously in an effort to conceal their panic and annoyance. Nettie grabbed what looked like a package of some sort from the floor, a jiffy bag maybe, and nonchalantly popped it into her kit bag. She had control of herself now and offered to help Miri search for the glasses.

"Oh well. Maybe I didn't bring them after all," said Miri. "I hope you didn't damage your parcel. Nothing fragile, I hope," she added. Sarah stared for a few beats.

"Oh, no. Nothing fragile." Then she approached. "You know, Miri, if this is not your thing, we won't be offended if you decide not to continue, will we Nettie?" Nettie shook her head. "There is a lot of interest in the village, and we are only insured for so many, so just give it some thought."

"Oh, I will, Sarah. I will."

Darkness had fallen, but the sky still retained a few striations of gold, enough to highlight the thatches, hedgerows and garden gates as Miri gathered her thoughts. Jack Whitlock certainly didn't do himself any favours, she thought. He had set himself up as the ultimate scapegoat for any unpleasantness in the village, simply by being there and speaking his mind, rather like his ancestor. Shel's theory that kids were guilty of setting him up had resonated with Miri, but the systematic and repetitive nature of these events was uncharacteristic of children and teenagers; they would have been bored after one or two incidents and moved onto the next thrill. No, if Jack Whitlock was being set up, and it was by no means clear that he was, it was not the work of a child. As for Nettie and Sarah, they were hiding something for sure; hadn't she just been given the brush-off? They would be on their guard at Pink Pilates from now on. Miri must find another way of rooting it out.

Chapter 15

"Witches? Darling, you can't be serious!"

"You don't know, then?"

"Of course not! If I'd known I would have gone to the class; it was only the Pilates that was putting me off. Is that bit compulsory? Really! Mrs. Duggan of all people. I just don't believe it. I must go, I simply must."

Edie was beside herself with indignation at having missed a trick, images of glamourous pink ensembles floating around in her imagination.

"I shall be quite unique."

"Really?" said Miri, innocently.

"But of course! No boring tracksuit for me, Darling."

Miri knew from experience that there was no point in contradicting her when she was in full creative flow. Instead, she considered how she might use Edie's newly discovered enthusiasm to her own advantage.

"I suspected something of the sort was going on there."

"Did you, Darling? How jolly clever of you. You don't think there's a link with that horrid raven thing, do you?" Edie paused and Miri allowed Edie the time to reach her own conclusion. "You know, they could be up to all sorts of things underneath all that pink and pastel." Miri looked at her as she sipped her coffee and raised her brows in agreement.

"How do you fancy going undercover, Edie?" said Miri quietly after a long pause. The air between them crackled with Edie's boundless excitement, and for once she couldn't speak. Miri could barely hide her amusement and retreated into her mug, awaiting the inevitable outburst.

"Do I? Do I? Oh! What a marvellous idea! I'll be the very soul of discretion, Darling." Miri seriously doubted that, but she trusted her friend's sincerity completely. Most of the villagers underestimated her, too shallow to look beyond her eccentricities, so her reputation as the batty old posh woman with her wigs and makeup was the perfect cover, and while the Witches of Eastwick were distracted by theories about Edie's sudden appearance, Miri would be free to do some real investigating.

"Mum, for God's sake!" said Joe, later that day over dinner. "It's hardly the crime of the century. You've sent Edie on a mission to uncover signs of the dark arts, which may or may not be linked to a Pilates and self-awareness class, all because of a dead bird! It's like a plot from Murder She Wrote. Let it go, Mum."

"I agree," said Will, resurfacing briefly from his plate of pasta, much to Joe's surprise.

"Now look what you've done. You've made Will agree with me."

"There's something going on, Joe. I know it," said Miri leaning forward, arms folded. "They won't drop their guard while I'm there, but Edie will be my eyes and ears. It's perfect." Miri chose not to elaborate any further, fearing the barrage of objections that would inevitably ensue, particularly from Joe.

"But some of your friends were there weren't they? Shel, for example. Are you saying they're all practicing black magic or something?"

"No, Joe. I'm not saying that at all. I saw really positive results in fact, especially for Clare."

"Well then."

"I'm just not convinced that what I saw is the extent of the activity, that's all. Sarah Clarke seemed false somehow, too polite and gushing. And those eyes." The veiled threats remained unspoken.

"That's it then," said Will, who had finished eating and was therefore able to join in the conversation. "A polite leader with unusual eyes. That's just the sort of crap that led to innocent women being burned at the stake." Joe nodded, thinking of Lavinia. Then he thought of Jack.

"Well maybe there's no harm in keeping an eye out," he said tentatively. Will groaned and escaped upstairs to catch up on some emails. Miri stacked the dishwasher in silence, mulling over what the boys had said, and Joe wandered into the sitting room in response to a message on his phone.

"That was Zoe," he said. Miri looked up and raised her eyebrows, smiling at her son's pleasure. "She wants to launch Halloween week with a garden party at the vicarage, weather permitting. If it rains, she'll open up the house, I guess."

"That sounds fun," said Miri, waiting for the reason she had texted Joe about it.

"Oh, she has asked me if I'll help her to organise it," he added, blushing slightly. "I suppose she needs some muscle to move tables, string lights up, you know the sort of thing."

Miri did not want to embarrass her son, who was clearly excited about being asked, so she continued clearing up and agreed, reluctantly, with his assessment of Zoe's needs, though privately she did not buy the 'damsel in distress' call for one minute. The jury was still out as far as Zoe was concerned, but Miri had enough to think about. The garden party would go ahead whether she worried about it or not, so she pushed it to the back of her mind and focused on the latest email attachment from Shel, a superb colour coded spreadsheet detailing the dates, times and venue of rehearsals, along with the names of the children involved and their respective parts. A further attachment listed costumes and scripts required for each child with a red dot next to the ones for which Miri was responsible. Miri shook her head in admiration. What an absolute marvel she was. In her imagination, Miri saw an attachment spreadsheet detailing colour coded spells, ingredients for potions, their proven effects, intended victims, incantations and a results column. She smiled at herself. Maybe the boys were right. She was just being foolish. When she met with Shel the following morning, the Pilates class was bound to be mentioned, so she could simply ask her what she thought of their activities. If Shel had witnessed anything unusual, she would be sure to confide in Miri, as she had, so bravely, once before.

In the meantime, there were costumes to plan and scripts to prepare. Joe and Will had plans of their own for the evening, so Miri was free to accept Edie's invitation to an early supper, followed by an evening rummaging through Edie's archives and remnant baskets, for inspiration.

***

Miri always enjoyed Edie's company and the evening they had planned together was no exception. Edie was still excited about 'Operation Broomstick' as she called it, but once she had shared her sketches of the pink all-in-one she was going to 'run up in no time, Darling', and turned her attention to the mushroom risotto she had prepared, she was back to her usual self. Almost.

Miri felt like a child with an enormous dressing up box to explore, revelling in the vast array of colours and textures at their disposal, haphazardly strewn across the sparse fittings and wooden floor of Edie's workroom beneath the eves. She had already sifted out the oranges, blacks and reds from her enormous collection, so it wasn't so hard to select suitable pieces from the silks, velvets and brocades now pooled around their feet. The whole of the year six class had been invited to take part in the play, so Diane would need to order a much larger quantity of the fabrics on Miri's short list. Fortunately, Edie had kept a meticulous list of suppliers and batch numbers so if a particular shade had been discontinued, Diane would know where to source something similar.

After much deliberation and a shared bottle of red wine, a basket of remnants was packed ready for Diane and her team to work on. They had decided that the three witches, the main focus of the scene, would be kitted out in black cloaks with red hoods, the rest of the class, the chorus, would be in orange cloaks with black hoods. "So much easier," Edie said. "No need for fittings, one size fits all, and the block colours are simple and striking. Easy to run up too, which will make Diane's life easier. They can wear their own clothes underneath, their own black boots or shoes, and the makeup will do the rest. Result. Who is doing the makeup, by the way, do you know?"

"Brilliant, Edie. The makeup? I think," Miri replied with a frown, trying to remember. "A friend of Shel's? Yes, I seem to recall her telling me that she had sorted the makeup. I'll check. Let me write that down. By the way," she continued casually, "have you seen any more of Dex, I mean Bill?" Edie looked down to hide her emotion and busied herself with packing away the discarded fabrics.

"Just to pass the time of day, Darling. I enjoyed the evening in the pub with you all there, but I certainly don't intend to make any further overtures. You might as well know, Darling," she continued, "he dumped me rather unceremoniously when I was young and vulnerable and although a lot of water has flowed under the bridge since then, I can still feel the smart, as keenly as if it were yesterday." Tears welled up in Edie's tired eyes and Miri's heart went out to her.

"I'm so sorry," she said, giving her a hug. "The last few days must have been very difficult for you. I suspected that you had been quite close."

"Oh, don't worry," said Edie, with a theatrical sniff, wiping her eyes with a piece of damask silk. "I hated him with a vengeance at the time, naturally, but I think I probably had a narrow escape, all things considered. Looks to me like he has a drink problem, probably lost his driving licence, and who knows what other sort of trouble he's got himself into over the years. I wouldn't want him to know I was so upset though, even after all this time. He didn't refer to it and neither did I. He probably doesn't even remember. Even if he does, he's not the type to consider the effect his behaviour may have had on me all those years ago. There were plenty of young girls willing to fall under his spell, only to be cast aside after the curtain call, I'm sure. He was very handsome."

"I'm sure you're right, Edie. I think you're behaving wonderfully well under the circumstances, and I promise never to leave you alone with him, whether he likes it or not," she added mischievously.

Edie laughed and Miri was relieved to see that she had regained her customary control. She too doubted that the feelings of others would have much impact on Dexter Steele, but Miri kept her opinion to herself and as she helped to fold up the last few swathes of fabric, she wondered just how much his treatment of the young Edie had affected the course of her life in the years that followed.

***

Shel had left a message for Miri, to ask if she would mind meeting at her house the following day, instead of the school. There was a teacher training day, and it would be a good excuse to get away for an afternoon, she thought. Miri had readily agreed and spent the following morning baking scones to take along. She decided not to mention Pink Pilates outright but was very curious about what Shel made of it all, and also her role within the group; maybe the subject would arise naturally. As she turned into the small close of new semi-detached houses on the edge of the village, Miri was taken back to the day, only a few months before, when she and Constable Jane Peters had met there and interviewed Shel about her suspicions regarding the activities in the new schoolroom.

"I'm supposed to be on a diet," said Shel as she spied the cake tin perched on top of the files in Miri's arms.

"Nonsense. We'll need some reinforcements along the way."

Shel's house of chrome and glass was every bit as immaculate as Miri remembered it, and all the paperwork they needed in order to make progress was set out ready. The coffee machine was blipping merrily, and Miri made herself comfortable, taking the lid off the warm tin and closing her eyes, the better to appreciate the smell of vanilla and spice.

"We'll probably get more work done; no cuts and bruises, no lost P.E kits or forgotten lunches. Right. Let's get started."

"Oh, before I forget. Edie mentioned makeup yesterday." Shel raised her eyebrows and they both laughed. "No, not her own makeup, for once. Arrangements for the kids to be made up on the night of the performance and possibly a trial run if there's time. Do you know anything about it or is it something we still need to organise?"

Shel picked out a scone from the tin, sat back and crossed her legs. Miri thought this was a bit odd as they had barely started, and Shel was anything but a slacker. "Well," she said and hummed with pleasure as she devoured the first mouthful. "I can trust you, can't I Miri?"

"Of course. What is it?"

"You were there the other night. You know that there's more to the Pilates class than exercise."

"Well, yes."

"Yes, of course you do. You're a very perceptive lady, Miri. Not much escapes you, I'm sure." Shel smiled, popped the rest of the scone into her mouth and reached for a serviette. "Thing is," she continued, "most of us are there for exactly what you saw, self-help, grounding, confidence, all the stuff you know about already. Miri nodded. But," she added, pausing to pour coffee, "there are one or two members of the group who like to dabble more deeply into the whole witchcraft thing, outside of the class. A sort of sub-group, if you like. I didn't dwell on it when you asked me before because you never know who's listening." Miri remained silent. She didn't want to interrupt Shel's flow with her own suspicions and was wondering how all this was going to link up with makeup for the play. She tucked her feet up onto the chair and waited for her to go on.

"There's a young woman who lives on the other side of the crescent here, called Suzie Cooper. Very pretty. Blonde. Good figure. Petite. She's a single parent and works as a mobile beautician. You may have seen her little van around the place? She's out at the moment, otherwise you'd be able to see it from here," said Shel, craning her neck to look beyond the window.

"Would that be, 'Glamour on the Go'? I've seen it, yes."

"She does eyebrows, lash tinting, facials, waxing, wedding makeup, that sort of thing. It's very popular with women who don't want to go to a salon, and the prices are good because she works from home. Anyway, I digress," she said, judging by Miri's silence and vacant expression that she was unfamiliar with most beauty treatments. "The point is," she continued, "Suzie volunteered to do the makeup for the kids play, oh, about a week ago, and I said I'd pop over and discuss it with her." Shel paused, leaned forward and lowered her voice. "When I got there, last night it was, and she opened the door, my God! Her face and hands were completely covered in red blotches, raised and sore. Nothing on her arms or chest, just her face and hands. Poor thing was in tears, her baby was crying, mess everywhere. Terrible." Miri frowned. "I stayed with her, cleared up a bit and settled the baby, but I had to leave her to it in the end, of course. I offered to call a doctor while I was there, but she wouldn't hear of it, so I suggested Nettie Hopkins, the district nurse. You know her, I believe?" Miri nodded, slowly. "She completely freaked out when I suggested Nettie, sobbed her heart out, mumbling something about an allergic reaction to a new face cream she was trying out and that she didn't want any fuss. Of course, it will have a devastating effect on her business."

"Hmm," said Miri. "And you think," she added slowly, not wanting to put words into Shel's mouth.

"I think that Suzie is afraid of Nettie and I think I know why."

"Because she's a witch?"

"Because I think she's been having an affair with her husband," she said slowly. "And because she's a 'witch'," she added, more quickly, with comic effect.

"This is a two-scone problem," said Miri.

"Agreed. I'll make a pot of tea."

Miri had lots of questions. She knew that Shel was not a fanciful woman, it was unlikely that she believed in magic, but there was plenty of evidence in the real world to satisfy her. Shel's husband, Geoff, worked with Tom Hopkins, and had hinted to Shel that he might be playing away, but wouldn't say where, probably for fear of losing his job, letting his mate down, any number of reasons. "Of course, I've got no actual proof. It may be just Geoff getting the wrong end of the stick. Wouldn't be the first time. Or a bit of male bravado on Tom's part, you know?" Miri remembered how shifty Tom had looked during Zoe's sermon, and her own initial surprise at how handsome he was; a man you would keep an eye on if he was yours. Of course, Geoff had told Shel to keep his suspicions between the two of them, it was none of their business after all, and she had done just that, until now, and only then because of this latest development.

"You don't think that this rash is the result of a spell do you, Shel?" Miri laughed uneasily. "Surely, if it is Nettie's doing, it's more likely to be something related to her role as a nurse? Easy enough to pop something nasty into one of Suzie's pots; they both visit people in their homes, remember?"

"Yes, I thought of that," said Shel. "But there's something else, Miri. My Geoff says that Nettie has been spending quite a bit of time with young Adam." Miri looked up. She knew the Hopkins' were keeping an eye on him, but she still felt responsible in some way and she had made that clear to Nettie. "She grows plants and herbs in his patch behind the cottage."

"Yes, the boys mentioned something about that. They said she makes drinks."

"Drinks? Potions more like."

"That's a loaded word though, Shel. A mixture designed to create an illness or allergy, can be used in all sorts of ways. The word 'potion' suggests witchcraft."

"Well, maybe it is. I've heard her talking with her friend Sarah Clarke about it. They're always getting their heads together and laughing in secret after the sessions. I wouldn't put anything past either of them. She's too much under the influence of Sarah if you ask me. It's not like they were ever real friends, as far as I know. This is a recent thing, as if they have hooked up for a reason."

"It's probably a combination of Nettie's medical knowledge and Sarah's, well, just Sarah," Miri said, thinking about her recent encounter. "It's interesting though. If there is a purpose, as you say, I wonder what their motive is. If they are responsible for Suzie's rash, it sounds like they may be launching some sort of campaign. I know you don't agree but I'm keeping an open mind about the raven incident. Who knows what they may be capable of..." Shel looked thoughtful and nodded slowly. "I'm due to visit Adam soon anyway. I'll keep my eyes open."

"Well, be careful. Whatever they're up to, you wouldn't want to cross 'em."

Shel said she'd check on Suzie and make alternative arrangements for the makeup if necessary, and the rest of the afternoon was spent ticking off a range of things on Shel's 'to do' list and deciding what each of them could most usefully do next.

"I'll check how the costumes are getting on, collect and deliver the decorations for the trailer," said Shel.

"And I'll drop in on one of Dexter Steele's master class rehearsals tomorrow, I'll be around that way visiting Adam."

"Be careful." said Shel.

"Oh, I'm not afraid of Nettie Hopkins."

"I wasn't thinking of Nettie."

Chapter 16

"Okay, everybody!" Dexter Steele clapped loudly using a rhythm he had taught the children, and the effect was instantaneous.

"Look at them all," said Tracey, the year six class teacher. "I've had this class for over a year now and it takes me at least five minutes to get them where I want them to be. In sweeps Oscar bloody Steele and he has 'em eating out of his hands in half an hour flat."

"Dexter," said Miri.

"Whatever."

"You should be proud of them, Tracey. They're excited about the whole experience, working with a real actor. You can't blame them. The novelty would soon wear off if he was here full time. He is very professional though; he's doing a proper warm up just like they do in the theatre." Miri was teasing but she was genuinely impressed.

"Shut up!" said Tracey, playfully. "Of course, I'm pleased for them. It's a marvellous opportunity. It's just that when he's gone, regular class is going to seem so dull."

"Not necessarily. You could get a whole term's work out of this. Milk it. Copy some of his techniques."

At that very moment, Dexter was creeping silently around the hall, demonstrating how to be scary using his face and body language alone, as the class looked on in awe.

"Hmm. I don't think so." said Tracey, standing up and straightening her skirt. "I must get on Miri, but thanks for all your help. See you soon."

Miri had arrived shortly after morning break, much earlier than she had planned, the visit to see Adam having been short and sweet, but by no means fruitless. She had hoped to do a bit of sleuthing, find out what had been planted in Adam's garden for example, drop a few hints to Nettie about allergies so that she could gauge her reaction, that sort of thing, and although circumstances were not entirely in Miri's favour, she'd had plenty to occupy her thoughts en route to the rehearsal.

Adam had been working alone, clearing paths and repairing fences, and although he had been pleased to see her, waving to attract her attention and greeting her with his usual wide smile, he had said that he needed to carry on because he still had a lot to do.

He had seemed anxious to Miri, who knew him well, and once his initial pleasure at seeing her had passed, he had looked around nervously, as a child does when they are hiding something. Adam loved nothing more than to be busy, so there must be another reason for the tension she sensed in him; his movements had been jerky, his dribbling profuse, and there had been a noticeable deterioration in his speech pattern. Miri hadn't pressed him, of course, but she wasn't going to let it go. She had seen Tom walking towards the storage sheds at the bottom of the field and wondered whether Adam was afraid of him. Maybe he had seen her coming and was deliberately avoiding her too? Only when she was near to the perimeter fence did Miri spot Nettie leaving Adam's cottage, a basket nestled in her arms, a can of paint, or something similar, hooked over her elbow. Adam's cottage was not his own, she was sure of that, and he was the perfect victim; abused from an early age, abandoned into the care system and used by all and sundry on the Frankland Estate as a decoy for their crimes. If there was anything sinister going on, with Nettie and Sarah at the heart of it, where better to set up than Adam's cottage? The only person who ever went there was Miri. Nettie hadn't noticed her and Miri chose not to attract her attention; the last thing she wanted to do was give Nettie cause to change whatever it was she was up to.

Dexter set the children a group task based around fear and as soon as they got started, he made his way towards Miri and re-introduced himself by way of a theatrical bow.

"Something wicked! Something wicked! Something wicked! Something wicked!" The children chanted as they crept around the hall.

"Looks like it's going really well," she said. "They're loving it."

"Indeed." he said, hands on hips, paisley waistcoat open revealing a violet shirt. "I'm enjoying it too. It never ceases to amaze me how therapeutic drama can be, my dear."

"Yes. I don't doubt it," said Miri. Role playing came very close to some of her work as a psychiatrist and she understood the process of unlocking feelings in this way. Maybe she could do some follow up work with Tracey after Halloween, using Dexter's themes to tackle any residual fear hanging over from the murder of Melanie Crew. She would give that some thought.

"How far have they got with the actual scene, Dexter?"

"I'm still laying the foundations, as you can see. I'm a firm believer in building blocks," he said, his deep resonant voice accompanied by an expert mime. "When we get to the scene where the witches cast their spell, these kids will have learned the techniques already and it will be a breeze, lovie. An absolute breeze."

The kids were totally absorbed in their task and as soon as they heard the clapping tune, they broke off and gathered at Dexter's feet, eager to make the most of this larger-than- life character and his expertise. Even the shy and reluctant ones were doing something and would have their part to play. Miri was pleased to know that everything was going to plan. She had doubted Dexter Steele, half expected him to be drunk or hungover, but he clearly knew and loved his craft. Now all she had to do was reconcile this impressive professional with the young buck who had broken her friend's heart to the extent that it still brought forth tears some forty years on.

Miri texted the boys with an offer of a pub lunch and gathered her thoughts, as she so often did, during her walk back to the village. The solitude and peace improved her ability to process experience and consider her next steps. The drama class had been great, but her visit to see Adam was gnawing away at her. Whatever was in that package that had been passed from Sarah to Nettie when Miri had interrupted them at the end of the Pilates class, was connected in some way with recent unexplained events and Adam's behaviour that morning, she was sure of it. Tom had reasons of his own for not wanting a conversation with her no doubt, and Miri wondered whether he knew about Suzie's rash.

Over lunch, Joe and Will shared their own news and Miri took the opportunity to forget about the whole business of witchcraft, illicit affairs and facial rashes, at least for now. Joe was full of plans for the vicarage garden party. He had spent the morning with Zoe, and they had come up with some great ideas, including a fancy-dress competition and a bat hunt for the kids. "Gavin and Craig have agreed to provide a barbeque, and I'm going to see if I can get a decent sound out of that ancient p.a. system in the village hall so some of the locals can get up and do their stuff. We can do all of that, outside or in, depending on the weather." Will and Miri raised their glasses in support. Will had been spending spare time with Kate and, though he didn't give much away, it seemed to Miri that their relationship was inching its way towards the next level. So far so good. The boys were happy, busy and above all, Joe especially, suitably distracted from the Whitlock business.

The afternoon was becoming unseasonably warm for the time of year, a huge honey coloured sun casting a comforting glow over the fields, highlighting the spectacular russets of the fallen leaves. The air was thick with the scents of the fruit harvest, the pungency of rotting apples, the sweetness of berries. Dexter Steele, conspicuous in his ruby red jacket and jet-black cap, was making his way back from the school to the Kington, where he had decided to stay until the event was over, just as Miri, Joe and Will were passing the church. He waved elaborately to attract their attention and Miri, having seen quite enough of Dexter for one day, waved politely but kept on walking, pausing briefly to exchange a few words with Michael, who was working at the edge of the graveyard. The boys went on ahead. In the distance, Jack was sitting in his yard on an old barrel, both hands buried and busy, deep inside a basket on his lap, staring out towards them, grim faced and still.

Miri, having finished her exchange with Michael, noticed that Jack had not resumed whatever it was he was doing, gnarly hands firmly gripping the sides of the basket, so she followed his gaze. Jack had spotted Dexter Steele, who had paused to light a cigarette. Bill Tanner. The last surviving member of the family who, Jack believed, had been the cause of Whitlock poverty and ill luck ever since the Middle Ages. He must have heard that he was coming to the village, but this may well have been the first time he had seen him for decades.

"Hi Miri!" Nettie Hopkins broke the spell and Miri turned to respond to the call. She had pulled up on her bike, doing her rounds, Miri presumed, a halo of pale frizzy hair expanding in the wake of the breeze; a striking image. "Sorry I missed you earlier. We are all so busy with the fruit harvest and all. Tom said you'd been." She hesitated momentarily, unsure of her next move, maybe. "See you next week at Pilates?" Miri knew she wasn't going to be there and made a non-committal gesture. It would have been foolish to show any sign that she was potentially onto something, and it was clear that Nettie was trying to find out if Sarah had succeeded in putting her off, so she quickly turned her attention to Dexter, and Nettie pedalled away. Had he recognised Jack, she wondered? He certainly looked shaken. Quite pale in fact. It had all happened so quickly and Dexter had not moved an inch since lighting his cigar.

"Are you alright, Dexter?" said Miri, backtracking a few paces.

"Oh yes, m'dear. Quite alright," he said, backing away with a polite wave. No, you're not, thought Miri. No, you're not.

"Strange chappie. I knew his father," said Michael, rejoining Miri, leaning on his broom. Miri was not in the mood to engage in any gossip, so she adjusted her shoulder bag and briskly buttoned up her jacket. "I must go, Michael. The boys will be home by now."

"Still," he said, ignoring the hint. "Not as strange as some I could mention." He nodded in the direction of Jack, still sitting on his barrel and rummaging around in his basket. Miri walked slowly away but Michael fell into step beside her, refusing to let the opportunity pass. "Just look at the silly old bugger! Whittling his bloody straw dollies. Every year's the same. For the Halloween decorations, he says." Michael tutted and shook his head. "Never speaks. Never goes anywhere. Then every year he makes a bloody great pile o'dolls out o'straw, like his father before him. Now that's strange, for ye! He tries to sell 'em sometimes, but because he keeps the money for 'imself, folks don't bother with 'em." Miri looked back over Michael's shoulder. He had gained her interest.

"Where does he put the ones he doesn't sell?"

"Ha! Sticks 'em all over the truck an' the like. All over the place, really. Never says a word about 'em, they just appear. Some 'ave 'ats. Some 'ave jackets. Even boots." Michael wiggled his finger near to his temple and laughed. "Bloody nutcase."

"Must go, Michael. Really." She waved as he turned, and walked quickly home, her brain, having slipped into neutral over lunch, buzzing away against her will. She would ask Jack if he would make some dolls for the play prop box. They would be perfect for the little witches to hold while they were performing their lines. Perfect.

Chapter 17

The final dress rehearsal was over. The trailer, temporarily parked in the school playground, had been duly decorated with bats, pumpkins and an array of spooks made by the younger children. Strings of orange and red lights were in place against an ink black backdrop, and a huge cauldron made from a repurposed stockpot, stood proudly centre stage, spilling over with plastic toads, squishy eyeballs, drips of theatrical blood, spiders, snakes, yellow teeth and gruesome fingers. The effect was spectacular, and Miri stood back in admiration, hands on cheeks, smiling with pleasure.

The rehearsal had gone badly, much to Dexter's delight. "Bad rehearsal, good show!" he boomed, twirling his director's 'wand' and puffing himself out like a toad. Several children had trodden, either on their own, or another child's cape, (causing a comical domino effect which reminded Miri of the old Keystone Cops movies), a large boy had inadvertently dropped his sandwiches into the cauldron and would stop at nothing to retrieve them, and a pale faced girl had started to cry, declaring a hitherto undisclosed snake phobia.

Dexter had been required to prompt three times during the scene, ('Fillet of fenny, not 'fanny' sweetie. Really!') but the lines had been distributed among the group to make it easier for them to learn. Most children only had a line or two, the three around the cauldron, the most articulate and reliable, taking on most of the learning.

*'By the pricking of my thumbs,
something wicked this way comes.'*

"On the day, you see, the little darlings will already be on the trailer ready, so there'll be no tripping hazard, Billy won't have his sandwiches, hopefully, and Prue can stand at the back away from the snakes. Voila! As long as none of the little dears says the word 'Macbeth' before the performance which, as you probably know, is a curse to all actors, we should be fine." Dexter concluded with a theatrical bow and backed away. Thank goodness he had decided not to perform a solo speech from the play, Miri thought; the village was definitely not ready for that. She smiled her encouragement, however, and hurried across the playground to the office.

Shel agreed that the costumes looked wonderful. Diane had stitched the hoods onto the capes to minimise the chance of them falling off or getting lost, and the colours had created a striking contrast with the backdrop. Two sixth form drama students from the local secondary school had stepped up to do the makeup, as Suzie was still indisposed with her skin rash, and the overall visual effect had been stunning. Satisfied that there was nothing more to be done, Miri checked the props box and mentioned to Shel that she may have access to some straw dollies, or poppets as they were called, for the kids to hold if they wanted to. Such tiny figures were associated with witchcraft after all, so it was entirely appropriate. She would have a word with Jack.

With only two days to go to the start of the festivities, everyone involved was keeping an eye on the weather and putting finishing touches to their arrangements. Gavin and Craig were busy scrubbing barbeques, erecting trestle tables and awnings, and marinating meats in delicious homemade sauces. The Aunt Sally teams were practicing in the pub garden and the bonfire was taking shape on the waste ground behind the pub.

Joe and Zoe had enlisted Will to help with their plans and he had suggested, true to form, a ghost hunt for the adults later in the evening, following on from the garden party. "The kids are having a bat hunt," he said. "Why not do something for the mums and dads? Everyone will have had a drink by then; it'll be a good laugh. I can do the spooky voices through the speakers you've set up Joe, and we can just hide a few old sheets in the trees and bushes with a clue attached to each one. Simple enough."

"Why not?" said Zoe, adding 'old sheets' to her list. "Are you happy to think up the clues though? I'm not very good at that sort of thing and I've got a christening to prepare for this evening."

"No problem. We can work on it tonight."

"I take it your detective is on duty tonight, then?" said Joe.

"She's not my detective. But yeah, she's on duty."

Joe grinned. "Better make the most of you while we've got you then. Now, is there anything else we need to do?"

"Nope," said Zoe. "Food and drink sorted with Craig. Helen and Beatrice have kindly offered to do some baking, and music and entertainment is sorted, along with fun and games. Decorations ready, pallets to sit on, flyers delivered and displayed. Done. All we need now is some decent weather, but there's plenty of room inside. I haven't even had chance to explore the place myself yet. So many nooks and crannies." Joe and Will looked at each other. When they were growing up, there was nothing they had liked more than exploring together, much to their mother's dismay. They were too polite to suggest rummaging around the vicarage now, but they both knew it would be something they would talk about later; 'nooks and crannies' was a magnetic phrase to them both.

***

The late afternoon sky was already turning to lead as they walked home. An hour of daylight had been lost since summertime had officially ended and the temperature had dropped. Will pulled his jacket tighter and increased the pace. The moon was almost full, keeping watch from behind a tangle of bare branches, pale and omniscient.

"Nooks and crannies, says Zoe. Well, maybe we could have a bit of a look round inside during the afternoon or evening, if things are going well. What do you think?"

Joe, whose thoughts had been running along similar lines, nodded and smiled. "Don't see why not. Probably just a few dusty old cupboards and rickety serving hatches from the Victorian era or before even; servants' hidey holes, priest holes, that sort of thing."

"You two look like you've got something up your sleeve," said Miri as they sauntered through the back door into the kitchen. As soon as her back was turned both boys raised their hands, palms up and looked at each other.

"How does she *do* that?" whispered Will.

"Must be all that psychic Pilates," said Joe.

"What's for tea?" asked Will, in an effort to deflect the conversation.

"I've had a busy day, so it's pizza and salad," Miri replied simply.

"You okay, Mum? You look a bit stressed," said Joe with concern.

"No, I'm fine. Well," she added after a pause. "If you must know, I saw Jack Whitlock today."

"What?" said the boys in unison.

"I wanted to beg or borrow some of the straw dollies he makes, for the kids' performance on Saturday."

"And?"

Miri hadn't had a specific plan for her encounter with Jack Whitlock. She had spotted him emerging from Bob's repair shop, the name often given to his re-purposed ancient cowshed, also known locally as plain 'Bob's'. Bob Whittle was the latest in a long line of Whittles to make a living on these premises and, apart from a smattering of post war machinery, Bob was proud of the fact that nothing much had changed since his grandfather's day, that his tools, lathes, anvils, vices and the like, still shone like trophies and worked as well as they had when they were new. 'None of the throw away rubbish they make today' he'd say, stroking the surface of a much-loved piece with affection. 'If they want to sort this bloody planet out, they should go back to 'ow things used to be. Blimey, to 'ear 'em all talk you'd think this recyclin' business was sommat new! I ain't throwed anythi' out for seventy year or more!'

Miri knew it to be the one place where Jack Whitlock could be sure of a warm welcome. He and Bob had been boys together and Bob interpreted the general attitude of the villagers towards Jack to be just another indication of how modern society had lost its way. He knew him, warts an' all, and accepted him. Jack never stayed there long, always chose a time when the barn would be empty and most folk would hardly be aware that he was ever in there. But there was always a battered old chair in the corner, a clean enamel mug on a shelf and the chance to pass the time of day with his old playmate.

Bob could turn his hand to anything, from welding broken toys, fixing bikes and lawn mowers to, sharpening knives. There was a hook for everything, natural grooves in the walls where centuries of capable hands had lifted and replaced tools, and the comforting smell of freshly shaved woodchip, oil and polish, permeated the walls. Bob's vintage style of brightly painted wooden toys were proving to be very popular with families in many of the surrounding villages and whenever Miri saw him pottering about, she always had the feeling that she was witnessing pure happiness, a man at peace with himself.

Miri had taken her chance. "Jack! Jack!" He'd paused, ready to scowl, but on seeing it was Miri calling, had settled his face into an indeterminate expression and waited. "Been shopping, I see."

"No, I ain't. Bob's been sharpening some knives for me, that's all." Jack had made to go, impatient at what he perceived as intrusion into his private life.

"Oh, I see. Do you use those for the dolls, Jack?" Miri had been almost jogging in order to keep up with Jack's loping stride.

"That's right," he'd said curtly, with his back to her.

"Well, I was wondering if you might donate a few for me to use to add to the set for the kids' performance of Macbeth? Would that be okay?"

"Don't see why not. Long as you keep hold of 'em. Don't want 'em getting' into the wrong 'ands." Jack had been halfway through his gate and it was clear he was going to shut it just as Miri caught up.

"What do you mean, Jack?"

"Nothin'. 'Ere. Take these," he'd growled, reaching down to a bench by the gate. "I made 'em yesterday. That's 'ow I come to need the knives doin'." He'd thrust a basket of dolls at Miri, no more than half a dozen, and turned his back once more.

"Thank you, Jack. But what do you mean about them getting into the wrong hands?" Miri had been forced to raise her voice to catch his attention while she still had the chance. He'd paused, halfway along the path, old Bess managing no more than a single thump of her ancient tail.

"Nothin'. I told yer!" He'd raised his arm high to signal the end of the conversation, dipping his head before disappearing and slamming the door.

Miri was not satisfied. She had her dollies, yes, but now she was in possession of another piece of the puzzle. Why would Jack warn her to keep the dolls safe? She knew they were associated with witchcraft, that's why she wanted them, so did Jack know something about how else they might be used? Was Jack himself trying to cast suspicion elsewhere? Or was he just living up to local gossip? What game was he playing?

"Told you he's weird," said Joe, when Miri had finished. "Forget it, Mum. More important things to do. All sorted for the garden party tomorrow, weather's looking good. Nothing can go wrong now, unless you count the local entertainment, which could go either way. Just relax and enjoy."

What Miri didn't mention, not because she was being deliberately secretive, but because she would need to be sure of the significance, were the new details about Jack that she had also learned from Bob Whittle. He had been outside his workshop as Miri made her way back from her encounter with Jack, and she had taken advantage of her basket of dolls to strike up a conversation with Bob.

"No wonder Jack's knives needed sharpening with all this work. Look at these. Aren't they beautiful, Bob?"

"Yep," he'd said, pushing back his oily cap and wiping his face with an old rag. "I remember his mother and gran makin' 'em when we was kids."

"Really? What were they used for?"

"Well, the skill had been passed down since before anyone can remember, from the witch hunt days they say, but they was used for good luck charms, fertility offerings and the like in mine and Jack's day. If you left a corn dolly out all night, you'd get a good harvest, that sort o' thing. Folk will make of such things what they will, I expect." Bob had looked around, trying to re-establish his rhythm.

"I can't believe how much ruddy knife sharpening' I been doin'" he'd said, half to himself, scratching his head as if trying to solve the biggest mystery ever.

"Must be that time of year."

"Let me see now. There's old Farmer Truelove, he wanted the blades on his old scythe doin'. Bless him. Still uses a hand-held thing on the small pasture." Bob lay his hands on his hips and shook his head affectionately. Then there's that young Sarah whatsername, with her rare collection—" Miri's ears had burned.

"Sarah Clarke?"

"Ay, that's 'er. Nice stuff, but a bugger to sharpen. I dunno why she can't just keep 'em as they are. They're worth a lot of money, she says, so she wants 'em kept in tip top nick. Won't trust no-one else but me to do it, she says. She always gets round me." I bet she does, Miri had thought.

"What do you think about Bill Tanner being back in town?" Nothing ventured, nothing gained, thought Miri.

Bob's face had clouded as he removed his cap and wiped his forehead. His skin was leathery and streaked with fine powder, several of his teeth were missing and his features were flattish, like a tombstone.

"Don't think nothin'," he'd said quietly. " 'e were a bit younger than us. I remember 'is dad more, old Sam Tanner. Died before 'is time in a terrible accident out in the field, poor bugger. They found 'is body all mangled up in one o' them new-fangled combine 'arvesters. Course, everyone says it was the curse." Bob had taken a step forward. "Jack knows all about it. The Tanner menfolk will all die a terrible death before their time."

Bob's voice had faded away and it had taken him a few seconds to rally and look Miri in the eye. "By all accounts, last thing Sam said to young Bill before 'e went to the field that morning, was that 'e didn't approve of 'im wanting to be an actor and that 'e should do a proper man's job. Bill was never the same after that. 'e left before the funeral. Came back to see 'is mother laid to rest, but apart from that, nothin'."

"Have you seen him, Bob?"

"Can't bloody miss him, can ye? Same old swagger that turned the 'eads of all the girls in Kington! 'Dandy Tanner' we used to call 'im. Wasn't till 'e left that the rest of us got a look in. Stole my girl an' all when we was lads." He'd turned his face away. "Well, water under the bridge," he'd added with a half-smile and a vague wave of his arm. He'd turned and lifted another knife to sharpen, a clear indication to Miri that the conversation was over.

***

The following morning was fine, chilly but clear and still, the waxing moon secretly suspended, waiting in the wings to make a dramatic entrance, in all its glory, on Halloween. Then it would be a full moon for the second time in the month; a blue moon too, the star of the show.

Miri, Joe and Will spent a lazy morning lingering over a cooked breakfast, catching up with emails and preparing themselves for the day to come. Edie called round to walk with Miri to the vicarage, the boys having gone ahead to help Zoe with the preparations. She looked charming in a silver woollen suit with pale pink accessories, and Miri hoped that she would not be thrown off course by the presence or behaviour of Dexter Steele. She had been thinking a lot about Dexter and how awful it must have been for him to have been rejected by his father on the day he died, never having had the chance to put things right, the weight of an ancient curse on his back. No wonder he left. She imagined the dashing youth, destined for the stage, swaggering out of the village, determined never to return, fuelled by raw regret and pain.

"Anything to report from Pilates, Edie?" Miri asked as they walked.

"Not really, Darling. Much as you described it. Don't seem to be getting any fitter, if that's what you mean. But I do think you're right about Nettie and Sarah Clarke. They're very close and they always seem to be deep in conversation after the session. Last week was about herbs. Nothing I don't already know really, but it was nice to see the ladies sharing what they had grown." Miri's ears pricked up. "I might take some cuttings along myself, next time."

"I don't think Nettie and Sarah are using them for hearty casseroles, Edie. Nor do I think they'd be particularly interested in parsley or thyme." Miri went on to explain about her suspicions in relation to Suzie's skin condition. Edie, suitably shocked, promised to keep her ear to the ground.

"They haven't bothered you at all have they, Edie? I mean, tried to put you off or threaten you?"

"Good Lord, no Darling! Why ever would they do that?"

"Because they have probably twigged that you are there on my behalf and—"

Edie laughed. "Really, Darling! I really am quite used to blending into the background, you know. They're barely aware of me, I'm sure."

Miri and Edie were among the first few to arrive. Will was there on the gate collecting the modest entrance fees, and the vicarage grounds looked superb. Michael had been a great help clearing the garden, setting out the pallets and fixing the lighting for when darkness fell, and Craig was already shrouded in smoke behind the barbeque. He was not one for the front of house, so hiding behind the plume and paraphernalia of the catering corner suited him. Suzie's little van was parked in the far corner, advertising her business, and the girls who had stepped up to do the make-up for the play were filling in for her now, offering face painting for the kids and fake tattoos for the Mums and Dads. Joe, self-appointed master of ceremonies, was busy checking the sound system, and a local folk duo were trying out a couple of numbers in preparation for their full set later in the afternoon when floor singers, confidence fuelled by drink, would be offered the opportunity to strut their stuff. Zoe was encouraging everyone to mingle, directing the children towards the games. 'Yes, isn't it great that the rain is keeping off,' and 'the portaloos? Just over there.'

"Phew," she said to Miri. "This hostess lark is exhausting. By the way," she added more quietly. "There'll be a small gathering afterwards for friends if you're interested, Miri. Just a drink and a chat. A kind of housewarming, I suppose. I thought while you're all here—" she continued.

"Well," Miri cut her short. "It's a big day tomorrow with the play and everything so I'll probably give it a miss. Thanks anyway. I'm sure the boys will be up for it though." Zoe smiled and scanned the garden to check all was going well as the guests continued to stream in, encouraged by the dry weather and prospect of some family fun at last. Miri scanned the scene. No sign of Jack Whitlock, or his dolls.

She reflected on how far she had come since her move to the village earlier in the year, the many people she recognised, the many friends she had made. She chatted with Diane and Clare, Shel and her husband, a few of the teachers and of course Dexter, local celebrity, dressed down for the occasion in a cobalt blue pure woollen suit and pale lemon cashmere sweater. His skill at engaging anyone and everyone in conversation was most impressive and Miri could hear him from wherever she was for almost the entire afternoon. 'How charming you look!' 'Really? Yes, I think I know him.' 'Emmerdale? Well, yes of course!' Miri kept an eye on him to make sure he didn't bother Edie, but he appeared not to have noticed her and, to her credit, she did nothing to attract his attention. Maybe his mind was occupied by more pressing matters? He was certainly full of enthusiasm for the event, and confident that the play would be the highlight of the following day. "It will be remembered for many years to come, lovie. Mark my words!" And so it was.

DS Kate Woodley arrived, on duty. "I was due the afternoon off, then someone called in sick so Mike drafted me in." Kate was seriously put out, evident in both her words and her face.

"Oh dear!" said Miri sympathetically. "And when the boss calls-"

"I don't mind really. I'm in the area at least, but it's not the same. I won't be able to stay long. Still, Will says there's a party inside later. I'll be off duty by then."

"Good. You'll be able to relax. Is Jane coming?"

"She's over there, waiting for the barbeque to start." Kate smiled affectionately in the direction of the smoky haze and there was Jane in her civvies, plate balanced on her forearm, can of lager poking out of her bag. Nettie, hair bobbing and frothing, was also in the queue, looking a little pensive, Miri thought. Tom was standing alone at a distance, shuffling his feet awkwardly, clearly out of his comfort zone. Whenever Miri saw them together, they were never actually near to one another. They might as well have been strangers. Miri wanted to ask him where Adam was but thought better of it. She didn't want to be dragged into their domestic troubles; she would ask him herself. Where was Nettie's partner in crime, she wondered? Too embarrassed to make an appearance maybe, in case, against all odds, Suzie had turned up after all? Keeping a low profile? Sharpening her antique knife collection?

The event was a great success. Food was duly consumed, kids' faces were painted, games were lost and won, bats were unearthed, music was played with varying degrees of aplomb, and a good time was had by all. At around seven o'clock, long after the string lanterns had studded the vicarage with their pastel haloes, families with small children began to drift home and Joe announced the ghost hunt. So that's what they were up to, thought Miri. She'd heard the printer whirring while she was reading in bed the night before. Now she knew why. Well, it was one event too many for Miri, so she gathered Edie, said her farewells, complimented Craig on the catering and prepared to leave.

"Mum!" Joe called. "Don't wait up for us. We'll be here till late. And don't worry if—"

"I know. Enjoy yourselves and take care." She hugged her son and took Edie's arm.

A moon, fat and stark against the dense black backdrop, hovered like part of a stage set, pre-lit, hanging from imaginary wires and surrounded by random clusters of miniature fairy lights. It lit their way home and, having wished Edie goodnight, cast a spotlight on Miri's back doorstep as she left her cottage; a moon that swelled and drifted as Miri made her way over the field towards Adam's cottage. This was an ideal opportunity to encourage Adam to confide in her. Most people were at the party and he was sure to be indoors by now.

A twig snapped as Miri approached the perimeter fence. The sound was unnaturally loud, the still air causing an echo. Someone coughed. A clattering. A mumbling. A figure in a long dark hooded coat stumbled out from behind Adam's cottage. It wasn't him; Miri would know his gait anywhere. She waited for whoever it was to disappear, heading towards the road which ran alongside the manor house. This was her chance. She crept along the perimeter to the cottage and tapped gently.

"Adam. It's Miri. Can I talk to you for a minute?" No response. She tried again and eventually Adam's pale face appeared at the upstairs window, not much higher off the ground than Miri herself. Once he had confirmed it was Miri, he came downstairs, fully dressed, despite having been in bed, opened the door and looked around before beckoning her to go inside. Miri apologised for calling so late and managed a smile, despite the urgency of her mission. Adam, not without reason, appeared bewildered and tense.

"Did you have a visitor tonight, Adam?" said Miri, as casually as she could. He shook his head violently. Too violently. "If you are worried about something, Adam, you should tell me." Adam looked down. Miri was the only person in the world he could trust and it wasn't long before it all came spilling out.

***

Will had hidden torn sheets adorned with crude facial features, along with accompanying clues printed in a spooky font, in various semi hard to reach places around the grounds; tucked amid forked branches, draped around door knockers, and hanging from drainpipes. Joe explained the rules, blew the whistle, and the contestants scattered in all directions like ants, whilst Will made spooky sounds and provided a blood curdling voice over. The winner, a burly young farmer with tight curly hair and full ruddy cheeks, lifted his prize, a keg of ale, as if he had won an Oscar, and strutted back to his proud family, wide smile showing no sign of fading. It was a fine end to the afternoon.

"Well, that's that," said Zoe, falling dramatically onto her low squidgy sofa in the sitting room when the last of the villagers had gone. "Here's to a successful day. Thank you everyone for helping to make the afternoon so enjoyable. And thank God for the lovely weather," she added, raising a glass to heaven as an afterthought.

It was a small gathering consisting mainly of those who had played their part in organising the event. Michael chose not to stay on, unsurprisingly, but a couple of his young helpers were there, and Kate had returned, off-duty now and ready to enjoy herself. As the wine began to flow and the last of the barbequed food had been consumed, Joe shot a glance at Will and, one by one they left the room, unnoticed.

"We'd better not be too long," said Will, mindful of not missing an opportunity with Kate. "They'll miss us."

"Yeah fine," said Joe. "We'll just have a quick look round, that's all."

They climbed the first staircase they found, Will looking back to check his bearings.

"I bet some of this oak panelling dates back centuries, Joe."

"Yeah, but some of these wall coverings, here and here, have been added," he whispered. "I was reading about it last night. During the dissolution of the monasteries, all sorts of hidey holes were built into the structure of buildings like this, to hide priests and anyone connected with the church. Some of the National Trust sites allow visitors to go inside them apparently. You tap the wall to see if it makes a hollow sound, like this. Nope. Like this. Shit! I've found one!"

"Don't be daft, Joe. Come on, let's go. I've had enough of enclosed spaces for one year."

"It's loose. Look. I can see the outline of a tiny door. Give me a hand, Will. It's jammed but there doesn't appear to be a lock of any sort."

They used their fingertips and Will's penknife to prize the tiny door open, and peered in. The stale smell knocked them both back and Will gagged, memories of his sojourn in the cellar beneath the institute still raw.

"There's a winding staircase. I'm going down for a look. Coming?"

Will knew he wouldn't be able to persuade Joe to leave it alone and he couldn't let him go by himself.

"Wait while I secure this door wide open."

They crept down the few spiral steps, deep and barely wide enough for them to pass, the yellowing walls rough and damp to the touch. There was another small door at the bottom, unlocked, slightly ajar, at least six inches thick and strewn with ancient cobwebs and dead spiders.

He'll want to go back now, thought Will. He won't go near those spiders. He was wrong. Joe's curiosity had got the better of him and he tentatively pushed the door. It caught on the rough dirt floor and creaked as it inched forward.

"There's a room here, Will. Look. It was dark obviously, but there was enough light from upstairs for them to view the space, once their vision had become accustomed to the change, and they both stared in astonishment. This was no bare cellar or dungeon; it was packed from floor to ceiling with works of art, antiques, valuables of every conceivable shape and colour. The door creaked again.

"Two for the price of one. You won't be so lucky this time, mate. We'll be back." And the door banged shut.

Chapter 18

Miri woke early on Halloween and after a luxurious shower under the eaves in her bedroom set about preparing breakfast. Edie, who had timed it to perfection, brought over coffee and her homemade shortbread. They both agreed that the garden party had been a huge success, that Zoe had done a solid job for the church, and that the stage was set fair for another great day.

"Dexter will steal the show when everyone sees what a marvellous job he's done with the kids," said Miri, thinking aloud.

"Just the way he likes it then," said Edie, curtly. "Pompous ass, strutting around the garden in his finery, soaking up adoration from the usual star-struck soap addicts."

"Well, to be fair Edie, he couldn't very well ignore people, especially the parents; it goes with the territory." Edie shrugged and as Miri cleared the table, they arranged to meet outside the farm shop later, where the trailer would be parked ready for the performance.

"Miri! Miri!" It was Kate, in relatively glamorous clothes, banging on the kitchen window.

"Hey, hang on!" said Miri, wiping her hands and smiling. Edie opened the door.

"Is Will here?"

"No, why? I thought he was with you, Kate. Joe's not here either. He'd said not to expect them back."

"They're missing, Miri." Kate slumped onto the nearest chair, tears overflowing. Edie and Miri stared at each other and tried to process what Kate was implying. This was uncharacteristic of Kate. She always had her emotions under control; this must be a personal matter.

"No, Darling. They'll have gone off somewhere together. Don't worry, they've probably gone foraging or whatever it is they do. Now calm down while I get you a drink."

"You don't understand!" Kate shouted. "Will was going to stay with me at my house. We'd all had a few drinks and I must've fallen asleep on Zoe's sofa. When I woke up at about four, they'd both gone. I checked every room and all around the grounds. Number one," continued Kate, gaining control and moving into professional mode. "Will would not go off like that. I just know it. He would have woken me to say he was going home or whatever. Number two, their stuff is still there, bags, phones and coats, exactly as they left them; even their drinks were still there, half empty. It's like they suddenly just disappeared into thin air. Will would never go anywhere without his phone. I don't expect Joe would either, but they must've taken them out of their pockets when we were relaxing, you know?" Kate's voice broke down and she paused to take a deep breath.

Miri's heart was hammering as she tried to hang onto the thought that they had gone exploring somewhere and forgotten their phones. They would turn up any minute, late to the show and full of earnest apologies for any worry they may have caused.

Kate's phone rang and she fumbled blindly in her pocket, back on red alert.

"What is it, Mike?" She closed her eyes. "What?" She stood up and paced the floor. Miri and Edie looked on, still as statues, open-mouthed and pale, following Kate's every move. "I can't come now, Mike, I'm sorry. I'm in the middle of a personal crisis of my own, a possible police matter." Miri could hear the detective chief inspector raising his voice in response. "Just give me an hour, sir? Please! Get Peters or Meadows to cover for me. I'll explain later. I'll be there as soon as I can." Kate hung up and turned to face them, slightly trembling with emotion.

"It's Dexter Steele. He's been murdered." Kate managed to reach Edie and steer her into a chair just before her legs gave way. Miri knew that she herself had reached the limit at which she could bear no more, and clutched the edge of the worktop, reeling with, what? Relief that the victim was not one of her sons, or fear that the next one, or two, might be?

Kate, on automatic pilot and momentarily distracted from her own fears by duty, rubbed Edie's cold hands and arms vigorously and encouraged her to drink some sweet tea, cool in the pot but better than nothing.

"Dear God," said Edie eventually. "Dear God."

Miri waved away Kate's offer of assistance, took a few deep breaths and gulped some fresh cold water. She shook her head slowly, bewildered and unsure of how to proceed. What should she mention first, her sons or poor Dexter?

"I don't know any details," said Kate, sparing Miri the trouble of asking. "All I know is, I've got one hour. Edie, can you manage here by yourself while Miri and I go?"

Edie nodded firmly, swallowed hard and raised her pallid face. "Of course, dear. It's just the shock. I'll be fine. Miri, may I stay here?" Miri hugged her in response. "I do so hope you find them," she said, her weak voice breaking, fresh tears spilling.

"Think, Kate," said Miri as they left the cottage. "Is there anything at all that either of them said, however insignificant, that might give us an idea of where they may have gone?" Miri voiced a fleeting thought that they may have decided to prank Jack Whitlock in a drunken fit of bravado and come off the worst for it.

"I doubt it," said Kate, scanning the paths and fields for any sign. "It's too near where the boss wants me to meet him, so they would have been seen if they were anywhere around there." Miri looked up, unclear as to the significance of what Kate had just revealed. "Sorry. I didn't say before because of Edie, but Dexter was found with a knife in his back, draped over the grave of Lavinia Whitlock. They've removed the body but forensics will be hard at work there by now."

"Oh, the poor man." Miri closed her eyes in a vain effort to eradicate the image.

"And," Kate added, quickening her pace as they neared the vicarage, "the grave had been disturbed."

Kate had rung the bell three times before Zoe came trudging to the door. She looked terrible. Her hair was matted, she hadn't changed her clothes and her pale face was crusty with sleep. She covered her eyes and screwed up her face as the daylight hit her full on. "My head," she said. "What is it? Can it wait?" Kate pushed her way in and took Zoe's shoulders firmly in her grip. "Ow! What's going on? Hey!" she said, trying to wriggle away.

"Listen to me! Your bloody hangover will have to wait. Do you understand, Zoe?"

"Yeah, but—"

"Will and Joe are missing," she said, loud and in monotone, as if giving instructions to a small child. Kate had her attention. "Now think! Can you remember anything that happened last night that may explain where they might be?" Kate gave her shoulders a quick shake. "Think!"

"No. Have you checked all the rooms? There's so many nooks and crannies here I don't know my way around myself yet."

"What did you say?" said Miri, pushing past Kate. "Say that again. Zoe." Zoe repeated her words and Miri took Kate to one side, leaving Zoe rubbing first her shoulders, then her head as she watched them charge up the stairs.

"Nooks and crannies, Kate. If they had heard Zoe use that phrase, they would have gone exploring. I know they would. They've done it before. They're trapped somewhere here. I know it!" Kate didn't look convinced but Miri was their mother. She knew them. It may be a long shot but worth a try, surely. Kate was fully prepared for failure and was already thinking about a strategy for the inevitable wider search.

The two of them started calling, flinging closet doors open, banging the backs of wardrobes, Kate blowing her whistle frantically. Every few seconds they paused to listen in case of a response. They repeated this process in both wings of the house. Nothing. Kate pulled out her phone, ready to initiate what she thought was a more realistic plan. "I'm not waiting any longer, Miri. We've been looking for over forty minutes. We're wasting precious time."

Miri touched her arm. "Listen," she hissed. "I heard something, a distant echo." Both women stood perfectly still, ears close to the wood panelling.

"They're in there somewhere!" Kate said. Neither of them could see the entrance point, nor did they think there was any point in consulting Zoe. Almost by instinct they began tapping the wood, just as Joe had done the night before, and the same hollow sound alerted them to the hidden door.

"Get me a knife or something, Miri. Quick!" Miri tore off in search of the kitchen, almost knocking a bewildered Zoe over as she flew back up the stairs.

"Right. Get ready to ease this edge back as soon as it becomes free. Good. Now!"

The tiny door gave way and Kate ordered Miri to stay where she was. Miri didn't argue. This was Kate's area of expertise and she knew she was right not to take any chances. Kate crept down the short narrow staircase carefully and banged on the second door for all she was worth, shouting as loudly as she could. It was locked and she could tell by the muffled sound from within, that the door was thick, much thicker than the one hidden in the panel upstairs.

"Miri!" she called. "They're here!" Kate knew that most of the local uniformed officers would be out on the murder investigation and there was no signal on her phone down here, so she crept back up and made the call.

"Jane. It's me. Have you been called out yet? Oh, good. Listen carefully, Jane. This is an emergency. Yes, another one." Kate went on to explain the situation, added a series of instructions and waited with Miri on the stairs until officers arrived with the special equipment needed to take the door down.

"Jesus!" First to enter the subterranean dungeon was one Phil Watkins, young, fit and eager. He had entered the police force because he had thought it would be exciting. This was just up his street. "Woah! Look at all this, mate!" His 'mate', a more experienced officer in her thirties called Marie, had pretty much seen it all, and was checking Joe and Will for signs of injury or illness, an obvious priority as far as she was concerned. They were exhausted, dehydrated and cold, but otherwise okay, and overcome with relief. Will was close to tears and both were silent. They had hugged each other when they'd heard Kate shouting. She'd seemed miles away, and although they'd known from that point on that they were going to be rescued, that the next person they saw would be there to save them and not murder them, the fear that they had lived and breathed throughout those interminable hours would stay with them for the rest of their lives. They had been expecting the 'heavies' who had locked them in, to return at any minute, and they had no way of alerting anyone. Even though they hadn't come back, they had both feared that, once everyone knew they were missing, after a cursory look around the vicarage, the search would have moved elsewhere. Joe thought they had turned up because one of them had forgotten to lock the door, having got wind of a party; they'd be keen to silence them at the first opportunity.

Zoe had gone back to bed once she knew the boys were safe. "No use to man nor ornament," Kate muttered. She was already late for her meeting with Mike, so she spoke her private words to Will, squeezed Miri's hand and promised to call later. She would report the discovery of the stolen goods to the DCI, knowing that he would make the link to Tripley, Burton and their gang. It was exactly the evidence they had been looking for. At least something positive had emerged from all this. Good police work, she told herself. She'd deal with Will later.

Joe and Will sat in silence, looking down, wrapped in blankets, a bottle of water each in one hand, an energy gel in the other. Miri had called Edie, who had cried afresh at the news, and she was only just beginning to recover herself, yet again, from the agonising fear of losing one or both of her precious sons. But Miri was angry too. It was so typical of them to pull a stunt like this, to go poking around, expecting everything to be fine. They both knew their mother was angry and genuinely felt awful for putting her through this ordeal, especially Joe, who had lectured her about taking on too much work and stress.

"We're really sorry Mum," said Joe quietly. "We weren't to know that someone was watching the place, or that the place was full of stolen goods. We thought they were going to come back and kill us!"

"It's the 'not knowing bit' that prevents most people from crossing the line, Joe," she said firmly. Will remained silent. He knew the extent of the stress his mother had endured when he had been kidnapped in the spring and left to die. She was near to tears again, so she turned away and said she'd see them at home later.

As a way of distracting herself from her fragile emotional state, Miri decided to find out if the play was still going ahead. She was not sure how much help she would be either way, but she hoped, if possible, the children should still be allowed to perform. It was what Dexter would have wanted; Miri was sure of that. She called Tracey to find out if a decision had been made and to her relief, and indeed surprise, a sensible idea had been suggested and agreed. The play would be allowed to go ahead because they had put so much work into it, but the trailer would remain in the playground, far enough away from the murder scene, the audience restricted to parents of the performers. Tracey offered to take responsibility for the children. They would be told for now that Mr. Steele was poorly, but that he wanted them to do their best.

Tracey's voice broke as she said these words, but she was a professional and she would make it work. "Looks like your counselling skills are going to be needed for some time to come, Miri. Isn't it sad? Who on earth would do such a thing?" Miri didn't have an answer for that but offered to help with the play.

"Thank you for staying strong," she added, before making her way home.

Edie was still there, relieved beyond measure for Miri but still shaken by the news of the murder. "I called him a pompous ass," she said miserably. "I can think of a few people who might have wished him dead, poor fellow."

"Really, who?"

"Oh, I don't mean it that way, Darling. No-one specific. You know, disgruntled husbands, bitter ex-lovers." Edie obviously hadn't made the connection to herself, so Miri didn't either. Neither did she share the gruesome details that Kate had revealed earlier, but after Edie had left, she thought about it a great deal as she made herself a well-earned pot of tea. The grave had been disturbed. That was interesting. Was Dexter caught defacing the grave of Jack's ancestor? Had Dexter challenged some vandals and been stabbed for his pains? He wouldn't be the first to meet with such a fate. Had he challenged the thugs who had threatened Will and Joe? Or was he murdered for some other reason and the graveyard just happened to be the place where he was attacked? A macabre setting for sure, the link to the grave undeniable.

Miri would keep her promise to Tracey, but she had no intention of going anywhere or doing anything else for the rest of the day. The evening events would surely be cancelled anyway under the circumstances. She tried to kid herself that she was thinking of herself alone, but in her heart, she knew that what she wanted more than anything was to see her sons fed and properly rested. They had been let go after making their statements, arriving home just as Miri was sitting down to eat.

"There's plenty left in the pot," she said. "Help yourselves." Without speaking, they ladled out a dish full each and sat down. Miri broke the silence. "Have you heard about the murder?"

"Yes," said Will. "Kate rang. Poor Dexter. Just can't believe it."

"And do you know where he was found?" They looked up and nodded. Joe in particular seemed deeply affected. "I'm sorry you have been dragged into this, both of you."

"And we're sorry too Mum," said Will. Miri said nothing for a while.

"Looks like you've solved the mystery of the stolen goods anyway. Mike was sure there was more hidden away, stuff that Vic Burton and his network of thieves have been collecting. He was telling me about it a few weeks ago at the pub." Miri was trying to be her usual self, but the conversation was stilted and unnaturally formal. They knew she was upset. "The police may want to talk to you both again. Did you recognise the voice, the one who threatened you, Will?"

"Not really. Be one of Vic's gang. They probably all knew about the kidnap and saw it as a perfect opportunity for revenge. They knew me."

"Correction. They know you. And now they know you as well, Joe." Miri collected the dishes from the table wearily, told them she would be out for a couple of hours helping with the play but when she turned round to offer them a drink, they'd escaped upstairs to shower and change.

***

Tracey was talking to the children when Miri arrived. They were gathered in costume in front of the trailer. Mums and dads had started to arrive, unnaturally subdued, conscious that anything they said might be inappropriate or misconstrued.

"So just do your best and 'break a leg' as Mr Steele would say." Miri's eyes filled up. It was so strange not to see him there, fussing, encouraging, making the kids laugh. This was the culmination of his work, a tribute really, and at some point the children would have to be told that he was dead. If any of them knew already, they hadn't let on.

The children filed onto the trailer with Miri's help. There were no trips, no flying sandwiches, no tears, no-one fluffed their lines and there were no costume malfunctions. The makeup was spectacular, and the main characters delivered the longer speeches with real skill.

'Double, double, toil and trouble;
Fire burn and cauldron bubble.'

Each chorus grew louder and more menacing than the last, just as Dexter had directed. "Dexter would have been so proud, Tracey. Well done." Tracey, tearful, congratulated the children and thanked the audience for their support, especially under the circumstances. While the children were back in school changing Tracey suggested to the parents, who were milling around and whispering in small groups, that they should tell their children as much of what had happened as they felt appropriate. "Miri and I will do some follow up work next week when we know a bit more about the circumstances of Mr. Steele's death. Thank you." Miri helped Tracey to clear up, then excused herself, promising to contact her soon to plan the next steps.

"How did it go, Mum?" Joe asked.

"The kids were wonderful, Joe. They really pulled out all the stops, as if they were doing it just for him. It's the aftermath I'm concerned about. The shock."

"Try not to think about it now, Mum."

"Have you heard anything else about it?" Miri asked.

"Not about Dexter, but Kate has messaged us to say that the stolen goods are being removed from the vicarage as we speak. I suppose I'll need to check on Zoe though. Wonder if she knew about it?" Joe looked abashed.

"Hope they're careful with those antique vases," shouted Will from the kitchen, breaking the tension. "I peed in two of 'em."

Chapter 19

As Miri had anticipated, all Halloween evening events had been cancelled. An announcement was made on local radio, the parish website, and more effectively by Mrs. Duggan, that all planned activities were cancelled until further notice, though a decision was yet to be made regarding bonfire night. Miri was relieved. She knew that the main reason for the decision was to preserve the authenticity of the murder scene, but she was pleased that the hideous witch burning ritual would not go ahead after all, and any fun and games at the pub would be in bad taste. Of course, there was nothing to stop private parties from going on and there would be many families celebrating with their children, dressing up, carving pumpkins and so on.

After darkness had fallen, Miri leaned against her back door frame with a glass of wine and looked at the sky. The much anticipated full moon was watching over the village, periodically smeared by high drifting fingers of cloud, causing the outline to glow and blur mysteriously.

"And what did you see?" Miri whispered aloud. "What did you see last night at the graveyard? Who killed Dexter Steele?" The moon emerged suddenly from its transitory shroud, and a cone of light brought the garden into relief, greys and blacks merging like ghosts; a spotlight on nature's stage. A hedgehog ambled across the lawn to steal its moment of fame. The moon had been fully exposed during the whole of the previous evening. Miri remembered Edie commenting on it. Somebody must have seen something.

"Mum?" said Joe gently. She smiled as he placed his hand on her shoulder and she covered it with hers. "Will says Kate wants to come over. Are you okay with that? We can put it off till tomorrow if you've had enough."

"No, that's fine."

"She's on duty apparently, so it'll be about the murder."

Miri, energised by the prospect of an update from Kate, immersed herself in various light domestic tasks as the stress of the day finally began to subside. She surprised her sons who were watching a film and keeping a low profile by kissing their heads before disappearing upstairs to freshen up.

"We're forgiven," said Will.

***

Kate arrived at eight o'clock and Miri welcomed her warmly. She had been distraught when the boys went missing, had stopped at nothing to find them, and had found the strength not to allow her emotions get in the way of what needed to be done. Kate might well have saved their lives.

After the initial enquiries about how everyone was feeling, they sat around the table. Kate refused a glass of wine in favour of tea, grateful for the refreshment. "I've barely stopped all day," she said, rubbing her eyes. "And it's not over yet. I need to ask a few questions, I'm afraid. Hope you don't mind. I know it's been a long day for you too," she added, looking around the table. Miri pulled down the blind. She rather hoped Edie had decided to have an early night.

"Of course, we don't mind."

"Mike has set up an incident room at the village hall. Again," she added with meaning. "So, if you think of anything else after I've gone and I don't respond, you can always call in and add to your statement." Kate was very business-like, even with Will, and it was clear that she wanted to get home for a good night's sleep as much as anyone.

Kate went over the events of the previous afternoon, timings and so on, with particular emphasis on their recollections about Dexter, who he had spoken to, for how long and so on. Joe and Will had been busy the whole time and barely noticed Dexter at all. It was impossible for them to say if there was anyone there who was not part of the community, because they were visitors themselves and only really knew Miri's friends.

"And you didn't see any activity around the landing where the secret door is, either of you?" They shook their heads.

"No-one went in as far as I can remember," said Joe. "The loos were outside. There would have been no need to go in. That stuff had been there for ages, Kate. There was dust everywhere. My guess is that they came in later, taking advantage of the fact that we'd all had a drink. The front door was probably open. Maybe they'd come to check the stuff, check the door, or take a few pieces away.

They may not've even known about the party, just turned up on the off chance. They're bound to know about the new reverend and it wouldn't take much to tie Zoe up."

"Not if she was already unconscious, certainly," said Kate, making no effort to hide her disdain. Miri supressed a smile. "Mike's got someone working on Burton and Tripley in prison, to try and get them to reveal the names of their partners in crime. That's probably why the blokes who threatened you are keen to get their hands on the stuff sooner rather than later; they know those two would shop their own grannies for a fiver. Can you describe them?"

"Not really," said Will. Joe shook his head. "It was dark, and they were only there for a few seconds. They both looked tall, but then the door is really small. I could probably recognise the voice if I heard it again though," he added, hoping this might be useful.

Miri had been at leisure to be rather more observant and relayed her memories of Dexter's behaviour as well as she could, grateful that so little time had passed and she could still remember.

"Nothing unusual, really. He was just being himself, playing to the crowd, larger than life. You saw him in action at the pub when he first arrived, Kate. He was just like that, but I don't think he was drinking much, probably wanted to keep a clear head for the performance today." Miri trailed off, feeling the sadness once more. "He has taken his responsibility for the children seriously, whatever anyone might think of him. He doesn't do himself any favours with his dramatic antics, but he has been an inspiration to the kids. I think some of the people he spoke to were parents of the year six children, so that would have been about the play. Other than that, I didn't spot anything that might indicate someone was out to kill him." Kate was making notes. "He knows Edie, as you've already gathered, but they didn't spend any time together. You might want to check that though."

"Yes, I'll be speaking to Edie tomorrow."

Oh dear, thought Miri, hoping all the probing wouldn't open old wounds again and make Kate think that Edie had a motive for murder.

"When was the body discovered, Kate? Or aren't you allowed to tell us?"

"I can tell you because the boss has given me permission to keep you informed," she announced with mock grandeur. "Something to do with you having a bit to do with solving the murder of Melanie Crew." Kate winked at Will and Joe.

"A bit!" said Miri with exaggerated shock. "You bet I did! I'm flattered," she said more seriously, "and hope I can be of help again."

"He didn't say anything about you two though," Kate added, flicking over a fresh page of her notebook.

"Oh, come on Kate," said Will. "Mum'll tell us anyway. Won't you, Mum?"

"No."

Kate laughed. All three inadvertently leaned forward and gave Kate their complete attention. "The body was discovered by Michael, the gardener who looks after the churchyard," she began quietly. Miri sighed. Poor Michael. "He turned up for his usual shift at half past seven this morning. He likes to make an early start apparently, especially at this time of year when there's a lot going on. He doesn't have a mobile, so he ran to the pub and banged on the door for all he was worth. Gavin says he was in a dreadful state, shaking and shouting something about a curse." Joe looked at Will. "Anyway, Gavin called it in, took care of Michael as best he could and then the scenes of crime officers moved in to do their initial assessments."

"Is he okay? Michael?" asked Miri, replenishing their drinks and mentally trying to tally the time of Dexter's death with the time it would have taken Adam's mysterious visitor to get back to the village. Adam had revealed that Nettie was using his garden to grow unusual plants and herbs, that much she knew. It had crossed her mind that she may be growing something illegal and that the package she had seen at Pilates had contained a delivery of some sort, but she couldn't see any connection between that and Dexter Steele, unless he was a notorious drug dealer, which she doubted. The mysterious visitor must have been Sarah, though Adam had only seen her outside collecting plants. Who else could it be? Everyone else was at the vicarage, she must have been leaving just as Miri had arrived. Miri wanted to find out more before she told Kate or Mike, there was always a chance that this whole thing would just lead back to Tripley and co. Adam had also revealed that he had been told to keep quiet about anything to do with work. This is what had frightened him more than anything because he had been afraid of making a mistake and getting into trouble. He had taken it literally of course, and it had taken a great deal of skill on Miri's part to get him to tell her anything at all. He had told her, in passing, that he had heard Tom and Nettie arguing a lot and that it scared him.

"He's been treated for shock but otherwise okay, I think. He has someone with him." Miri nodded and waited.

"The body was slumped face down in a horizontal position across Lavinia Whitlock's gravestone. It's the one in the corner."

"We know where it is," said Joe quietly. "Next to Jack Whitlock's cottage."

If Kate was surprised, she didn't show it. "He was dressed in the same clothes he had worn in the afternoon, jacket and all, and there was some sort of long, thin knife sticking out of his back. According to the pathologist, he'd been dead for several hours, but we'll know more when we get the results of the post-mortem."

"You said the grave has been disturbed, Kate?"

"Oh yes," she said. "That's a curious feature of this case." Again, Joe and Will exchanged a glance. "The stone itself had clearly been moved or looked as if it had." Kate drew a quick sketch in her notebook to illustrate the point. "Not pushed straight back, as you might expect from some sort of struggle, the stone was always crooked anyway, but sort of lifted to one side like opening a door. See?"

"How do you account for that?" asked Will.

"No idea. That's for the forensics bods to puzzle over," she said with a yawn.

"And what about the knife? Anything significant about that? Miri asked. If Kate detected a hidden motive for the question she was too tired to process it, raised her hands, shook her head wearily and yawned again.

They sat in silence for a minute or two mulling over the facts so far and formulating their own private questions. "The next few days will be spent interviewing everyone who attended the garden party," Kate said, breaking the silence, "and the house party afterwards, of course. We may even be able to find a link between Dexter's death and the thieves who threatened you two, if the timings tally. Who knows?"

"You mean Dexter may have stumbled upon them hanging around the vicarage, trying to break in or whatever, interfered, and they stabbed him to death? Nah, what would Dexter be doing hanging around at that time? Why leave him slumped over a grave? A significant one at that! The person who did this knows the history. Unless the thieves are locals."

"'Significant grave'? What's so *significant* about it?" Kate, although she knew the village well, did not live there and knew nothing about the church or the inhabitants of the graveyard. She had heard Mike refer to Jack Whitlock, who lived on the edge of the churchyard, as a bit of a crank who had a grudge against the world, but other than that she'd had no reason to concern herself with it. So, although she felt like she could sleep for a week, she knew she wouldn't be able to settle until she knew what Will had meant.

Joe spilled everything, his visits to Lavinia's hypnotic grave, the time he'd spent at Jack's cottage, the back-story about the Whitlock's and the Tanners, and above all, the curse. Will chipped in with details he thought Joe had missed out, so between them an accurate account was beginning to take shape in Kate's notebook.

"Wow. Well, that puts Jack well into the frame. Explains old Michael's ravings as well. I'd dismissed that. Motive and opportunity. I wonder what the pathology report and the forensic investigation will throw up. It takes a while though. Painstaking stuff." Kate was getting to the point where complete sentences were becoming a struggle, so she hauled herself up from her chair and promised to keep them all up to date. Will grabbed his coat to walk with her to the car and Joe and Miri wished her a well-earned good night's rest.

"There was one other weird thing I heard though," Kate added, an afterthought as she buttoned up her coat. "Meadows was one of the first on the scene, reckons there was some sort of toy or doll thing next to the body. Quite strange."

Stranger than you might think, thought Miri, but now was not the time to say. She had no wish to be the one to hammer the last nail down on Jack's coffin. Not yet. Joe had also picked up on its significance, but he too had the good sense to keep it to himself.

Chapter 20

DCI Mike Absolom paced slowly back and forth at the front of the temporary incident room in Kington Village Hall, rubbing his buzzcut for all it was worth. Nadya, always on hand for matters relating to the hall, plus a few volunteers from the WI, had swept the floor and laid out tables and chairs. The blinds were lowered against the slab of low autumnal sunshine, and a brass tea urn blipped and steamed in the corner. The committee had invested in large portable magnetic white boards the year before with money raised from a jumble sale, and Mike had already pinned up several enlarged photographs of the crime scene, shot from different angles, the dead body of Dexter Steele, ungainly strewn across the grave of Lavinia Whitlock.

"Morning everyone!"

Mike's team perched disparately on the nearest available table or chair, wound up their conversations, stifled their yawns, crammed in the last of their warm pastries, bought from the village bakery on the way in, and silenced their phones. Kate took her position at the front, ready to contribute as required; Jane Peters, Meadows and the rest of the support team, eager to play their part, notebooks at the ready. This was the second violent murder in the village this year and the mood was one of sombre determination.

Mike made eye contact with every single member of his team. It was a technique he used, not only to get their attention, but to make them feel valued. Jane, hoping to pop another mini pain du chocolate in before the briefing started, was caught like a rabbit in the beam of a headlight, big brown eyes flickering, crunchy paper bag.

"The body of the actor Dexter Steele, as he was known, was discovered early on the morning of Friday October 31st by one Michael Swain, gardener and maintenance man responsible for the churchyard, amongst other things. The body has since been formally identified by a neighbour in Oxford." Mike spoke slowly and deliberately. He didn't want his audience to miss anything, but also liked to give himself the opportunity to gauge their responses so that he could allocate each task to the most appropriate officer. He already knew their strengths and weaknesses of course, but every case was different, and this was an unusual one in many ways.

"For those of you who don't know already Dexter Steele was the victim's professional name. He was born William Tanner and grew up here in Kington before leaving to pursue a career as an actor. Anyone who has any local information which may be relevant, family members who knew him and so on, please inform DI Woodley after the briefing." The ripple of whispers that ensued here and there, suggested that there would be more than a few leads for Kate to follow up.

"Many of you will be aware that Mr. Tanner had been staying at the Kington Arms. He began his stay on October 20th having agreed to a request from the parish council to return to the village, as a favour I believe, and help produce a school production for the Halloween celebrations. Now," Mike continued, moving towards the photographs. "There are a few things I want to point out about the body, initial findings, theories and so on, before you have the opportunity to ask questions and I divvy out the jobs."

This was the important bit and everyone in the room was concentrating. They all knew, as with any investigation, that there would be a variety of jobs to do, ranging in tedium from research in the office, data trawling and form filling, to the more interesting stuff out in the field, interviewing suspects and following up on clues arising from the forensic scientists and the pathology report.

"We already know that Mr. Tanner was killed sometime between midnight and two a.m. We're hoping for a more accurate time when we get the report. Initial impressions indicate that death was caused by a stab to the back, here. The knife has a black handle, as you can see here, and the blade is long and thin." Mike leaned in and pointed to the images, sleeves rolled up, lack of sleep beginning to take its toll. "Initial research places it firmly in the category of a particular type of knife called—" Mike paused to consult his notes, "an Athame, which is associated with the element of fire in modern witchcraft," he quoted, followed by a slight cough. The revelation of this unusual aspect of the case caused quite a stir; those who were standing shifted from one foot to the other, those who were seated exchanged meaningful looks as they eased themselves into a more comfortable position. Mike allowed time for the atmosphere to settle again.

"The position of the body suggests he fell forwards due to the impact of the knife, but analysis of the angle of the knife, the depth of penetration and pattern of blood spatters will tell us more. Hopefully, by briefing tomorrow morning I'll be able to give you some detail on that. There is another link to witchcraft which you can see on this enlargement here. It's a tiny figure made of straw known sometimes as a poppet. This one was found next to the body and as you can see," he continued, directing a pointer to the detail, "there's a miniature knife in its back." This was a shock to many in the room and there was a sharp intake of breath. "Many of you will know that Jack Whitlock makes these doll things every year. It does not mean he murdered Mr. Tanner," he said firmly.

"Now, look at these pictures here." Mike directed everyone's attention to a series of enlarged photographs of the grave itself pinned to a separate board, taken after the body had been taken away. He explained where the grave was situated, who was buried there and as much about the history of the Whitlock family as he wanted them to know. Mike knew better than to put any more ideas about curses, witches, ancient family feuds and revenge into their heads at this stage than necessary. For now, it was facts and facts alone and he was keeping everything his Detective Sergeant had told him about all that to himself, much of which he already knew. Jack was an obvious suspect, but he didn't want opinion to influence the meeting.

"Most of the blood was on the body and soaked into the clothes and you can see clearly that the gravestone looks as if it has been moved to one side, here. We know this because the earth is fresh underneath, plus we have a photo of the grave as it was before, here. I'm sure Michael will confirm this when he feels up to it. We already have a statement, but I will be speaking to him again. In addition to that, and here's the interesting thing, there's a dip in the earth just below where the body lay, also free from growth, the earth turned over like a molehill. Here, see?" Everyone leaned forward to get a better view, puzzled brows furrowed.

"What can it mean, sir?" said Meadows slowly, who had been thinking aloud and blushed at the realisation that he had actually spoken.

"Indeed," said Mike to spare him further embarrassment. One or two older members of the team mimed ghostly apparitions, accompanied by the usual sound effects, and Mike allowed it to run its course.

"Forensics are running tests on the fibres of Mr. Tanner's clothes to establish whether he might have been killed somewhere else and taken to the grave for reasons we don't yet know. The ground may have been disturbed by Mr. Tanner himself as he lay dying, or it may be that the grave was deliberately defaced in order to make it look like a different kind of killing, for example. We simply don't know yet so please don't speculate further." Mike put his hand up to deflect further comment.

"In the meantime, the area is cordoned off and will remain so until the painstaking work at the scene is complete. Every blade of grass will be searched for clues, every indentation measured and logged, footprints, fingerprints, every scientific test available carried out, till we get our man. Or woman," he added, mindful of the on-line 'equality awareness' course he was under pressure to complete before the end of the week. Nor was he likely to forget the recent arrest of Constance Fielding.

"Any questions? Yes, Huntley."

"I'd like to know who invited Mr. Tanner here in the first place, sir. Might be significant?"

"Yes, good. As far as I'm aware, the parish council came up with the idea, but they may have been swayed by someone with a motive." Mike took refuge in his buzzcut. "Sergeant. Check that out?" Kate nodded.

"Sir?" Meadows again, his pale young face almost phosphorescent in the cold light. "Why did Mr. Tanner stay in the village? I heard he lives in Oxford; he could have commuted."

"Yes, that's true, Meadows. The original plan, according to Gavin at the Kington, was that he would do just that, but Mr. Tanner made the decision to stay on. Gavin would like to think it was because of the hospitality, and that might well have had something to do with it, but it's more likely to be linked to the fact that he didn't drive. He did employ a driver, and he owned a couple of very nice cars, but all the toing and froing must have proved a bit of a nuisance after a while so he gave the driver some time off, according to Gavin, and stayed put; that way he could be on hand for rehearsals whenever it suited the school. I think he probably enjoyed the whole thing more than he was expecting to. This is his native village, remember? Perhaps he was just enjoying being home."

"Do we know why he didn't drive, sir?" Jane Peters asked.

"Not at this stage, constable. I've got someone looking into Mr. Tanner's background." Jane nodded and made a note.

The room fell silent, and Mike moved onto allocating the jobs necessary for the next stage of the investigation.

"Constable Huntley, you have a child in the school, I believe? Good. Take statements from all staff concerned with the play Mr. Tanner was producing, and any other adults drafted in as helpers; costume, makeup and anything else you can think of. Want to see some initiative here Huntley, okay?"

"Sir."

"Peters. There's no next of kin that we know of, so you won't be delivering the tragic news to a grieving widow or anything like that." There was some low-level muttering in the room as everyone processed the fact that there were no loved ones. "Just goes to show," someone whispered. What it showed was not elaborated upon, but it was generally acknowledged by a network of significant looks and nods of agreement.

"So," Mike continued, "I'm putting you and Meadows in charge of taking statements from everyone who attended the garden party at the vicarage, not forgetting the ones who were invited to stay on afterwards." At this point Mike turned to address everyone in the room. "You may be aware that the vicarage was also host to some uninvited guests on the night in question, resulting in a very narrow escape for two young men." Kate blushed slightly and dived into her bag for an unnecessary pen. "We think the culprits were there to retrieve stolen goods hidden in one of the cellars, but there may be a link to the murder. So," he continued, looking directly at Jane and Meadows, "don't forget to ask if anyone saw anything else suspicious, strangers hanging around, trying to get into the party, that sort of thing. Halloween is always a favourite cover for burglars, all that fancy dress and makeup. Murderers too it would seem." The two constables made notes and smiled at each other. This was important stuff, and they couldn't wait to get stuck in. "There'll be a lot of door-to-door stuff, so if you need help, let me know. We're all allocated at the moment though so make a good start and we'll take it from there. You can argue between you as to who gets Mrs. Duggan, the village gossip. She might actually be a useful source of information, for once." The two officers pointed to each other and shook their heads.

"Kate, you'll be interviewing the Reverend Zoe Deans, the Sinclairs, and their neighbour, whatsername."

"Edie, Sir."

"Yes. She was a friend of the deceased, I believe. Oh, and the landlords at the Kington. They'd have been busy I know, but they might have noticed something. They may be able to shed some light on his personal life, day to day habits, you know the sort of thing."

"Sir."

"Go!" Mike shouted and clapped his hands, striding round the room.

"I might be done sooner than you think, sir. Zoe won't remember a damn thing." Kate's dislike of Zoe was evident, and Mike reminded her to keep an open mind. He wasn't yet aware of Kate's relationship with Will; if he had been, he would have given her a different brief. She'd tell him in her own time, confident that she would never allow personal feelings to interfere with her investigation.

"I'll be paying a visit to Mr. Whitlock," he announced, gathering his things together and removing the photographs from the boards. "I'll be very interested to hear what he has to say for himself. After that, I'll be dealing with the press here at 4.30."

"Shall I come along, sir?"

"Certainly, if you're finished."

I will be, she thought.

Press conferences were one of the aspects of police work that Mike liked least, along with breaking tragic news to families, attending post-mortem examinations, and on-line courses. An interview with Jack Whitlock would be a walk in the park, right?

Chapter 21

Kate planned to leave her car at Miri's cottage and then walk to the pub for her interview with Gavin and Craig. After the briefing, she took a short walk to the vicarage, grateful for the opportunity of some fresh air, to record a statement from Zoe. From there she would drive to Miri's, giving herself an excuse to return later when she was finally off duty. Zoe, as Kate had predicted, had neither seen nor heard anything unusual, had fallen asleep on the sofa sometime after midnight, and the next thing she'd been aware of was the rude awakening caused by Kate and Miri banging on her door, 'at some ungodly hour'.

"Gone ten, you mean?" Kate said unsympathetically. "Think hard, Zoe. Dexter was murdered sometime after midnight. Are you sure you didn't hear anything unusual? Or anything related to the business with Will and Joe?"

"I've told you. We had music on. We'd all had a few drinks. You were there. Did you hear anything?"

"I'm asking you."

"No. I wish I could be more helpful. How're Joe and Will?"

Kate ignored the question, snapped her notebook shut and gave Zoe her card.

"If you think of anything, call me. By the way," she added, as if the thought had only just occurred to her, hand on the doorknob. "Did you know about the hidden staircase and the cellar below?"

"Of course not!"

"Any other secret hideaways we should know about?"

"I told you, I can barely find my way around yet. What are you implying?"

Again, Kate ignored the question, strode down the long drive, and tried to account for her disproportionate dislike of the Reverend Zoe Deans.

At Miri's cottage, things started to get more interesting. Although Kate considered the family to be her friends, when Miri asked if it would suit her to have Edie round to be interviewed at the same time, Kate politely declined. This was a murder investigation. She wanted to conduct the interview with Edie in private.

"There just might be something Miri, something that springs to mind when there are no distractions, that crucial piece of information we need to build up a more accurate picture. And I hope you won't be offended Miri, but I want to interview you all separately as well, for the same reason."

"I understand," said Miri. There were tea and cookies, but the tone had been set. This was no picnic, and Kate was in professional mode. Full throttle. Bringing criminals to justice was Kate's motivation for remaining in the police force. A couple of thugs, associates of paedophiles and thieves, had threatened people she cared for with murder, and she had no doubt that they would have carried out their threat, given the chance. At around the same time, a man had been butchered on a slab. She already knew some details about recent events and she had relayed them to her boss, but she needed to get all that clear now and more. Kate pressed her lips together firmly.

"Right," she said. "Miri?"

Miri went through everything she could think of that may have some bearing on the case; the dead raven, Tilly Clarke's unwitting revelation about her mother, Pink Pilates, her own growing suspicions about Sarah with her knives and veiled threats. Nettie's control over Adam and the goings on at the Estate, and Shel's suspicion that Nettie, with or without Sarah, was somehow responsible for Suzie's skin condition, she decided to keep to herself, for now. Kate had made it clear that she wasn't interested in anyone else's theories anyway. Regarding Dexter himself, Miri could only speak from experience. "I always found him to be professional, enthusiastic and totally committed. The kids were loving the experience, even the less engaged ones, and they tried so hard with the performance when he wasn't there. I must admit to a certain scepticism to start with, especially after that first night in the pub when he was clearly the worse for wear, but I was wrong. He was a perfect gentleman when I saw him at rehearsal, and the staff spoke very highly of him too." The memory of the rehearsal she had attended sparked another, fleeting though it was. "I don't know if this is significant Kate, but I saw Dexter walking back from the rehearsal that day and he had a sort of funny turn, near the church. He suddenly went very pale and shaky, and I remember asking him if he was okay. I saw Jack Whitlock staring at him from his garden and wondered whether that was the cause. Joe will tell you more about the situation between them, which will make it clearer, I hope."

"What day was this?" Miri checked her diary for the rehearsal date.

"Fifteenth of October, about two weeks before the performance, mid-afternoon. It did occur to me some time later that Dexter might have been thinking of his own family; presumably his ancestors are buried there. Maybe something in his own personal history caused him to react like that?"

Kate made notes, forsaking her trusty notebook for a new tablet.

"Hmm. This dead raven thing. You're not the only one to get one of those as a gift this year, Miri." Miri didn't know whether to be relieved or not, so she merely raised her brow and waited for Kate to elaborate. "We've had a number of complaints from all over the village. You probably haven't heard anything about it because, like you, folks decided to keep it to themselves in case the campaign, or whatever it is, went up a notch. Might sound trivial if they were isolated incidents, but when you put them together, it tells a different story; rats chasing around in gardens, cats crying like babies in the night. Like I say, not unusual incidents in isolation, but when half the village is talking about it... And before you ask," said Kate, anticipating Miri's next question, "we don't know who is doing it or why. We think we know how though, and I don't mind telling you that, if you're interested?"

Will and Joe, who had heard most of the conversation from the sitting room, sidled up and leaned on the door frame.

"We know," Kate began, addressing them all, "that the ravens were poisoned before being stabbed; that's how they were caught. We did some tests on one of the birds and it had a chemical in its system that is commonly used in sheep dip." Will and Joe looked at each other, clearly surprised by this revelation but still unclear as to how it got into the birds' digestive systems. "We think that a carcass, drenched in the stuff was left out in a field somewhere as bait, and when the birds fed, they died instantly."

Will made a vomiting noise. "Sounds like a good theory to me," he said. "There must be gallons of the stuff on the farms around here."

"Yeah, well we've got officers asking around to see if any of the local farms have had a break in, noticed anything missing, that sort of thing. Nothing so far. My own opinion, for what it's worth, is that the whole raven thing is designed to deflect attention and cause confusion. There doesn't appear to be any connection between the victims, for one thing."

"Might be a way of framing someone too," said Joe. "You know, making it look like someone's out to destroy, using things associated with witches and rituals." Kate nodded. "Well, it's a piece in the jigsaw, for sure."

The interview with Will was much shorter. He confirmed what Joe had said about Nettie's herb garden and Adam's revelation that she 'makes drinks'. His account of the secret door and stolen goods stash was spot on. So far so good. Kate was pleased with her progress.

"Be gentle with Edie," said Miri as Kate prepared to leave. "It's been quite a shock for her, poor thing. She and

Dexter were close once and, well she'll tell you herself, I'm sure."

"Don't worry. I'm a pussy cat really," she said, flexing her fingers to prove it. Miri doubted that but wished her luck all the same.

An hour later, as she escaped down the garden path and onto the track towards the Kington, Kate blew hard into the stiffening breeze as she reflected on what she had learned. She knew Edie, of course, but the intensity of the interview had drained her, and she was looking forward to a break. Edie had spoken of her trepidation on learning that Bill was coming back to the village. "It opened up old wounds, you see, Darling," she'd said. Kate didn't have the heart to ask Edie to address her as Sergeant Woodley. I am a pussy cat after all, she thought. Edie had been a little miffed that Dexter had practically ignored her at the garden party. "Too full of his own importance, as usual." Edie had shed a tear or two when she had recalled their youthful romance, but Kate had no reason to suspect that Edie carried any more significance than an old flame, reliving powerful memories of, what was to her, an intense and lost love. She was grieving as much for her lost youth as for the loss of Bill Tanner, and Kate seriously doubted that Dexter had remembered the romance with anything more than a roll of his roving eye. But there had been something else. Something that Kate was mulling over now, in the luxury of her solitude.

"So, no-one else really knows or remembers Dexter then, apart from you, Edie?" Kate had asked.

"No, Darling. Just me, and Bob, of course, his old school friend. The only other person who has any connection with him is Carol Sterling." Kate had looked puzzled and waited for Edie to continue. "She's on the parish council and her father was a councillor, I believe." Edie had paused, clearly trying to dredge up anything that might be of help to Kate. "Yes, I believe there was some talk about a business deal with a production company that Dexter was involved with, ooh, decades ago now. It brought considerable financial ruin to the Sterlings, I believe, but that's as much as I know, and it may not even be true, Darling."

Kate had heard Carol Sterling mentioned in the wake of various council issues. She would speak with her. Someone must have proposed the idea of inviting Dexter back to the village. Her father, Trevor Sterling, was still alive, according to Edie, though retired from duty, and financial ruin was as good a motive as any in Kate's experience.

November had brought with it an overcast sky, a wetness to the tree trunks, and a slippery viscous quality to the last of the fallen leaves. It was with particular appreciation, therefore, that Kate searched out a chair by the log fire and scanned the specials board; she was on expenses so what the hell.

"When do you want us, love? I still haven't taken it in," said Gavin.

What is it with people today? Kate thought. "I'm on duty, Gavin."

"Sorry, love. Sergeant."

Kate gave up. "After lunch, one at a time. In the meeting room?"

"Fine. Anything we can do. What will you have? The fish is good today, and I can recommend the chilli."

"I'll have the fish please, chips and side salad. Thanks."

Kate bought a coke from the bar and sat down to observe. The regulars were in, leaning against the bar or settling down at a table for a ploughman's or a sandwich. Tom Hopkins was among the crowd of men from the estate, utility belt hanging low from his waist, boots caked with mud, curls falling in clusters around his rakish face. Miri had said that he seemed unusually subdued at the garden party. He looked as if he was enjoying his pint and platter today. Maybe he just hadn't wanted to be at the party. That would be enough to account for his mood.

Kate, fortified by an excellent meal, signalled to Gavin, who called the barmaid in from the kitchen to cover, and followed him into the snug.

"Well! Here we go again. So soon after, you know. Another one bites the dust. So sorry about Dex. He was such a sweetie, he really was. Awful." Gavin crossed his legs and prepared for the interview, reminded of the importance of the situation by Kate's tablet and her official manner. Kate asked Gavin to tell her about his impressions of Dexter Steele as a guest, first of all. "Was he a creature of habit, for example? Did he take regular meals? That sort of thing. I'm trying to find out about him as a person. It helps us to establish some background and hopefully deepen our understanding of his life. Someone hated him enough to kill him, Gavin. This is very important. Don't be afraid of betraying any secrets; you can't hurt him now."

"Well, we try not to be intrusive with our guests, but we do get to see them at their most relaxed, so we can't help noticing a few things," Gavin began by way of apology. Kate smiled patiently. "He liked a drink," he continued. "Often had a nightcap in his room. Or two," he added, rolling his eyes. "I think that's one of the reasons he decided to stay on, you know, so that he could drink late in the evenings, take his time in the mornings and be on time for his commitments."

"Would you say he was an alcoholic?"

"Oh, I don't know about that, love. Sergeant. He was never drunk during the day to my knowledge. Although he did look a bit pasty one afternoon," Gavin went on, slowly, trying to dredge up the details. "Yes, I remember that because he usually had lunch when he'd finished a morning rehearsal, but on that day, he just went straight up to his room."

"When was that? Could you work out the date?" Gavin poked his head through the door into the kitchen and asked a girl called Lisa for the date of her sister's wedding.

"October 25th," said Gavin triumphantly. "I remember because we were short staffed, and I was working on the bar when Dex came in. He looked like he'd seen a ghost. Walked straight past and up the stairs like a zombie. We were very busy so I didn't get chance to check on him, but he came down for dinner later on, back to his usual self, so I left it at that."

Kate went on to ask about the vicarage garden party and Gavin told her everything he could remember, but there was nothing of any significance. He knew everyone there, he hadn't seen anything suspicious at any point, and he had been too busy to talk for any length of time to any of the guests. Craig corroborated Gavin's account of the day although he was even less likely to have noticed anything, tethered as he was to the barbeque, but he confirmed the date of Dexter's missed lunch and endorsed Gavin's general opinion of him. They had both agreed that they hadn't seen him after the party. So much for separate interviews.

"We didn't think anything of it at the time because we had extra staff on for the day and we weren't really around much, were we Gav? Clearing up at the vicarage, that sort of thing, you know? We just assumed he had ordered his usual from one of the girls and gone to bed. I texted each of them as soon as I knew about Dex, naturally. No-one remembers seeing him. That's not to say he wasn't here, but his bed hadn't been touched, I can tell you that. His room had been serviced as usual, and nothing was out of place. I'll show you. No-one's been in, only me and Gav."

Kate was building up quite a detailed picture, but it was early days and there was nothing so far to link anyone with the murder. Almost anyone had the means and the opportunity, but who had the motive? If Dexter was killed at the grave, she reasoned, he must have been lured there. Why else would he have been wandering around there at midnight? The ghost hunt had finished at around eight and by the time everyone had left and the revellers had gone inside, it must have been only about nine. There was an outside possibility that Dexter was somehow mixed up with the stolen goods case, but Kate couldn't quite square that up; he had been invited by the parish council who, as far as she knew, had no connection with Burton's gang. If he was killed somewhere else, then the killer must have had the help of an accomplice. Kate was mulling things over thus, arriving at the village hall in plenty of time for the press conference.

"Glad you could make it, sergeant. How did you get on?" Mike asked, steeling himself for the inevitable insinuations of incompetence from the press.

"Good, sir. We'll talk later, when this lot have gone."

"We certainly will," said Mike, steering her to one side. "Just got the post mortem report through. William Tanner was poisoned."

Chapter 22

Mike Absolom revealed nothing of the post mortem results during the press conference. Keeping his comments general and concise, he answered predictable questions with predictable answers, and excused himself and Kate as soon as it was politically polite to do so. There were times when the press could be very useful to the police in an investigation; circulating photographs of people who had disappeared without a trace, advertising rewards for information and so on. In this case, however, because Dexter Steele was a celebrity of sorts, representatives from the various tabloid newspapers were more interested in gossip and sensationalism, endeavouring to find the link with one of Dexter's most famous roles, to coin the cleverest headline: 'Dexter Steele, Emmerdale's Heartbreaker, Dies at the Hands of Disgruntled Lover.' 'Backstabber Steele, Stabbed in the Back!'

"You didn't give much away, sir," said Kate, amid the dismantling of cameras and the withdrawal of microphones.

"Don't worry. They'll make it up anyway, no doubt. We've got more important things to think about." Mike guided Kate to a table at the side of the hall and invited her to sit down, Kate eager as ever to learn about this unexpected new development.

"The post mortem report confirms that Tanner was stabbed, and the considerable amount of blood spilled proves that he must have still been alive just as, or not long before the knife went in, otherwise the blood would have already started to pool around the organs and in the legs, away from the heart. With me?" Kate was fully aware of the effects of death by stabbing, she had been on a case once where there was barely any blood at all from a stab wound because the victim had died the day before from a totally unrelated cause.

"But," Mike continued, "we also know from the toxicology report that there was enough poison in Tanner's system to have killed him anyway. The stabbing was unnecessary, an act of violence and, or ritual."

"What sort of poison was it, sir?" Mike flipped his notebook open.

"A substance called wolf's bane, or monkshood. There are various other names for the same thing, but those are the most common. I've a picture of what it looks like in flower, on my phone, here." Kate looked. She'd seen it before. "According to the lab, it can be ingested or absorbed through the skin but in this case, there was a considerable quantity in Tanner's stomach and minute traces on his fingertips. So," said Mike, hoisting his trousers up over his expanding waistline and stretching his fingers, "we are looking for a murderer who knows a thing or two about poisonous plants and carries enough of a grudge to stick the knife in, to make sure of the job. Oh! That reminds me. I found out something else about that knife." Kate looked around to make sure everyone around them was still busy and not listening in.

"What's that, sir?"

"You already know it's a kind of ceremonial blade, associated sometimes with witchcraft, Sergeant?" Kate nodded. "Well, I got 'em back at the station doing some research, and apparently this particular knife represents the element of fire." Kate looked up. Fire. An obvious reference to the burning of witches, death and destruction. Fire burn and cauldron bubble. "There's a whole raft of paraphernalia that goes with it, like a chalice, a sword and so on," Mike explained, scrolling through a series of pictures, "but in this case, it's the knife that played the crucial part in this grizzly murder. There are a couple of nice fat fingerprints on the handle of the knife as well, for our convenience, and I think I know who they belong to. Come on. Be good to have you along for this one."

"Yes, and 'for our convenience' is right, sir. I'm always a bit suspicious about fingerprint evidence," Kate said breathlessly as she strode behind Mike. "They're so easily planted, deliberately left somewhere, or completely faked, all to frame somebody else."

"Yes, I know. But there will always be a link, Sergeant, and it's as good a place to start as any. The trail starts here." Mike rubbed his hands together and flashed his eyes. This was his favourite part of the investigative process; the chase, the puzzle, the brain work. It was with great relish, therefore, that he lifted the rusty latch of the gate that separated the gravestones from Jack Whitlock's back yard.

"I've been expecting you," Jack mumbled. "Only a matter of time, I said to old Bess 'ere." The poor old dog looked up with rheumy eyes and flopped to the floor, resigned to whatever fate awaited them and just as powerless as Jack to do anything about it. Kate lifted her scarf up over her mouth and nose from time to time; the acrid smell in the kitchen was uniquely overwhelming.

Jack barely gave Mike time to question him; he'd been through the process many times before, usually in the wake of a complaint about an aspect of his behaviour. His tone was resigned and weary, his mouth appeared to have drooped since Mike last saw him, and he was using an old, gnarled stick to get around.

"I was 'ere all day and all night as usual," he began, turning his back to search for a stool amongst the clutter to perch on. Then he turned and glared at Mike and Kate in turn. "I been waiting for this day all my life as a man." He was barely audible, and Kate was obliged to ask him to speak up. "The day when the curse on the Tanners is fulfilled," he continued, ignoring the request. "I ain't going to go through all that, it's common knowledge. And I've know'd all along that it would 'appen, without any 'elp from me. That's what a curse is. So now you need to ask yourselves, why would I go to the trouble of killing someone who I know was already taken care of?"

"Nobody's accusing you of anything, Mr. Whitlock," said Mike, aware of the logic of Jack's point. "We're here to ask you a few questions, that's all."

Jack laughed, his chest rattling in response to the unaccustomed experience. "Help with your enquiries?" he added with a sneer. "What do you take me for?" Jack's voice was gaining strength. Mike and Kate knew they needed to tread very carefully.

"Mr. Whitlock," said Kate gently. "I'm going to show you a photograph of a knife. Please can you tell me if it belongs to you?"

Jack took a cursory glance and confirmed that it was his knife. "Don't prove nothin'," he growled. "That knife's been in my family for hundreds of years, since 'er day." Jack clarified his meaning by nodding towards the grave of his ancestor. "If I was goin' to stab somebody, I'm not such a fool as to use that! I want it back, d'you 'ear?"

"How do you know Mr. Tanner was stabbed, Mr. Whitlock?"

Jack glowered. "Stop playing yer games with me!" He was becoming agitated, and a violent coughing fit caused Mike and Kate to share a glance. Mike took a back seat. The classic 'good cop, bad cop' was unlikely to be effective with Jack.

"Please try to remain calm, Mr. Whitlock. We are trying to establish the facts." Kate found a box, tested its strength and sat near to Jack's stool. Jack was able to look down on her. "No, it doesn't mean anything Mr. Whitlock. That's right," she said soothingly. "So, can you help me by trying to remember if you noticed the knife was missing recently?" There was a long pause during which Jack decided whether it was in his best interest to co-operate.

" 'Ard to tell in 'ere, my yard be tidier than the kitchen, but yes, I did look for it, last Monday it were." Jack had mellowed. Kate was winning him over. "I know it was Monday 'cos old Fred were out deliverin' to the shop there, and it was the day I 'ad my fall in the yard." Jack lifted his stick to illustrate the point and Kate looked up to encourage him to elaborate. "I wanted it to skin a rabbit an' it's the best I got for the job, but I couldn't lay 'ands on it. I didn't think nothin' of it cos I often forgets where I put things, but I ain't seen it since. I just thought it'd turn up like usual."

"I see. You do understand that we will need to take your prints."

"What, again? Ain't you still got 'em from the last time you lot blamed me for summat I 'adn't done?"

"If they are still on file we won't need to bother you, Mr. Whitlock."

Jack grunted and looked from Kate to Mike and back again, re-assessed them both and came to the conclusion that Kate was definitely the brains behind the duo. From that point on, he addressed his comments exclusively to her. "As if I'm in any shape to go round stabbing people," he said, pointing to his leg with a trembling finger. "Specially a big bloke like Tanner! I can barely get around my own place." Mike launched himself forward from the sink where he had been leaning with his arms folded, watching the scene develop.

"What about," he said, startling Jack, who had almost forgotten he was there. "What about if a big bloke like Tanner was drugged first, or poisoned even? That would make it easier, wouldn't it, Jack?"

Jack looked genuinely surprised, as if he'd been told he'd won something, and it was just about the last thing he was expecting to hear. "And I suppose I done that as well, did I?" Jack raised his trembling hands, palms up in grubby fingerless gloves to illustrate the folly of the notion. Kate looked at Mike, leaving him in no doubt that she was angry at his intrusion, raised her hand slightly and stepped back in, keen to re-establish her rapport with Jack. Mike rolled his eyes but retreated and allowed Kate to take control again.

"We think Mr. Tanner may have been weakened by a drug before he was stabbed, Jack. You might be able to help us identify the plant. We've got pictures of the flowers if you are happy to have a look?"

"Ha! Like hell I will. Soon as I say I know what it is, you'll cuff me! Bastards! I ain't so far gone that I'll fall for a trick like that. Ha!"

"Lots of people will know what it is, Jack. That is not what this is about." Kate gently manoeuvred her tablet screen towards his lap, low down so that he wouldn't feel it was in his face. "Take it Jack and have a look. See the purple flowers?" Jack's curiosity got the better of him and he pulled the tablet up closer and squinted.

"It's wolf's bane," he said simply and thrust the tablet back towards Kate. "I got some in my garden. Satisfied? And my prints will be all over the knife. It's my knife. If I was planning to stab Tanner, don't you think I'd 've wiped the bloody thing? Ha!"

"Thank you, Jack. We know it doesn't mean you did it. We know that." Jack looked down at his hands and Kate thought he was going to weep. Despite her revulsion at Jack's living conditions, Kate found her own eyes filling up, just as Mike eased the stable door open and went to search the garden.

"Best tell 'im it don't flower till June," said Jack, and Kate smiled.

"Did you hear anything that night? Anything unusual?"

"Nah. I'd 'ad a pint or two." Kate nodded.

"By the way, Jack," Kate said casually. "We found one of your straw dollies near the body." Jack looked up, like a child searching for someone to understand, his chest wheezing weakly, all the bluster gone. He had nothing left to say. "Best get that leg seen to, Jack."

"I'm alright. Nettie Hopkins fixed me up with some ointment. I don't want no doctor pokin' about."

Fresh air had never tasted sweeter. Mike arranged for a lab check on Jack's fingerprints, assuming they were still on file, and arranged for a specialist to take samples of wolf's bane from the garden. Mike was withdrawn and Kate needed to find a way of getting back into his good books. She knew he was under pressure to make an arrest as soon as possible but she also knew he would not wish to make a mistake. Mike's approach had got them nowhere. Kate was just thinking of a way to placate his male ego by pretending the whole approach had actually been his idea and he should be justly proud of the fact that the interview hadn't broken down completely, when the shrill scream of a fire engine cracked the skies wide open, rendering Kate's forays into psychology, totally unnecessary.

"What the—?"

"Hold on, sir. There's a message. House fire in The Glades. Number six."

Kate knew about the crescent of new homes called The Glades from Miri's account of her visit to Shel Cavendish's house, and her suspicions about the relationship between Tom Hopkins and a beautician whose name she couldn't remember. Suzie something. Kate's stomach dipped. Surely this couldn't be her house, suggesting that the cases might be linked? Or Shel's?

It was neither. The house belonged to a young divorcee called Serena Barker and she was still in there, according to a neighbour at the scene. There was substantial damage to the property, both inside and out, and as the flames spurted out of the upstairs window, a firefighter emerged from the blackness with Serena over his shoulder. Neighbours who had gathered at a distance, looked on, hands over their mouths, shocked and bewildered. Serena was alive, just about, and was treated with oxygen on site before being rushed to hospital with severe burns. According to the fire officer at the scene, initial evidence suggested that the cat, a black tabby, had knocked a pot of faux flowers into the gas fire as she'd crept along the mantlepiece. The cat had been sitting on the garden wall when Mike and Kate arrived, meticulously and rhythmically cleaning shreds of material from her jet fur, unblinking; mission accomplished.

Chapter 23

Miri had two jobs planned for the following morning. The first, requiring no preparation at all, involved a visit to Shel in the office, ostensibly to tie up loose ends left over from the Macbeth performance, but more importantly to get her take on the circumstances of the fire. She had called Miri and suggested a catch up. They needed to discuss storage of costumes and props, she'd said, which was code for, 'I've got something interesting to tell you.' The second job of the morning would take all the care and foresight Miri could draw upon.

There was an acrid taste in the air, even now, hours after the fire, as Miri left her cottage, stubborn battalions of cloud pushing freshness firmly back behind enemy lines. Miri had heard nothing further about the investigation into Dexter's murder since the interviews and assumed it wouldn't be long before the compass needle hovered and settled rigidly in the direction of Jack Whitlock's cottage. Who else would want to kill Dexter? Edie's half-hearted theory of ex-lovers or revengeful husbands would hardly be relevant now. There was no close family, and his theatre friends were, by his own admission, 'just ships in the night'. There was his chauffeur, of course, but he hadn't worked with Dexter for very long and was a newcomer to the area. It had crossed Miri's mind that there may be an aspect of

Dexter's life that would remain totally private and, though painstaking to unearth, may hold the key to his death.

Jack, on the other hand, was an obvious suspect, his story was well known and his hatred of the Tanners legendary, and as Jack had no relatives or champions to support him, Miri knew his position was weak. Mike's team, despite the professionalism of the individuals, would be under pressure to get a quick result, and the residents of Kington would be glad to be rid of Jack; he'd upset nearly everyone in the village, his cottage was a public health hazard, and his land was valuable. Miri understood from professional experience that it had been the easiest option for Jack to fuel the myth that he must be some sort of witch. His obsession with Lavinia's story, his lifestyle and behaviour all pointed to it, and he had done nothing to counteract it. He had used it as the perfect excuse not to seek out the company and intimacy of others, so that generation after generation had shunned him. Miri wondered if there had ever been a lover, if he had ever felt valued by a parent, what he had lost that had made him such an outcast.

Under normal circumstances, Miri loved spending time with her friend Shel. She was always well prepared for any official business, thus allowing plenty of time for more personal matters. Today, however, the fire began a conversation that was dominated by fear and speculation. Will had gathered some details from Kate, and Miri had been shocked to learn that the fire had occurred in the Glades. The smoke and sirens had given the impression that it was much further away, maybe because of the wind direction. It was from Shel, however, that Miri was to learn the most interesting aspect of the case.

She picked up her inevitable to-do list and prepared to tick them off one by one with Miri's help. 'Decorations returned to class teachers for display. Tick. Costumes stored in drama cupboard. Tick. And so on. Such were Shel's organisational skills, that if someone had entered the office unexpectedly, they would never guess that there was a highly sensitive conversation taking place at the same time.

"Kate told Will that the fire was caused by a cat," said Miri.

"Yes, a big fat black tabby. Interesting, isn't it?" Shel, a member of Pink Pilates, though not the 'inner pinkies' as Miri thought of them, shared Miri's suspicions, about Nettie and Sarah in particular; they'd had many conversations about it.

"You're not suggesting that a cat was obeying some sort of instructions? Shel! I'm quite happy to acknowledge that there are certain 'pinkies' who feel empowered by crystals and affirmations around a candle, but what you're suggesting is the actual culmination of a spell! Next, you'll be telling me that Nettie has transfigured into a cat!"

"If it's good enough for Shakespeare!"

Miri laughed. "Well, yes but that's—"

"What? Who knows what powers some people may have? And the cat is supposed to be an agent of the witch, isn't it?" Shel was serious. "Listen, Miri." Shel lowered her voice, pen in hand, one eye on the door. "The victim, in this case, is Serena Barker. I don't think you know her."

Miri shook her head and frowned. "She's young, attractive, divorced and available," Shel continued with a meaningful look. It took a few beats for Miri to catch up.

"Tom? Another one? He gets around, doesn't he? Are you sure? How do you know, anyway?"

"He always makes it look as if he's delivering something, logs or sacks of something for the garden. I didn't think anything of it at first. I certainly never bothered to check how long he stayed and I'm sure I wouldn't be suspicious at all if my Geoff hadn't put the idea in my head about Tom playing away in the first place. Like I said before, there's no proof of anything and Geoff would kill me if he thought I'd been gossiping like this. It's only because it's you, Miri. Anyway, whether it's true or not, I bet Nettie believes it. Maybe a coincidence, I suppose," Shel continued more seriously, "but it does seem odd, doesn't it? First Suzie with her rash, now this. She could've been burned to death!"

"Well one thing's for sure," said Miri. "Keep your suspicions to yourself. If Nettie is dabbling in some sort of witchcraft to teach her husband a lesson, or at least using it as some sort of cover for criminal activity, you'd do well to keep a low profile." Miri spoke in a light hearted tone, but both women were intrigued by the web that was beginning to stretch across the village, and the flies who were being caught up, one by one, in its sticky trap.

By the time Miri emerged from the office and out into the reception area, there had been a marked deterioration in the weather. A fog had drifted in and settled over the village, and the air had a sense of stagnancy and suspension about it. Had it not been for the importance of her next appointment, Miri would have headed straight home. It was still early though, and Miri reasoned she would be home by lunchtime at the latest, so she pulled her scarf up over the lower half of her face and turned onto the track that would take her to Adam's cottage. Last time Miri had seen Adam formally, and they had fixed up this appointment as a final wrapping up meeting. They would still be friends of course, but there would be no professional obligation for Miri to monitor Adam's progress any longer, and Mike was happy that the victim support targets had been met. However, he had been agitated when she had visited him on the evening of the garden party and she wanted to check that he was settling down again, despite the tensions around him. It was to be a celebration of sorts and, though the day felt anything but optimistic, Miri did not want to let Adam down now, after all that had happened.

Visibility across the field leading to the cottage was appalling, and Miri was forced to navigate by means of the extreme perimeter fence which prolonged her journey considerably. The damp fog clung to her face in the silence. No one was working the land. Nothing moved. Even the hedgerow wildlife had scampered to the safety of their respective habitats. The soft ridges of ploughed earth melted beneath her feet and it was hard going. Miri half hoped that Adam would have forgotten the arrangement, so that she could set off for home without delay.

The row of tied cottages loomed into view suddenly, muted colours and frayed edges in the filthy air.

Exhausted, her boots caked in mud, Miri leaned on the nearest gate post to catch her breath and unravel her scarf. The fog was patchy here, but tendrils of mist swirled and swooped around Miri's legs as Adam's beaming face loomed phosphorescent and hovering above the dividing wall.

"Gosh! You gave me a fright!" she said, one hand on her heart. Adam laughed, confident that Miri would forgive him, at ease in her presence.

"Come in! Come in! Hot drink." Adam was enjoying playing host and Miri accepted tea gratefully, her hands soaking up warmth from the enamel mug. He seemed more relaxed than he had been for a long time and when Miri asked how things were at work, he told her that he was being left to get on with things by himself and that no-one had been near the cottage. Adam's mood was affected by the way he felt at that moment; he had forgotten his anxieties because they were no longer there. Miri suspected that Sarah, if indeed it was her, was keeping a low profile. She may know that she had been spotted on the night of the garden party, and by whom, Miri thought with a shudder.

They exchanged pleasantries about the turn in the weather and the way the new season was affecting work on the estate. As ever, Adam was full of news about the wildlife, the animals who were hibernating and how he was looking after them. He was proud of having relocated a nest of hedgehogs away from danger, and he treated Miri to an imitation of the screech of a bat and the scream of an owl. Miri covered her ears and Adam swayed with joy. He hadn't mentioned anything about the murder or the fire so Miri didn't either. It was possible that he simply hadn't heard, though Miri's guess was that he *had* heard, but because he hadn't known the victim, he had processed the events as if they were taking place in another world, like a soap opera, ironically.

"So," she said, "from now on we can be the best of friends, Adam. I will come to visit you if you'd still like me to, and you will always be welcome at my cottage. Will and Joe are staying for a while longer and they would love to see you." Adam nodded wildly. "You have my mobile phone number so if you need me to come for any reason, just call. Okay? Promise?" Adam nodded again. "Now, there's one more thing, Adam. Listen carefully." Miri leaned forward. "Do you remember when you put something precious in my pocket for me to find? To help me work out who killed the little girl?" Miri knew she was opening up painful memories but there was no other way. Adam started to rock, the smile left his face abruptly and he dropped his head. "I know it's hard to think about. You've done nothing wrong." Adam looked up. "I know the pendant is important to you because I've seen the photograph and the words inside. I would like you to take it back, Adam, so that you can wear it again. What you did was very brave and now you can have your reward. Here." Miri slipped the pendant from her purse into Adam's hand, and he immediately fell to smoothing it, rhythmically and intensely, just as he had done when he wore it around his neck.

"Who is Melissa?" asked Miri gently. "You don't have to tell me."

"My sister. My sister. My sister." Adam was rocking, clutching the pendant to his cheek. "They took her away. Away. Secret."

"Why is it a secret, Adam?"

"N-ettie! N-ettie said!" Adam was becoming distressed, the very last thing Miri wanted to see. This was supposed to be a positive meeting, a celebration of Adam's progress and she was losing her grip.

"Okay, young man!" she said with a flourish. "I'll make a deal with you." Adam looked up, alarmed at the change of tone. "You wear that pendant for me, and I'll see what I can do about your sister. That'll be our secret. How does that sound?" Adam put the pendant on, his big rough fingers fumbling with the clasp, the smile back on his face.

"Don't tell N-ettie!" Miri crossed her heart. "She wants her sister b-ack too. Says why should Adam have sister an-and not Nettie!" Miri struggled to conceal her distaste. Was Adam saying that he had confided in Nettie about his sister, but she had rejected him out of spite because she had lost her own sister? Surely Nettie should have been the very person Adam could have counted on, having been through a similar trauma herself? Miri decided not to question Adam about it; he had his pendant back, she had managed to bring him back to a positive frame of mind, the rest could wait. She would do some research about the circumstances surrounding the death of Nettie's older sister first. Maybe that would shed some light on why Nettie had rejected Adam's confidences with such cruelty. Poor lad. And how had she wheedled such a personal matter out of him in the first place? Miri may have finished her formal mentoring programme, but she had not finished caring for Adam. Not by a long way.

***

Miri was pleased to see Kate with Will and Joe back at the cottage. The fog had lifted a little, but the afternoon was destined to remain dark. No one was going anywhere. An afternoon round the table near the warmth of the aga suited her just fine.

"Perfect timing, Mum," said Will, indicating a pot of aromatic curry and a dish of steaming rice.

"Smells wonderful," she said. "What a treat! I wonder whether Edie—"

"She's on her way," said Joe, just as Edie popped her head round the kitchen door.

"I say! How divine! Hello everyone. Here, Darling, take this dish."

No one spoke of the murder case, or the fire. Kate was off duty and they were all sensitive to the fact that she of all people needed a break. The bonfire party was still on for the following night, so at least there was some sort of normality on the horizon, even in the midst of a murder investigation. The curry was perfect, as was Edie's mango sorbet, and everyone seemed to relax for the first time in days. Miri kept her plans to investigate on her own, firmly under wraps.

"Did you go to the church service on Sunday, Edie? I meant to ask," said Miri.

"Yes, I did. Quite sombre as you can imagine, but Zoe struck the right chord, I thought. Talked about everyone pulling together, that sort of thing. There weren't as many there this time which didn't surprise me, but I think there's a lot of support for what she's trying to do."

"Good. I'm glad," said Miri. Kate made no comment. She had no tangible reason for disliking Zoe, apart from her initial jealousy when Zoe had been so close to Will in the pub, and disapproval of her drinking habits, and she didn't want to be accused of not being open minded.

"Well, it's going to take more than prayer and platitudes to solve this case," she said eventually, to break the silence. Again, no one pressed her. If she wanted to tell them anything, she would. "It gets more complicated by the minute. This morning at briefing, and this is not especially confidential, it'll be in all the papers soon enough, Mike told us that a tiny bare footprint, size two or something, was found just to the left of the gravestone where the body was found."

"Size two?!" said Will. "That's a child's, surely? Some kid at the party, I expect."

"Possibly. There's more though. Some fibres found clinging to Mr. Tanner's clothing have been analysed and found to be consistent with that of an ancient type of calico cotton. Could be four hundred or so years old, according to the lab. Mike told us that there was something that looked like a molehill underneath the body, as if the earth had been churned."

"Well maybe the kid with the size twos was dressed in an old calico cloak or something and was messing around there earlier in the evening? And the molehill is probably a molehill. Come on."

"Yes, but it's the fibres themselves that are ancient, not just the type of fabric. And they were embedded in the jacket, as if Mr. Tanner had somehow been in contact with the material beneath him."

"One doesn't come across calico very often now, certainly," said Edie, "but it is possible for fibres to migrate and wind up in dust and soil, you know. When I did my training, I learned all about that. It's possible that fibres from the clothing that Lavinia Whitlock was wearing when she was buried, most likely peasant material such as calico, have travelled in that way, especially if there was no coffin. The stone wasn't put there till much later, so I imagine she was buried, what was left of her, with very little ceremony. Might be worth testing for signs of burning, charred fibres, you know." This was a very uncomfortable thought, but Edie was keen to be of use; she'd already broken down in front of Kate and she wasn't about to do it again. Her tone was always serious when she was talking about fabrics; no-one in the room doubted her expertise. Will raised his eyebrows, affirming his acceptance of Edie's theory. Joe pursed his lips, deep in thought.

"That's interesting," said Kate. "There's more work to be done on the footprint cast anyway. If, as you suggest Will, it belongs to a child, then it shouldn't be too difficult to track the little one down."

Joe had been quiet during this conversation, feeling a stirring of the passion he had experienced when he first saw the grave, and absent-mindedly twisted a fork between his fingers.

"And if you don't?" he said.

Will would normally have taken this opportunity to pull a face and create a spooky monologue on the spot, but Joe had confided in him, and Will recognised the sensitivity in his brother's tone of voice.

"They will, Joe," he said. "They have to."

Chapter 24

Six o'clock, the last of the fog had retreated from the valley, and the sky obligingly provided a dramatic backdrop for a clear, starlit evening. The bonfire celebrations were inevitably going to be low key given the circumstances, but the fire was built, the kids were excited and the whole event would take place within an enclosed area behind the pub to minimise disturbance. By the time Miri, Edie, Will and Joe set out, the fire was well underway. Kate was on duty elsewhere, and enthusiasm for the event was generally low. "I don't think we'll be staying long, Mum," said Joe. "Just enough to support the event and watch the main display. I've got some prep work to do for a recording project anyway."

The flames were visible from the lane beyond the crime scene area, tongues of fire leaping and dying at once, exotic patterns living on their retinas before fading forever. There was quite a crowd, Miri guessing that young families would be quick to disappear once the display was over. Most of the committee members were there with their families, and Gavin and Craig were doing their utmost, as ever, to keep everyone's spirits up with hearty welcomes and hearty fayre. Jacket potatoes with their earthy scents and caramel skins were duly turned in the huge cast iron oven, thick burgers and fat sausages spat and sizzled on the griddle, and onions shrank crispy in a pan. The boys made a beeline for the queue and ordered pints from Gavin, who was taking orders from a hatch. "Things are looking up!" said Will. Joe was looking down, scuffing his feet on the gravel, lips pursed in concentration. "You're not still brooding on that bloody footprint are you, Joe? It'll be some kid! You can't seriously be considering the possibility that the size two belongs to a woman who's been dead for five hundred years."

"Nah, 'course not. Weird though isn't it, planted right next to the grave like that? The fibres as well, ancient bits of cloth, close enough to the surface to bond with Dexter's clothes. Come on, you must admit it's spooky."

"Yes, but there'll be a rational explanation for it all, Joe. You'll see. There always is. Edie explained about the fibre stuff."

"Hi there!" Zoe called, striding confidently towards them in double denims and a baker boy cap. "How are you all?" She was in good spirits, and her infectious energy gave a well needed boost to Joe. "What a day!" she went on. "I've had a team of police round all day, searching the place for hidey holes and any stolen goods they might have missed the first time round. My predecessor and the other thug have had the good grace to drop their pals in it, you'll be pleased to know, right up to their necks, so now I can confidently say that my house is clean. The charmer who locked you up was Rev Tripley's right hand man apparently; nasty piece of work I hear. He must have been in a good mood that night. Most of his victims end up in intensive care, according to the police. If ever you fancy a game of hide and seek just let me know!"

"No thanks," they said in perfect unison.

"For the first time, I'm actually beginning to feel at home there. If it wasn't for the murder in my back yard, I'd say I was totally at peace."

"Can you see the graveyard from any of your windows, Zoe?" asked Joe, steering her away from the crowd.

"Well, yes. But I didn't see anything that night, the police have already asked me about that. Kate in fact. I don't think she likes me, you know."

"Yeah, she does. She's hard to read at the best of times. I think she was just a bit miffed when she saw you and Will cosying up in the pub, that's all." Zoe was about to object but Joe interrupted her. He placed his hands on Zoe's shoulders, so that she would know he was being serious. "Is there a good view of the graves from any of the upstairs rooms?"

"Well, yes, from the side landing window. It's long and thin and you can see right down into the churchyard from there. I've seen Michael working there, not recently of course, but I—"

"Could I come round later and have a look?"

"Yes, but why?" said Zoe, puzzled.

"Just curious," said Joe. "I've got some work to do on a film score, and a scene like that might give me the inspiration I need. If I could just pop round about half eleven? Would that be okay?" This wasn't strictly true, the project Joe was working on having precious little to do with film, but it was the nearest to the truth he could come up with.

"Well, that's a bit late, Joe. I've had a busy day. I was planning a hot bath and an early night after the fireworks.

There's a wedding coming up in the village and I'm meeting the couple first thing in the morning."

"I won't stay long, I promise."

"Well, okay. As long as you aren't offended by fluffy slippers and princess jammies, and your intentions are honest." Joe laughed. "I won't say a word."

A sudden crack, followed by a frothy cascade of silver, signalled the start of the main display. Everyone stayed where they were, ended their conversations hurriedly, looked up and marvelled at the fizzing sprays and fountains of colour. Tiny hands held manic sparklers, gasps of delight punctuating the bangs and pops, whizzes and hoots. Craig, in his infinite culinary wisdom, had created a tub of soft toffee and as soon as the display was over, a queue formed of children and adults alike, holding apples on sticks ready to dip and drip.

At about nine o'clock, the fire began to collapse and die down, great planks and boxes withering and melting, caves of pure orange gaping open in the void. With full bellies, red faces and tired eyes, people began to slowly drift home. Miri stood by the edge of the far wall, beyond the serving hatch and contemplated the fascinating dichotomy around fire, how it is both a saver and destroyer of life. She had already gathered her things, but as she looked around for Edie, she was distracted by raised voices, aggressive and urgent but just about under control. Miri was in shadow, the voices coming from behind the remains of the fire. She listened.

"How do you explain this then, Nettie?" Tom was circling round his wife.

"Don't be ridiculous, Tom! It's just one of the cards we use after the Pilates class! What's your problem? Not like you ever bother to walk me home. At a loose end, are we?" Nettie's voice was hushed but full of menace. She was backing away, eyes flicking in all directions, hoping for an opportunity to melt away into the darkness.

"It's a fire tarot, Nettie! I'm not bloody stupid! I found it next to one of your crackpot moon journals and your other mumbo jumbo shite! You did something to start that bloody fire in The Glades, didn't you? Didn't you?!" Tom's heavy hands descended onto her shoulders. She wriggled.

"Get your paws off me! And keep your voice down! That temper of yours will get you into trouble, if it hasn't already."

"What do you mean by that? What do you mean, you witch?! I swear I'll—"

"Stop it! I didn't think you believed in witchcraft, Tom. How do you reckon I could start a fire with a card and a bunch of words? Ay?"

"You 'ad something to do with it! I know you did! You could've killed her. And it was you who put Suzie out of action an' all, wasn't it? Wasn't it?"

"Get your hands off! You're hurting me! And why would I want to do these things, Tom? Tell me that?" Nettie was crying now.

"I don't bloody know! I suppose you've been listening to that batty bloody Sarah and her poisonous gossip! Stupid cow! According to 'er I've 'ad 'alf the bitches in Kington! Even my mate Geoff heard it! Wait till I get my bloody hands on 'er!"

"Yes, Tom. Everyone will see a different side to you then, won't they?"

"Now you just listen to me." Tom had passed the peak of his temper and his voice was low and menacing. "This is the last time. I know you've had a hard time in the past and I've tried to make allowances for that. I know you're afraid of losing people, but you've got to lay off! Do you 'ear? Just lay off!" Miri waited until Tom was out of sight. He had backed away, threatening gestures punctuating his words, leaving Nettie standing perfectly still, as if lost in a maze, unsure of which way to go.

"Coo-ey, Darling! Over here!" Miri reluctantly made her way towards Edie for the walk home. She didn't want either Nettie or Tom to spot her but they were moving away now, in single file. Joe had ditched his plan to catch up on some work in favour of a drink with his brother. It would be easier, he reasoned, to keep his arrangement with Zoe that way; he might even ask Will along, if he was in a receptive mood. A couple of pints should see to that."

"I thought you'd gone without me, Darling!" said Edie, pouting. Her bonfire outfit, red boiler suit and yellow wellies, would have rendered that option unlikely, Miri thought, but she simply smiled and took her arm. They both agreed that the evening had been a great success, considering the circumstances, and the walk home was pleasant, if chilly, beneath the clear navy sky and the fuzzy stars. Miri relayed the row she had overheard between Tom and Nettie, keen to hear what Edie would make of it.

"Well, Darling, it's just gossip after all. Tom may well be justified in his anger. I can't imagine a practical chap like that would have much time for the pinkies, with their crystals and potions!"

"Yes, but the tarot, Edie. What do you make of that? He may not like it, but he was suggesting that she had the power to do it, even supposing he meant that she had started the fire by some other means."

"You mean arson?"

Miri shrugged. "Of course, it could have happened just the way they described it, with or without Nettie's help. Cat on the mantelpiece accidentally knocks something flammable into a gas fire. End of."

Edie shrugged. "Maybe we'll never know. So handsome Tom Hopkins has a violent temper then? That's interesting."

"Yes, but he may have been pushed to the limit, Edie. Nettie can't be easy to live with, given her past traumas and insecurities."

"Well, speak as you find I always say, and I've always found her pleasant enough. She's a hard worker too."

By now they had reached the gate to their cottages and there was one more thing Miri wanted to ask before she decided on her next move. "Do you know anything about how Nettie's sister died, Edie?"

"No, I don't." Edie sighed and leaned on the gate post, trying to recall. "It all happened before I moved here, and I suppose it's a subject that people get used to avoiding when they know how much pain it has caused. Eventually, it just fades away, I guess."

"What, even in the village shop? I can't imagine Mrs. Duggan avoiding anything."

"Oh, you'd be surprised, Darling. She may be an old gossip, but she can keep a secret if something is important enough." Edie looked wistful and Miri remembered that Mrs Duggan had behaved with extreme sensitivity towards Helen Triplow and her cousin Beatrice Burton after their husbands were arrested.

"Can she?" said Miri. "How interesting."

***

The Kington Arms was buzzing after the success of the bonfire, and the two brothers were enjoying the remainder of the evening. The dying embers of the fire threw dancing shadows on the wall opposite their table and the logs in the inglenook glowed. Their clothes stank of woodsmoke and their hair was laced with soot.

"You must be joking!" said Will, in response to Joe's proposition, carefully placing two more frothing pints on their table. "It'll suit me just fine if I never set foot in the place again. What's it all about anyway?"

"I want to watch the grave. At midnight."

Will sprayed a mouthful of beer. "What the—?" he coughed.

"I want to see if anything happens around the grave." Joe was serious and Will recognised the signs.

"Like what for God's sake?"

"Well, we know the stone has been moved. Kate told us that. We know that something has been disturbed, otherwise how do you explain the ancient fibres and the churned soil?"

"Edie explained that."

Joe shook his head. "Hardly. The footprint?"

"I've told you, Joe. It'll be a child's. It's obvious."

"Right by a gravestone at the far end of the churchyard? What parent would allow that?"

"You know what kids are like, Joe. We'd have done it, no problem. Still doin' it."

"Come with me to the vicarage then. I thought you were supposed to be the reckless one? It's not as if I'm asking you to walk around the graves. Mind you, if you reckon there's nothing to—"

"Fine, I'll come to the vicarage. But on one condition. We stay there no more than ten minutes. Okay? I've learned my lesson, mate!"

"Come on then, it's gone half eleven already."

Wisps of clouds scudded across the sky in response to a strengthening breeze, freshening the smoky air and lifting the ash. A light shone like a beacon from an upstairs window in the vicarage and the boys skirted the crime scene tape to follow its guide.

The huge door was unlocked, so they went in and called up to Zoe, letting her know they were there and locking the door behind them. There was no reply so they filed up the stairs, gave the secret doorway a wide birth, and called again.

"The light must be coming from her bedroom," said Will. "Best try to find her. She may have nodded off. Bloody stupid leaving the front door open like that."

Tentatively, they followed the light and pushed the door. Zoe was lying on her stomach, in her princess pyjamas, width ways across the bed, eyes closed, mouth open, a red stain spreading across the white candlewick throw.

"Oh my God!" said Will. "She's dead! Someone's killed her!"

"Don't touch anything," said Joe. "Call Kate!"

"Hang on," said Will, inching nearer to the body. "She's not dead. She's just pissed! Out cold. This is wine, I can smell it. Look, there's the glass on the floor. Jesus!"

Once they were sure Zoe was alive and in a safe position, and had given themselves a few minutes to recover from the shock, they crept out, more sober than they were when they went in.

"Good job it's only us," said Joe. "Anyone could've come in."

"You don't think anyone else is lurking about, do you? I don't like this place. Let's go, Joe. We can come back another night. We could get arrested for this. Especially after what happened before. It looks like we've come back for some of that stash."

"Well, it's midnight now, we might as well have a quick look from the landing window while we're here. Then we'll go straight out. We'll need to secure the door somehow."

"Okay, here we are. Have a quick look." Will stood behind Joe and peered over his shoulder. A flake of paint from the window frame fell silently onto his hair, making him rub his head in confusion. A cobweb wobbled, sticky and soft, beneath the sill. Joe shifted his weight from one leg to the other. A floorboard creaked. For all his scepticism, Will was scared. The clouds were tangled around bare branches and the moon cast an eerie glow through the mist as it eddied around the gravestones and the temperature dropped.

"What's that knocking?" whispered Will.

"What? Sshh! Just the old pipes, I think."

An owl, somewhere far off, hooted.

"Look!" said Will. "Down there! The graves! Shit!"

Something was moving; a shape, pale and translucent like muslin, stretched long and low, curling in and out of the stones. In and out. The hour stood suspended and there was a humming sound, a vibration in their heads. They covered their ears, limbs heavy and slow, toes numb.

Someone pressed the fast-forward button and the brothers belted down the stairs as fast as they could, Will clutching Joe's jacket. Joe fumbled with the lock, his fingers clumsy and numb, leaving just enough time for Will to notice the tiny shoes and boots spread out along a purpose-built bench.

Chapter 25

Miri ate breakfast alone. Will and Joe had not surfaced yet, and she needed to call Shel in the school office early in order to rearrange her regular mentoring session. Miri hated doing this, she felt that she was letting the children down, but there really was no alternative. She had barely slept, going over and over what she already knew and, more importantly, what she needed to find out before her lunch meeting with Mike in the Kington at noon.

She slipped out quietly through the back door, hood up against squally wind and increasing rain. This was not the day for admiring nature or lingering to absorb the changing landscape. This was a day of urgency and Miri needed to be sharp of mind and fleet of foot.

She was heading for the village store. Her purposeful stride barely slowed in pace as she passed the churchyard, despite the fact Jack Whitlock was being led away from his home before her eyes. It was still early. There was no other audience to witness his arrest. Jack was flanked by two uniformed police officers as he limped slowly, stick in hand, head bowed, towards the awaiting vehicle. This was no surprise. Miri knew that once 'means, motive and opportunity' had been established, Mike would have no option but to arrest Jack. She looked back briefly, just in time to see Jack pause and spit noisily before getting into the car.

Miri stood aside to allow an elderly gentleman to emerge from the shop with his newspaper, before entering with a smile. The shop was toasty, a refuge from the rain which she shook from her raincoat and squeezed from her hair.

"Morning, my love. What can I get for you?" Mrs. Duggan had been especially friendly to Miri ever since her one and only attendance at the Pilates class. Miri presumed a sort of conspiratorial bonding had taken place on the part of Mrs. Duggan, and Miri intended to utilise it to maximum advantage.

"I'm not here to buy anything, Mrs. Duggan. It's more important than that. I need your help with the investigation into the death of Dexter Steele." Mrs. Duggan's eyes wobbled, her mighty chest rising like the prow of a ship.

"Good Lord," she said, placing a hand to her throat. "Whatever do you mean?" Something of the old hostility had returned and Miri needed to think quickly to keep this mission on track.

"Don't misunderstand me, Mrs. Duggan. I'm not here to ask questions; that's the job of the police. I need you to help me with some information that only you may know. I desperately need your expertise." That did it. Mrs. Duggan's over-inflated bosom was no match for her over-inflated sense of her own importance, and the hand at her throat moved quickly to her hair, which she patted coyly.

"Well," she said slowly, as if she would need to think long and hard about it, "you'd best come into the back. I'll get my Jennie to take over for a bit."

Miri had never been beyond the shop counter before and was pleasantly surprised by how cosy the living quarters were.

"This is lovely, Mrs. Duggan! I had no idea there would be so much space."

"Yes, it fools everyone. Oh, excuse my manners. Can I get you a hot drink? Tea?"

"That would be perfect. Thank you." Miri sat down and observed with pleasure the old-fashioned sideboard, the wooden mantle clock, the wobbly hatstand in the corner. Her strategic compliment about the spacious living quarters had done much to settle the atmosphere and Mrs. Duggan could be heard filling the kettle, rattling cups and saucers, letting the cat out and giving her orders to Jennie. Eventually, she blustered in, breathless and eager, with a tray full of charmingly mismatched crockery and a plate of digestives.

"Now then," she said, as she poured the tea and handed a cup to Miri.

"First of all," Miri began, "I want you to understand that everything that I say to you must remain a secret, at least for the time being." Miri was aware that she was following a hunch based on her instincts as a psychiatrist; there was no guarantee that it would lead anywhere, and her line of enquiry could create a lot of unnecessary pain if she was wrong. Alternatively, if she was right, then the secret would be out in the open all too soon anyway and there would be no need for secrecy. Mrs. Duggan shifted in her seat and rolled her eyes.

"I know everyone thinks I'm an old gossip Miri, but let me tell you something. I provide a service in this village, not just groceries either. People come to tell me their problems and I listen." She hefted one of her bosoms and took a sip of tea. "They wouldn't do that if they thought I couldn't keep it to myself now would they? I also know," she went on, without giving Miri the chance to reply, "that some of that information finds its way out. It finds its way out," she murmured, leaning forward, one psychiatrist to another, "because it's part of my plan to help people." Miri raised her eyebrows, waiting for the punchline. "If two people aren't getting on, let's say, because of a misunderstanding, then I can easily put that right by telling each of them what they want to hear from the other, indirectly like, even if it isn't exactly true. See?"

Miri sighed. "I'm sure your motives are very honourable Mrs. Duggan, but that kind of behaviour can cause all sorts of confusion, and there's a real danger that things can end up in a worse state than before." Mrs. Duggan folded her arms, raising the portcullis, literally and metaphorically. "But I'm not here to talk about the rights and wrongs of all that. I'm here because I need your help with a very serious matter. If people tell you things, as you say, you might have just the information I need. Will you help me?" Mrs. Duggan nodded majestically, as if she was doing Miri a great favour against her own better judgement.

"Right. Were you living here in the village when Nettie Hopkins' older sister died?" If Mrs. Duggan was surprised by the question, she didn't show it; years of honing her craft had enabled her to conceal emotion. How many times had she tucked away snippets of information about people, unnoticed as she packed their shopping and gave them their change?

"Well, 'o course, dear. I been 'ere these thirty-five years!"

"How did she die, Mrs Duggan?"

"Well, she was killed outright in a road traffic accident, up on the by-pass just beyond the turning into the village there. Terrible it was. Terrible." Mrs. Duggan hung her head as she remembered the incident, then looked up, curious about the link between this and the murder of Dexter Steele.

"Did you keep any newspaper cuttings about it? Don't be embarrassed about it, please. You sell newspapers, among other things, so it's only natural that you would keep important cuttings. We have the internet now and there'll be records of the accident somewhere in the archives, but I thought if you could lay your hands on something it would be easier and more personal; quicker too, probably." Miri would have bet her best boots that she was a harbourer of newspapers that featured local events, and as if on cue, Mrs. Duggan became very business-like suddenly, heaving herself out of her chair and bustling over to the old sideboard.

"Do you know, I think I have? I always keep important things about the village." Miri smiled. Of course you do, she thought. Mrs Duggan rummaged through several drawers, peeling off pile after pile; there was no system here. Eventually, she unearthed a folded article, fragile and yellowing. "Here it is. I knew I'd kept it. May 10th, 1996. Here."

Miri took the paper, taking care not to damage it, and read the headline:

'Sixteen-year-old Stacey Merrick killed instantly in hit and run, on Oxfordshire by-pass.'

There were additional details about Stacey and the family, but the interesting thing about the article, the thing that took Miri's breath away, was the photograph of Stacey. She was the image of her sister Nettie. The general resemblance was striking enough, but the hair, the distinctive plume of white frizzy hair, was identical.

"Of course, they don't say everything about it in there," said Mrs. Duggan mysteriously, lending weight to her importance as the hub of anything worth knowing.

"Really?" said Miri, with what she hoped was enough amazement to reel her in.

"I wouldn't want to speak out of turn, neither. I said I can keep a secret and I can." This was a tricky one. Now Miri needed to persuade Mrs. Duggan to reveal a secret, something that she had specifically asked her not to do.

"It's extremely important, Mrs. Duggan. If there is anything significant about that incident that you have kept to yourself for over twenty years, please tell me." There was a long silence.

"I can't help you, I'm afraid." Mrs. Duggan folded her arms. "Like I said. I can keep a secret, whatever them out there thinks. I'll not be tricked into saying something I shouldn't."

"It's really not about that," Miri said gently. She was tempted to touch Mrs. Duggan's forearm in the hope that she might soften her body language, but she decided against it, adopted a gentler tone and leaned forward so that she was looking up at Mrs. Duggan. Miri knew that if she was to win her over, the older woman must be made to feel that she was in control of the conversation. "It's about doing what is right in the face of a dramatic change of circumstance." Mrs. Duggan sat up straight and was about to speak. Miri chose this moment to touch her. "You might have done the right thing in keeping your secret up to now, Mrs. Duggan, but I promise you, you will be doing the right thing if you off load the burden to me today. I'll take responsibility from this moment on." Miri's final words affected Mrs. Duggan deeply; Miri could see how much of a weight the poor woman must have borne as her shoulders dropped and her face crumpled.

"Do you promise only to use this information if there is no other way?" she asked, reasonably, Miri thought.

"Yes, I do. You have my word."

"Well then. I can tell you that little Nettie Merrick, as she was then, saw the accident. The whole thing. She saw her sister killed," she said sadly, shaking her head, tears welling up. "She'd be about six or seven and she'd followed Stacey. She was sixteen. Nettie worshipped her. Stacey was going to meet a boy, they said, and she'd told Nettie to go home and leave her alone. You can imagine that, I'm sure." Miri nodded. "Well, little Nettie ignored it and followed her sister. They lived near the end of the lane, not far from the top where the main road is, and where Stacey's young man had arranged to pick her up." Mrs. Duggan wiped her eyes, sniffed and took a deep breath. "The little one must have been dodging in and out of the hedgerow so as not to be seen, and scrambled up the bank at the top, just as the car hit Stacey and left her dead on the verge." Mrs. Duggan was weeping openly, and Miri tried to comfort her.

"How do you know all this?" Miri asked when she had regained some control.

"I saw her scrambling down the bank, white as a sheet. She was sick on the road and unable to speak. In fact, she didn't speak for three years. We all tried to bring her round but she seemed to be locked in a little world of her own. She never smiled and she had a sort of faraway look about her. As time went on, everybody just sort of got used to her being like that."

"Did you tell anyone?"

"No, I didn't," she said softly, her voice breaking, "because I thought they'd take her away into care, you see. Her poor mother wouldn't have been able to bear it, rest her soul, not to mention the child. I'm going back decades, remember, and there was a scandal at the time about children being taken away from their parents for no good reason."

"Yes, I remember something about that."

"So, everyone just assumed that she was grieving for her sister, which she was, and no more was said about it. Nowadays, there'd be help at hand of course, counselling, speech therapy and so on, but her father wouldn't have anything to do with social services anyway, said he wasn't having them poking their noses into his affairs. So, Nettie was left to her own devices, and I just did what I thought was right. I let her help out in the shop on Saturday mornings when she was about ten years old and her speech came back gradually, poor lamb, but then she had to deal with the death of her mother and all the rest of it. No one was happier than me when Tom Hopkins asked her to marry him. She was besotted by him, as you can imagine." Mrs. Duggan broke down again so Miri sat back to absorb what she'd heard.

"I'm sure you did everything you could. Please don't upset yourself. None of this is your fault, really it isn't." Mrs. Duggan wiped her face and rearranged herself into 'public facing' mode. "It can't have been easy carrying this burden with you all these years," she added, leaning forward and covering her hand with her own. "You've been a great help, you really have. May I take the cutting?"

"If you must. I want it back though. I'll get a plastic wallet; it's pouring down out there. I suppose I do feel a bit better now that I've told someone." She rubbed the wallet vigorously to make it open. "I hope I haven't caused any more trouble."

"I may have to pass on the information you have given me, Mrs. Duggan, but you knew that when I asked you about all this. There has been a brutal murder, as you know, and we must find out who did it, otherwise an innocent man may go to prison. None of us want that on our consciences."

"Everyone thinks old Jack did it."

"Do you think he did?"

"I don't know. He's a crabby old bugger, but I never had him pegged as a murderer, I must say. I told the

Inspector as much. Don't see what all this has to do with Stacey, though."

Miri smiled warmly. "Thank you again. I know how difficult this must have been for you. You've been a great help."

By the time Mrs. Duggan had resumed her rightful place behind the counter in her shop, she was back to her usual self, taking orders, exchanging pleasantries, immersed in her own particular brand of social work; listening to others, allowing them to offload, and chipping in with whatever tasty morsel she deemed handiest for the purpose.

It was still barely the middle of the morning and the rain had clearly settled in for the day, bouncing off the paths, pooling in the slightest dip and making a quagmire of the lane.

Miri did not want to wait another two hours before her lunch meeting with Mike; she needed to speak with him as soon as possible. He wasn't answering his phone, so Miri navigated the puddles and sheltered in the porch at the village hall. There was a briefing going on, as she'd expected, but she managed to attract Kate's attention through the glass panel of the swing doors.

"Hello! You okay?" said Kate. "You look a bit stressed. Mike's in full flow, so I can't hang about. What is it? Is it Will?" she added anxiously, grabbing Miri's arm.

"No. They're both fine. I think. I must speak with Mike, and you Kate, if you can make it. I have some important information that I think has a significant bearing on the murder case. I've a meeting planned with

Mike anyway at twelve, but if you can come to the Kington straight away after the briefing, I'll wait for you there." Miri put her hands on Kate's arms to emphasise the urgency. "Please, Kate. Quick as you can." Kate's face dropped. She knew that Miri was in earnest and promised to do her best. "Just get him out of there as soon as you can."

At the Kington, where morning coffee was being served, Miri asked Gavin if the snug was free for a meeting with DCI Absolom and DS Kate Woodley.

"Of course, love! I'll go and light the fire; it's freezing in there. About the investigation, is it?" Miri remained silent, taking off her coat and shaking the drips away. "Well, settle yourself in. I'll bring you a pot of coffee and a slice of fruit cake while you're waiting; you look like you need it. Such a day!"

Miri sat down in the inglenook by the fire, hoping that no one would disturb her while she tried to make sense of her fragmented thoughts, the image of Stacey Merrick as clear in her mind as if it was etched on the table in front of her.

Chapter 26

"Don't lift the blind, Joe. If Edie knows we're up, she'll be round, and I don't think I could cope, I really don't. Not today." Will sat with his head in his hands at the kitchen table, waiting for Joe to slip scrambled eggs on to their toasted muffins. "What shall we do?" he said with his mouth full as Joe joined him with his own plate. "Tell Mum?"

"Tell her what, Will? That we went to the vicarage after a few pints, thought Zoe had been murdered, but just before we called the police, we realised she was spark out on red wine? That we saw a ghost in the churchyard from the landing window, weaving in and out of the graves? That as we ran for our lives, we noticed that Zoe's shoes are really small, possibly about the size of the bare footprint found next to the dead body of Dexter Steele?"

"Why not? It's the truth, isn't it?" said Will, scraping his plate clean and reaching for the coffee pot. "We should be telling the police as well. That's what Mum will tell us to do next."

"You're gonna tell Kate we saw a ghost?"

"Well, we saw something, didn't we? It may have been fog or mist, I suppose. We'd had a few pints, Joe. Then there was the shock of thinking Zoe was dead. I don't see how it can help the enquiry anyway. We could keep that bit to ourselves."

"You've just talked your way out of it! What I saw had some sort of form; it wasn't just mist. Don't you think?"

"Yeah, I guess. I think we should tell them about the other things, though. Zoe's obviously got some sort of drink problem, which makes her an unreliable witness, and then there's the shoe business. If they're looking for a child's foot to fit the cast they made of that print, they might be wasting their time. What if it's Zoe's footprint?"

"What would she be doing barefoot next to that grave?"

"Exactly."

"You're not suggesting Zoe killed Dexter, are you? She's barely big enough to be seen behind the pulpit, even when she's standing on a box, Mum says. And she never left the room all night when we were at the vicarage. She was drinking then too."

"Maybe she had an accomplice, Joe. Anyway, that footprint could've been made earlier."

"Still weird."

"And don't forget, we were locked in that bloody cave for most of the night. Anything could've happened during that time. He was drugged, remember."

"Where is Mum anyway? I thought the meeting with Mike was at lunchtime."

"I'll call her." Joe left the kitchen while Will made a start on clearing up. Joe called down the hallway a few moments later. "She's already at the pub." He returned to the kitchen and leant on a chair. "Apparently, she's found out something important and asked Mike and Kate to meet her earlier. Oh, and Jack's been arrested. No surprise there. Do you think you should text Kate about Zoe's shoe size?"

"Dunno. Kate doesn't trust Zoe anyway. It might cause trouble."

"It's evidence, Will, whether we like it or not. I don't think Jack did it. It's not his style, all that straw dolly stuff. Who'd be that stupid?"

"S'pose. Go on then. It doesn't prove anything, anyway. I wouldn't want Zoe to know we'd done it, though. Hey!" he continued as he was texting. "What if she's Dexter's long-lost daughter, moved down here from Yorkshire, purposely to seek him out and kill him for abandoning her?"

"Shut up!" Joe threw a tea towel at his brother, almost knocking the phone out of his hand. "You're letting your imagination run away with you. Yorkshire! What the hell?"

"I can detect a Yorkshire accent, definitely. She's lived there at some point, for sure. Isn't that Emmerdale country, the soap that Dexter was in during the eighties?"

The boys were silent for a few minutes, registering this new possibility.

"One thing's for sure, Joe. What we saw last night in the graveyard wasn't our imagination. We saw something move and it scared the shit out of us. Nothing to do with Zoe either."

"Yeah, well I'm trying not to think about it, mate. I hope Mum's not going to go off on her own, following one of her famous hunches. Let's go for a walk, swing by the pub and check she's with Mike. Any reply from Kate?"

***

Miri didn't have to wait long. Mike came in first, moaning about the filthy weather and rubbing his buzzcut to shake off the drips. Kate was dressed for it, a perfectly dry ponytail beneath the hood of her waterproof Barbour jacket. While Kate was ordering hot chocolates at the bar, Miri gathered her things, signalled to them both that the snug was free, and Mike followed her through. The fire was blazing, and Gavin had moved three easy chairs and a coffee table near to it for their comfort.

"I know we're meant to be catching up about the various things I've been doing, Mike, with Adam and so on, but it'll have to wait. I asked Kate to bring you here because of the case you're working on now, the murder case."

Kate came in with a tray of steaming mugs and a dish of marshmallows. "Boy, I'm ready for this," she said.

"It won't take long, Miri. We've already made an arrest," said Mike, relaxing and picking up a mug. "We've got our man; 'means, motive and opportunity'. Jack Whitlock."

"Yes, I saw him getting into the police car early this morning."

"And you're here to tell me I've got it all wrong, I suppose."

Kate looked down, embarrassed in anticipation at the scene that was about to unfold. She knew that door to door enquiries had given them nothing else to go on. Nobody had seen or heard anything, not surprising really, given the location of the murder. Constable Stone had spent all day in the school, checking little feet against the plaster cast of the tiny print found at the graveside. No joy there either. 'Like bloody Cinderella, it was!' he'd said. Enquiries into Dexter's past had also revealed precious little more than everyone already knew, except for a few personal details from his actor friends and the chauffeur, which bore no relevance to the case as far as Mike was concerned. The lead regarding Carol Sterling and her father Trevor's financial loss had been a dead end too, apparently. Both had alibis, as did Bob, the repair man.

"Yes, Mike. I'm afraid I am."

Mike shifted in his chair and took a sip of his drink. Kate said nothing. She'd received a text message from Will which she wanted to follow up on her own, but that could wait.

"There's more to it than 'means, motive and opportunity' as you well know, Mike. That's all circumstantial anyway. The knife could have been stolen, the plant that was used for the poison grows all over the place, or could have been taken from Jack's garden, and as for the dolly? Well!" Mike sat back and let her blow herself out. "Lots of people had the opportunity and," she continued, leaning forward, "Jack Whitlock is not the only one with a motive, which is why I've asked you both here. You have to listen to me, Mike."

Mike listened. Twenty minutes later the three of them filed swiftly out of the pub without a word to anyone. "Well! Excuse me while I disappear, I'm sure!" said Gavin, slinging a bar towel over his shoulder. In the carpark, Will and Joe stood open-mouthed as Mike's car screeched away, Kate by his side, their mother in the back.

"What's going on, Gavin?"

"Who knows? Really! One minute the three of them are cosying up in my snug, the next minute they go all *Prime Suspect* on me and disappear without a 'by your leave'!"

"Well at least she's not on her own," said Will. "We might as well wait here now. Two mochas please, Gavin."

***

Mike's car pulled up on a discreet patch of rough ground behind the game-keeper's lodge. Adam was working nearby but if he noticed them at all, he retreated into his world and carried on with his task, head down, back against wind and rain.

"Wait here for a couple of minutes Miri, while Sergeant Woodley and I make the initial moves. We'll be needing you soon enough."

Miri sat in the back of the car and watched as Mike and Kate knocked on the door and waited. She was surprised to see Tom at the door. She had assumed he would be working. "Going somewhere, Mr. Hopkins?" she heard Mike say. "A short holiday, perhaps?" He was certainly not dressed in work clothes and Miri could just about see the edge of a holdall there in the porch, though the car windows were steamy. Miri was speculating on this possible new development and the timing of it, when the car jolted violently and a terrifying image, distorted in the rain, latched itself with a crack on to the rain-soaked window next to Miri's face. It was Nettie, having thrown her bike down, teeth bared and frantic, pulling madly at the door handles.

"What the hell do you think you're doing now, you bitch? Leave us alone! Where are they? Where are they?" The car had an automatic locking system which could only be released from inside, or with a key, so Miri, though jolted and scared, fumbling and shaking, had time to call Kate while Nettie scratched impotently at the glass, her sodden hair blocking Miri's view. Kate didn't answer at first, but Miri kept pressing redial until she got a response, terrified that Kate would go on ignoring the call.

"Quick! Nettie's out here going crazy! I'm trapped! Quick!"

Kate came flying out of the house, tackled Nettie to the ground, pulled her arm behind her back and stood on it while she snapped the cuffs on. Nor did she release her foot until she had called for backup. She nodded to Miri to let herself out and pushed Nettie, now limp and silent, unceremoniously into the house. Adam was nowhere to be seen.

Miri released the lock and opened the door, remaining seated until she had regained some of her composure. She took a few deep breaths and waited for her heartbeat to settle down. Slowly, she emerged from the car and walked stiffly through the rain to the front door.

Tom was standing in the sparse sitting room, his overcoat waiting to be lifted from the arm of a chair. Nettie was sitting on a threadbare dining chair, crying steadily and silently.

"Like I said, I'm leaving. I've been meaning to go for a long time. It's over between us. We both know it. Nettie with her bloody spells, clinging on all the time. I made allowances at first but there's a limit and I've reached it. You alright, love?" he said, turning to Miri. "Now you know what she's like." Miri sat on a stool in the background and watched.

"You're not going anywhere till I'm satisfied you were nowhere near the graveyard on the night Dexter Steele was killed," said Mike quietly and firmly.

"Well, of course I wasn't! Why should I be? And before you ask, I can't prove it." Nettie found the strength from somewhere, to laugh. "Nettie and me have separate rooms," he went on, ignoring her. "I was here, I tell you! I came straight home after the ghost hunt. We walked back together in fact," he added, looking down at his feet.

"So, you were here too?" said Mike, turning to Nettie. She nodded vacantly, staring at the coat and the holdall. She had nothing left to lose. Mike pulled up a chair so that he was level with Nettie, rested an arm on his knees casually, leaned forward and pressed her shackled hands gently so that she would know he wasn't going to lay into her. Kate knew the drill and pressed the record button on her phone.

"Tell me all about it, Nettie."

"Not much to tell. He killed my sister. I killed him." The backup cars pulled up noiselessly. Kate signalled to them from the window to wait.

"Do you mean William Tanner? Dexter Steele?" Nettie nodded. "How did you know it was him, Nettie? The driver of the car who killed your sister was never traced."

"I saw him." She stared ahead, blank and still. Tom had reached for a chair, mouth open, dumbfounded.

"But that was well over twenty years ago now," he said gently, "and you were only a little girl, Nettie."

"In the village. On my bike. He saw me. He went pale. He knew me. He saw my sister looking back at him. I knew. I think I must have blocked it out. I never recognised him on the telly, but in that moment I knew." Nettie's voice crackled. "The expression on his face was the same, the same as when he stood over her on the side of the road." Mike looked at Miri. She had shown him the photograph in the pub and explained her theory.

Miri had witnessed that moment. She had seen Dexter almost faint with shock, assuming that it was the sight of Jack Whitlock glaring at him that had disturbed him so much, or the graves of his ancestors, maybe. Then, when Adam had told her that Nettie had not wanted him to find his sister because she couldn't have hers back, Miri had realised that Stacey's death had triggered a pathological reaction. When she had seen the photograph of Stacey Merrick, she had known that it was the sight of Nettie Hopkins on her bike that had prompted such an emotional landslide. Miri had racked her brains over that moment, it had been one of the things that had kept her awake the night before she went to see Mrs. Duggan. 'If it wasn't Jack, then who was it?' she'd asked herself. She'd thought of Nettie in that moment and added all the other behaviours she'd noticed about her; the suspicions, the obsession with spells and charms, her bitter rejection of Adam and her desire to control him, the way her husband had needed to talk her down at the bonfire; it wasn't his temper that was the problem, it was hers.

William Tanner had done a terrible thing. He had left a young girl for dead on the side of the road and never reported it. Maybe he had been over the legal alcohol limit. Maybe he hadn't dared risk losing an already waning career. Whatever it was, it was unforgivable. There had been no witnesses and he had never been found out. Someone walking at a distance had reported seeing a car speeding along that stretch of road, which may have been grey or silver, but that was about it. A conversation with the actor friend who had identified Dexter's body, had revealed that Dexter had not driven since the year of Stacey's death and that he had developed a drink problem in the nineties. It would never be proven of course, but Miri knew it was true.

"Tell me what you did, Nettie."

Nettie had barely blinked. She didn't once look at Tom and sat perfectly still, eyes brimming with tears.

"I grow plants in Adam's garden. Sarah gave me a poisonous one. I didn't ask her for it. She told me to be careful with it because it could cause illness, or worse. There's one in Jack's garden. I saw it when I stole his knife, the day I went to see about his leg. I took a dolly that day too. He makes them for the children. I knew he hated the Tanners, so I made it look like he'd done it."

"Go on."

"On the night of the vicarage party, I offered to help Gavin a bit with the drinks. I laced Dexter's drink with the poison, just enough to slow him down and make him ill, but I didn't take it to him myself. I didn't want him to see me. I gave it to one of the barmaids to take it to him and watched to make sure he drank it. I timed it so that he would just be starting to react as everyone was leaving. He was dizzy and slurring his words, but everyone just thought he was drunk. I knew he wouldn't make it back to the pub. I walked home with Tom. We didn't say much. I didn't want to start an argument. I went straight to my room, then left an hour later and walked back to the churchyard."

"What time was this, Nettie?" said Mike gently.

"About half eleven." Mike nodded. "He was there, sitting on a wall by the churchyard, mumbling and sweating. I offered to help him and he came along like a child. Maybe he thought I was a ghost. His family are all buried there. I led him to the grave of Lavinia Whitlock, the witch, and pushed him down. It was easy. Then I stabbed him. Then I put the dolly there."

There was a long pause. Mike breathed deeply, knowing he'd got his confession.

"I'd like to ask you something, Nettie," said Kate. Nettie seemed to see her for the first time and nodded, just once. "Did you at any time remove your shoes?" Nettie shook her head. "Did you move the gravestone, deliberately or by accident?" Again, Nettie shook her head. "Did you dig around in the dirt before you pushed Dexter into the grave or when you placed the dolly there?" Again, a firm shake of the head. "And what about all the stuff that's been going on in the village, Nettie? The dead ravens, for example. Dexter wasn't even here then."

"That was nothing to do with it. I went along with Sarah. She said it was just a bit of fun, teach folk a lesson, especially them as gets above themselves." Nettie cast a look in Miri's direction that turned her blood cold. That's all it was. I knew Tom was playing around, so Sarah gave me some spells to try. I don't know nothin' else." Tom turned around, hands in the air, shaking his head. "It suited me. Made me think what I was doing must be right because everything would point to Jack.

Kate checked her equipment and went out, presumably to give orders to release Jack, but also to update the backup squad. Tom was pale and shaking slightly. Miri was near to tears, because as Nettie sat there, on her stool with her hands in her lap, she saw an innocent six-year-old child whose only crime had been to love her sister, who had seen and heard her bounce off a car and die in a matter of seconds on the roadside near her home. She also saw a young woman who had planned and killed in cold blood.

Chapter 27

"You poor thing! Look at you, Darling. You really must stop getting yourself mixed up in these things. Honestly!"

Mike had dropped Miri home. No one had wanted to discuss the case, least of all Miri, and she had said nothing throughout the short drive, except to acknowledge that they would be in touch soon and to assure them that she would look after herself. Kate mouthed that she'd be round later when she had finished her shift and Miri nodded gratefully. Joe and Will had given up waiting at the pub and sauntered home, just in time to see their mother being dropped off.

Edie, having established that no one had eaten lunch, put the kettle and the sandwich maker on and set about creating colourful toasties, with whatever she could find in the fridge.

"I got mixed up in it, Edie, because I knew Jack Whitlock was innocent." Edie knew when it was best to leave well alone and she did so now, busying herself with preparing lunch, while Miri explained what had happened and why. Edie was saddened, of course, to learn that her former lover had done such a terrible thing, but she admitted that it was in keeping with a part of his character that she had known. She was sad also, that Nettie had been traumatised to such an extent that she had become capable of a cold-blooded murder.

"I'm not happy about the outcome either, Edie. I feel sorry for Nettie in a way, but this killing was particularly brutal and I couldn't allow an innocent man to spend the rest of his life in prison for a crime he didn't commit. God knows what Mrs. Duggan will do; she'll never speak to me again, I'm sure of that."

"She'll understand, Mum. You had to do it." said Joe.

"Blood will have blood, they say," said Edie, quoting from Macbeth.

"It was her photograph that sealed it, though."

"You'd have found that somewhere else. You already knew what you were looking for."

"Yes. I suppose so. I must make sure she gets it back. I promised."

Miri, realising how hungry she was, ate well and thanked Edie for her help. Feeling restored enabled her to put matters into perspective. "I hope Tom stays on, for Adam's sake," she said. "Another shock for him, poor lad." She remembered now, with renewed resolve, her promise to him. There would be nothing standing in the way of that now and maybe Adam would be happier anyway, without Nettie breathing down his neck and invading his privacy.

Joe and Will had said nothing about their exploits at the vicarage the night before, or their concerns about Zoe, but had decided between them to confide in Kate and take her advice before worrying their mother about it.

"Bet you were scared out of your wits when Nettie attacked the car, though. Jesus!" said Will.

***

Kate came round just after four as soon as her shift had ended. Joe and Will were upstairs catching up with business of their own, and Edie had gone home.

"How are you, Miri?"

"Fine thanks, Kate. Good lunch, relaxing bath, short nap. I'm fine, honestly. How about you? And Mike?" she added.

"Good. Mike's pleased it's sorted out. I don't think he ever really believed Jack was guilty. I suppose he was hoping that something else would turn up during the trial, but he had to arrest him. I'm going to suggest giving Jane Peters the job of trying to rehabilitate Jack, integrate him into the community, you know? Someone to talk to."

"Tell her not to hold her breath, then."

"Actually, might be better if she did, from what I remember of his place," Kate said, remembering her interview with Jack.

Miri laughed. "Well, if anyone can win him round, it'll be Jane." She paused, her thoughts dwelling on how circumstances inform the actions of individuals. "I wonder if Nettie will get a lighter sentence because of the circumstances?"

"Maybe, with a psychiatric report," she said with a meaningful look. "Whatever happens though, I'd leave it alone for a bit if I were you; Mike's still licking his wounds."

Miri smiled. "He mustn't blame himself. He wasn't there when Dexter saw Nettie that day, and the effect it had on him; he would have come to the same conclusion as I did. Eventually." Kate nodded in agreement. "I need to see him about other things anyway," Miri continued, "so I'll mention it then. There's the meeting we should've had today," she said, pouring Kate a mug of tea, "and then there's the whole business about how to help the year sixes through it all. Tracey, the class teacher, has already started some work on it, which is good news, but it'll be a long- term thing, especially when news gets out about Nettie. Many of the kids know her. She's worked in the school sometimes, clinics and things."

"Yeah. What a year for the kids. We'll be keeping a close eye on her friend Sarah Clarke too, over the next couple of days, then she'll be brought in for questioning. We know she was egging Nettie on with the raven thing, causing confusion and suspicion in all the wrong places."

"Toil and trouble', in fact."

"Exactly! My hunch is that it was Sarah who convinced Nettie that Tom was having those affairs, whether he was or not, playing to her insecurities, the driving force behind Suzie's rash and the fire at number six; so easy to set up. Unless she really does have magical powers! Looks the sort. You heard Nettie say where she got the poisonous plant from."

"I wonder what her motive is?" Said Miri.

"We'll find out. God, what a year! I'll be glad when it's over!"

"Don't say that. It'll be Christmas soon enough."

"Oh, you'll love Christmas in the village, Miri. Jez always gets the choir doing loads of stuff; it's great. I don't even live here but everyone knows about the Kington choir at Christmas."

"I haven't been to the practices for a couple of weeks. I'd better get going again, then. Cheers to that," she said, and they clinked their mugs. "I wonder if Nettie's siblings will make an appearance. They've all left the village apparently, but even so."

"All that will be taken care of, Miri. Leave it to us."

Joe and Will came downstairs and suggested a pint at the Kington. "You up for it, Mum?" said Joe, secretly hoping she wouldn't be, so that they could talk to Kate.

"No thanks. Early night with a book. Plus, I don't want to be answering any questions about the arrest."

"You won't have to, not while I'm there," said Kate.

"Well, thanks, just for an hour then."

Will and Joe exchanged a look and reached for their coats.

News of the arrest had already broken in the Kington, but Gavin knew better than to question Kate about it; he'd been on the end of her professional persona before and he was sure she valued, and deserved, her down time as much as anyone else. No one else mentioned it either, for the same reasons probably, and the three of them settled down in a small corner alcove as far away from the bar as possible. The press would have their field day soon enough. For now, if there were any journalists in the pub, they wouldn't get very far with Kate; even Miri managed to get to the bar unmolested. There was quite a crowd in, no surprises there, but she was a little taken back by the appearance of Tom Hopkins; she wasn't expecting to see him with his freshly washed tousled hair and signature lumberjack shirt. She was just about to acknowledge him, when she realised that he wasn't looking at her at all. Miri followed his gaze behind her shoulder. Sarah Clarke. A spark flew across the room. An unmistakable electric current. Sexual tension. So that was it. Sarah had planned to get Nettie into some sort of trouble all along, encouraging her to create mayhem in the village, targeting Tom's so-called lovers, when all the time it was her. She was the lover! Miri couldn't be sure that Nettie had confided in Sarah about who Dexter was, she thought it unlikely on balance, but it couldn't have worked out better for these two. That row at the bonfire. Had that been set up as well to deflect suspicion from himself and Sarah?

"We don't have to talk about this if you don't want to Kate, but that text I sent you earlier about Zoe's shoes, remember?" said Will. Kate nodded.

"Yes, I've been thinking about that."

"It's not the whole story, Kate," said Joe.

"What do you mean?" she said, frowning and reaching for her glass of wine.

Between them Joe and Will went on to explain everything that had happened the night before. Kate was horrified.

"I knew Zoe was a drinker, but it sounds like she's got a real problem there. She needs help. I'll have a think about the best way forward; she can't go on like that, poor kid." Kate felt guilty about her recent attitude towards Zoe, deciding there and then to put it right.

"Yeah, well at least we know she didn't murder her long lost father, ay Will?" said Joe. Will threw a beer mat at Joe. Kate looked puzzled but Joe waved it off.

"Might have!" he said. "Good a theory as any!"

"Have you got any ideas about the footprint, Kate?" asked Joe.

"It doesn't really matter now, but if it is her print, my guess is that she'd been wondering about, earlier on in the evening of the murder, or even the night before. There had been no rain, remember, and when she's drunk, she may not be aware of what she's doing or where she's going. She might even have been sleep walking for all we know. We can check easily enough; we've still got the cast."

"What about the spook in the churchyard? What do you make of that, Kate?"

"We'll go and look. Tonight."

Will spat beer down his sweatshirt.

"Oh no, Kate. There's no need for that, really," said Joe. "Thinking about it now, it must have been the mist, wouldn't you say so, Will?"

"Oh, yes. Definitely. Mist or fog. Definitely." They nodded repeatedly to emphasise their conviction, trying, and failing, to change the subject.

"Another glass of wine?"

"You're scared."

"No, we're not. Are we, Will?"

"'Course not. Just don't feel like it, that's all. Right, Joe? Anyway, it's still a crime scene, isn't it?"

Kate was smiling broadly.

"Just a quick look around on the way back to yours. You wouldn't want me to go alone, would you?"

"Well, no 'course not," said Will, aware that this might be a pivotal moment in his relationship with Kate. Joe understood this.

"Alright then, a quick look," he said. "We'll be right behind you, won't we, Will? Shush, Mum's coming back."

The conversation had veered away from the murder case and Miri decided to keep her own counsel regarding Sarah Clarke. She finished her drink and gave in to the early night she had promised herself, glancing surreptitiously at the two heads at the bar, almost touching. One dark, one blonde.

As the wine flowed, both Joe and Will were hoping that Kate would either lose interest in the graveyard idea or forget about it altogether. Not so. Eleven thirty.

"Come on, then. Let's go. No torches, mind. It must be as dark as possible."

The crime scene tape had been removed, much to Joe's disappointment, but of course Kate knew that. The sky had cleared at last, so there was some light from the stars and the moon as the three of them stepped off the path and into the churchyard. The sense of desolation was keenly felt, a fitting place for the scene of a brutal murder. The ground was sodden, and because of the recent dry spell, much of the moisture was still lingering on the surface of the ground, yet to be absorbed. There was no way they would be here for long, Will thought, optimistically. Mud, watery and thin, had spread and splattered the stones in all directions. There was nothing to see on such a night as this, surely?

"Okay, dumb idea. Let's go," said Kate. They stood at the edge and watched from the relative security of the path for a while before preparing to walk back. Will and Kate went ahead, arm in arm, and Joe turned instinctively just in time to see a swirl of mist gather, and hear, what sounded to him like the soft rasp of calico on stone.

About The Author

Jane Hurst is a retired English teacher from the West Midlands. First introduced to the world of the macabre watching a vampiric Christopher Lee as a young girl, Jane has been a dedicated fan ever since. Alongside her hammer horror film collection, Murder Mysteries have always remained a staple of her literature diet, leading to her debut novel When Skies Are Grey. When she is not writing, she enjoys singing, spending time with her family, and recalling her claim to fame around the dinner table as a one time extra for Inspector Morse.

Printed in Great Britain
by Amazon